W9-BCL-477

Night Talk

Night Talk

BY

Elizabeth Cox

GRAYWOLF PRESS

Publication of this volume is made possible in part by a
grant provided by the Minnesota State Arts Board through
an appropriation by the Minnesota State Legislature, and
by a grant from the National Endowment for the Arts.
Significant additional support has been provided by the
Andrew W. Mellon Foundation, the Lila Wallace-Reader's
Digest Fund, the McKnight Foundation, and other
generous contributions from foundations, corporations,
and individuals. To these organizations and individuals
who make our work possible, we offer heartfelt thanks.

Published by Graywolf Press
2402 University Avenue, Suite 203
Saint Paul, Minnesota 55114
All rights reserved.

www.graywolfpress.org

Published in the United States of America

ISBN 1-55597-267-5

2 4 6 8 9 7 5 3 1
First Graywolf Printing, 1997

Library of Congress Catalog Card Number: 97-71190

Jacket Design: Julie Metz and Warren Bernard

FOR MICHAEL CURTIS

my husband, friend, and desire of my heart

ACKNOWLEDGMENTS

Thanks for support and friendship to Ginger Smith, Beth Graham, Betsy Gardner, Jessica Treadway, and to the Sally Brady writing group: Donna Stein, Alex Johnson, Elizabeth Berg, Mary Mitchell, Alan Emmett, Rick Reynolds, and Linda Cutting.

A special thanks to Beth and Michael, my children, and to my brothers, Herb and Coleman Barks, who have read my work and given helpful insights. My appreciation to Fiona McCrae and Anne Czarniecki at Graywolf Press. Thanks to my husband, Michael, for everything.

We two alone will sing like birds i'the cage
When thou dost ask me blessing, I'll kneel down
And ask of thee forgiveness; so we'll live.
And pray, and sing, and tell old tales, and laugh
At gilded butterflies, and hear poor rogues
Talk of court news: and we'll talk with them too,—
Who loses and who wins; who's in, who's out;—
And take upon's the mystery of things,
As if we were God's spies; and we'll wear out,
In a wall'd prison, packs and sects of great ones,
That ebb and flow by the moon.

King Lear

I

A LONG SEASON

PROLOGUE

Between the ages of eight and nine I prayed to the moon and thought it was God; then I turned ten and discovered the luminous flash of things. My father took me to the woods and to Corny's Pond almost every day. He showed me streaks of minnow and deer. He taught me to know birds by their songs. "Because," he said, "flash comes in more ways than sight."

Whenever we went out, my father asked Tucker to go with us. Tucker was my little brother, and he never really wanted to go. "Pay attention," my father told us, "and you'll see something you've never seen before." He was a tall man. His name was August Bell, and everything he said had weight.

"Watch where you put your hands; there'll be a whole world there." His hand hovered above a colony of ants, and he told us how they worked. When I pointed to a flock of geese going toward a field, he drew the shape of their bodies in the air. I wanted to miss nothing, to see everything August showed me. I called him August, but only behind his back.

August was a research biologist hired by the state of Georgia. He often traveled to islands to find and name new specimens of plants or insects. He was the first person in Mercy, Georgia to talk about ecology.

On our walks he urged us to look for something new. He told us that what we saw was a gift. "Sometimes," he said, "you see it only once, then you have to keep it in your memory." He made us feel lucky. "You have to come out here a lot to see the rare things," he said.

"Like what?" Tucker asked, wanting to see a rare thing, to even take it home and keep it in his room.

"Like a red-tailed hawk, or a grebe. Like a deer that we just walk up on." August took us to the pond every night after supper in the summertime, and late into the fall. He wanted us to look past the reflection on the water, into the mud where there was movement. He wanted us to be startled by the life hidden there.

At times he brought the world of mud up into a small net scoop that hung from his back pocket. He poured mud and water into a jar, then at night let us observe the drops under a microscope on the kitchen table. I could hardly believe the strange shapes changing before my eyes.

Leaning over the microscope, I could look beneath the water; but at the river I preferred the reflection of trees on the bank, the doubleness of their image—branches splaying out from bank and sky.

If August pointed to something under the water, I would pull back. "I can't see it," I said. In truth, I didn't want to see what lay in the mud of the pond.

Then one evening beneath the reflection of cloud and branch, I saw the clear delineation of a crawdad jerk toward something it hunted. When I saw it, a narrow slit in my mind ran down itself, widened. My head ran clean as slate.

The underwater world came alive—cobwebby with legions of spiky, quick tadpoles. Then beneath the grid of shallow water I saw a form half-hidden by a great basket of interwoven sticks. A tiny bird had fallen—nest and all. And I knew what August meant to teach.

"Don't turn away," August said. "Make your eyes hard." He pointed to a crawdad that nibbled at the bird's head. I felt large with sight. August knew everything. He knew everything except how to live with us.

I hid my face. "He's killing it," I protested.

"That's his food," August said.

I knew that. I knew it from health books with pictures of the Food Chain, but I had never seen what actually took place, and I realized that what I was seeing was life played out before my eyes.

During the next year something changed in our family. My mother grew short-tempered, and complained about how late August came home each night. Her face grew tight, and August stopped taking me to the pond on Sunday evenings.

After a while their arguments stopped, and my mother began to sleep in a different room. Then one night he left, and though I prayed for the moon to bring him back, he returned only for visits.

The day August left, Volusia and Janey Louise moved into our house. Volusia had already worked for us for two years, but now she moved in with Janey Louise and they slept in a room off the kitchen. We believed they would like it there.

Volusia lived with us for eleven and a half years. After six months (but sworn to secrecy) Janey Louise moved into the room with me. Volusia stayed in her small servant-room, and in all those years she let no one set foot inside. Now, more than then, I know there were places in her life where she would not allow me to go.

Volusia entered our life like a storm on wings. She took over the house: cleaned in corners and hung sheets on the line. She cooked meals and made the house smell like food. We came unhinged from our past, and moved constantly like those shapes under the microscope.

And I began, at age ten, to think of a moment as holding all of life inside it, like a pulse in the body. An impulse. I saw the flash of things even better when August was gone, because when he left I could see each moment with the knowledge that I might lose something, then gain something else.

1

What brought me back to Mercy was Volusia's funeral.

She had been sick off and on for a year, so news of her death was not a surprise. Still my body acted surprised. She had survived bouts of pneumonia before. Last summer my mother called to say that Volusia was in Erlanger Hospital. "Maybe you should come," she told me. She thought Volusia might not last through the summer, but by the time I arrived, Volusia was out of the hospital. I went to see her.

She sat in the rocker on the front porch of Joe Sugar's store. Volusia married Joe in 1961, and moved out of our house and into the place above Joe's store. She liked to greet people as they came in. She liked to make them linger.

"You got over the pneumonia without me," I told her.

"Nuu-mon-ya. Sound like the name of some little bitty girl. Maybe some girl too big for her britches. Like you." This is the way she talked to me when she didn't want me to know what she was thinking. She hugged me without standing up, and I leaned over to pull her head against my chest. I could tell how weak she felt. She had the smell of sickness.

"Maybe you came home from the hospital too soon," I told her. "Maybe you need somebody to look after you."

"And you think that's gonna be you?" she said, but she was smiling. "Volusia does all right." She held her mouth stubbornly, as though she had food in it. I kept seeing her mouth in that position when my mother called to tell me she was dead.

I had already told Volusia good-bye. On Easter weekend I had flown back to see her. She lay in bed, thin, struggling to breathe. She had lung cancer, the result of smoking Old Golds for thirty-five years. By Easter the cancer had spread to other parts of her body. She fought for each breath, begging us to relieve her of the pain she was suffering.

"Why are y'all keeping me alive?" she said. She really wanted to know.

We told her there was nothing we could do.

"You could do *some*thing," she said.

The first thing I noticed was that her hospital gown was starched and probably uncomfortable. I went to Belk's and bought her a satin nightdress. Volusia had always loved the feel of satin, and thought it was the material of rich folks. She unwrapped it and saw it lying pink and soft in the tissue paper. It had buttons down the front.

"Bless your heart," she said.

She sat up, and pulled off her hospital gown and put her lumpy arms into the satiny material. For the first time in my life I saw her body—her dark stomach and breasts. She wore panties but nothing else. She slipped on the gown and asked me to button it for her. When she lay back down, she was puffing as though she had run up a hill.

"I got no more breath," she said, embarrassed. "Somebody ought to put me out of my misery—like a old horse."

"You want them to shoot you?"

"Be good as what they're doing now. Be better!" She smiled, and touched the satin front of her gown.

I found I was praying (wordlessly, and with my eyes open) that she wouldn't die. But her own prayers asked for an ending. I imagined our prayers bumping up against each other as they traveled toward God.

"What you do to your hair?" she asked me.

"I cut it."

"That man you been living with like it like that?"

"Johnny." I said his name. "He likes it any way at all."

"When you getting married? I forget."

She wanted a specific date. She hadn't minded my divorce from Lowell Hardison, to whom I was married for only two years. She hated Lowell, though she adored Ty—who would turn seven next month. She liked Johnny, too, but she'd never approved of my living arrangement with him, and asked me often about my plans to marry. She was pretending I'd given her a specific date, and that she couldn't remember it.

"Soon," I said.

"Soon won't say *when*."

"Soon," I repeated, miffed at the turn the conversation had taken.

"I don't mind nagging you," she said. "A sick old woman can nag anybody she wants to."

An attendant brought her lunch in on a tray and she asked me to help her sit up. She told the attendant, a young girl and probably a volunteer, to look at her new gown. The girl smiled and said it was pretty.

I laid the napkin under her chin. "I want you to pray for me," she said, as I opened her carton of milk.

"I will," I promised.

"I want you to pray hard that somebody's gonna come in here and shoot me good. One time."

I laughed and lifted a spoonful of soup toward her mouth. She dabbed at her lips after each sip. I cut the chicken into tiny pieces and gave her bites of rice. I fed her slowly and with exaggerated care. I buttered her roll and watched her mouth take the bites, her tongue moving in and out like a baby bird's.

"That taste good?" I asked. She had fed me like this when I was young, when I stayed home sick.

"It's okay," she said.

"You want me to bring you something from home tomorrow?"

"You gonna cook it?" she asked.

"Yes."

"You any good at cooking?"

"Yes."

"That'd be nice. I'd like to have something with a little taste to it. I'd like to have a good piece of pie."

I knew that even if I brought in the food she wanted that she might leave it on her plate, might not have the appetite to eat it. But I promised anyway and her face brightened with expectation.

2

I looked forward to seeing Mercy in early June. Even returning for Volusia's funeral, I loved coming back to Georgia.

On the plane from Texas I sat next to a man old enough to be my father. He talked to me as though he had a daughter of his own and was pretending I was she. He told me about a trip he took, but I couldn't listen to him. We spoke of news and weather, but I didn't mention Volusia, or the funeral. I didn't want sympathy from him.

The plane's small window made my face enlarged and dark. If I closed my eyes I could bring back Volusia's face, and the smell of her—not the sick smell, but the odor of her arms, strong like overripe fruit.

The plane hit an air pocket and everyone jumped. Sunlight broke through a cloud. One thing seemed to cause another: the thought of Volusia formed an air pocket, made everyone jump; our jumpiness startled the sun, broke clouds apart, and the man beside me began to talk again.

We hit another air pocket, and the pilot spoke in his scratchy mechanical voice to say that everything was normal. We laughed nervously. The clouds formed themselves into the shapes of fish, then unformed.

I hadn't seen Janey Louise in three years. The politics of the seventies had pulled us apart. Her friends told her not to trust me, and mine were wary of us.

One holiday a year we returned to Mercy with our children. Jane had two sons—Max, (the same age as Ty) and Sammy, who was three years younger. Max and Ty looked forward to seeing each other at Christmas or Thanksgiving.

Three years ago we missed our holiday visit, so during the summer Jane came to visit me in Texas. Max and Sammy stayed at home and Ty was at YMCA camp.

When Jane got off the plane that day in Texas, her hair was pulled into a sleek bun at the back of her neck, and her skin shone like moonlight. I thought I looked pretty good myself, but I noticed something in the way she walked or held her head that set her apart from me.

She was pleased when I told her she looked sophisticated, and our whole first day together was comfortable, until we went shopping at Neiman Marcus.

We tried on nightgowns. We wanted to find something that would drive our men crazy. Jane was married to Bandy Johnson, a detective in the Chicago Police Department, and I'd been living with Johnny for two years.

As we tried on lingerie, we felt like girls again. We selected elegant but outrageous peignoirs. We said peig*noir* with exaggerated accents, and we moved into each other's dressing rooms to approve our choices.

But the saleslady kept checking on us. She hovered and counted our items endlessly, speaking in a polite, tight voice. Her name was Darla and everything she said sounded very proper.

Jane asked for another color and size in a particular gown. When Darla handed Jane the gown, she slammed the hanger against the door.

"She's being a bitch," I said.

"That's *not* it. If you think that's it, I don't even know who you are."

"What do you mean?"

"Let's go, Evie," Jane said.

"Wait! I have to get dressed."

Jane pulled her clothes on and left the room in a rush. She opened my dressing-room door.

"What're you doing?" I was still buttoning my blouse.

"I told you, let's go. I'm leaving."

"Come on, Jane. Don't do this." I wanted us to get back to having fun.

"Didn't you see how she kept counting everything? She watched us like a hawk." Jane wanted me to be sympathetic.

"Come *on*," I begged.

Jane walked away fast. I couldn't say what was in Darla's mind, but I knew what was going on in Jane's.

"Listen," I said. "You know how many times we've done this? I mean, I *always* leave with you. You know that. I just get tired of it."

She kept walking, but I caught up with her. "Remember that restaurant last time? I didn't want to leave that night. Bandy didn't want to leave either." I knew I was pushing her too far, but I'd already started on this track. "Sometimes you just get on your high horse."

"High horse? You're not looking around, Evie. You're not seeing what's going on."

"That woman was just as rude to me," I said. "Why does everything have to be about race?"

Jane stopped and held up a hand as if to demand silence. She looked like a woman I might have just met. "Everything *is* about race," she said calmly, as though she'd just returned from a rally.

"Not to *me* it isn't. Sometimes it's about being in a bad mood, or just scared, or sick. Sometimes it's about one person not liking another—no matter *who* they are."

"I can't believe you," she said. We were standing on the sidewalk in the middle of downtown Houston. "All of a sudden it seems like you've been stupid all your life."

Jane left the next day. We spoke to each other politely, but cooly. Then, right before she left, Jane asked if she could have a small piece of coral that I kept on my coffee table. On the night she arrived she had admired it, and Johnny told her we had picked it up off a reef when we went scuba diving the summer before. I cherished it, but couldn't refuse Jane's request to take it home. Even as a child she had been able to talk me out of small treasures.

During our first spring after August left, I showed Janey Louise a yellow moth I had found. It had two dark spots, like eyes, on its wings. I was letting Tucker keep it in his room. Tucker was almost seven and we looked up the species in one of August's old biology books. It was an Io moth.

I took Janey Louise to Tucker's room to show her the moth's markings, and she said the wings looked so beautiful it was hard to believe someone hadn't painted it like that. She asked Tucker if she could take it to school. Tucker said no.

Tucker said he had decided to start a dead-butterfly collection and to keep this as his first specimen; but Janey Louise told him this was a moth not a butterfly and that this moth was magic. She said we should keep it in a special box, then told us that she had such a box at her other house, the house on Latham Street where she really lived.

When Tucker would not give it to her, Janey Louise told him that both butterfly and moth collections could bring bad luck to people, and that she would keep the Io in a box next to her bed. We could look at it anytime we wanted to.

"You'll get the bad luck on *you*," Tucker told her.

"No, I won't," she said. "Because I know ways to keep the bad part out. Ways, if I tell, that could get me in more trouble than the moth."

She said that her brother Albert (before he went into the Army) had started a butterfly collection, "and in only a few days someone knocked him down and took all his money." She asked if Tucker wanted that kind of thing to happen to him, and Tucker said no.

I didn't believe what Janey Louise told us, but I never had the nerve to question her. She had a way of telling something that made a person not want to challenge her. She could take what she wanted in this way, and over the years was able to make me do things I didn't want to do. Once I stole three lipsticks from the five-and-ten-cent store on Foster Street. I think that even now, if Jane suggested something, I would do it to please her.

Our letters for the past three years had been absurdly polite. No funny stories about the children, no curiosity about each other's lives. Our questions were ones a stranger might ask of any family. Whenever I called her, I listened for a sign that the chill in her voice was gone; maybe she listened the same way to mine.

We didn't know how to be together anymore, and I wondered what seeing her would be like. I was afraid of saying something offensive, and no doubt she expected to be offended. We couldn't laugh at anything. I wished we could just be *us* again. I wished we could just be *us*.

3

The man beside me on the plane was asleep, but he awoke when the young, gangly stewardess offered us lunch. He began to talk, and I felt I ought to listen. A thin framework of light fell through the plane's small window.

The stewardess put our meal on the tray in front of us—pale meat, two vegetables, a roll, and two cookies wrapped in a neat package. The dishes were small, like doll's dishes. The meal didn't look real. To eat it was like pretending to eat and I found the whole experience very pleasurable, like a game. I asked for coffee and a glass of tomato juice. To have these things brought to me felt luxurious, and I pretended this could go on for the rest of my life.

Finally I told the man next to me that I wanted to sleep for a while, because I was returning for a funeral and would be very busy once I reached my destination. The way I said it sounded formal, as a teacher sounds.

"I'm sorry," the man said. "Was this someone close?"

I said she was close.

I dozed and dreamed about the day when August still lived at home, though in the dream I also moved into a later time, when he was no longer there.

We were in the house and August had come to kiss me good night. Tucker had not yet been born. August brought my toys upstairs, but didn't fuss at me for not bringing them up myself. He dropped them on the floor in a corner. He never cared if things were neat, something I loved in him.

Then he did a strange thing. He sang. He had never sung in real life because he couldn't carry a tune; but in the dream he sang several songs very well. Even in my dreaming I was surprised that he had such a fine voice.

When I woke, I remembered the song, and I began to wonder if August might return to Georgia for Volusia's funeral. The song was

"Dream a Little Dream with Me," which I'd sung many times before, not only with August, but also with Janey Louise on the street in front of the beauty parlor. Sometimes ladies came out and gave us dimes.

In our beds at night, after the lights were turned off, Janey Louise and I had whispered together about our fathers.

"My daddy died when I was real little," Janey Louise told me. "I think I wasn't even born yet. Mama says I was still in her stomach when he died. She said it was bound to happen, because of how he was."

"You mean to say you never even *saw* him?" I couldn't imagine someone not ever seeing her father.

"Seems like I did. Mama told me about him. Albert did, too. Albert was already ten by the time I was born." Janey Louise couldn't say anything without mentioning Albert.

"Albert showed me pictures," she said, "and he gave me a shirt that belong to him. Mama kept a picture of him beside her bed. I used to look at it. Now she keeps it above the stove."

I knew she was talking about her house on Latham Street.

"Can I see the picture sometime?" I asked. My voice went straight up to the ceiling, and Janey Louise turned toward me in the other bed. She didn't answer. "Could I go to the place on Latham Street and see it?" I was curious about her father, and about her house.

"We'd have to ride the bus there. It's two buses to catch."

"I never rode on a bus before," I confessed.

"It's no big deal. I do it all the time."

"You sit in the back like Volusia does?"

"I have to."

"Maybe if you're with me, we won't have to. Don't tell Volusia or Mama."

"I won't." Janey Louise rolled onto her side and sat up. "I have another picture of my daddy, in a uniform. He looks regular and good."

"Can I see that one, too?"

"I got that one here."

"You do?" I reached to turn on the lamp and saw Janey Louise lift part of her mattress. She took out a small photograph, fluted around the edges.

"This's even before he knew Mama. He's just eighteen." The large man stood beside a small, clapboard house. The yard was dirt and I could see the face of someone, a woman, at the window.

"Is that *his* mama?" I asked.

"I don't know."

We studied the picture a few moments without speaking, then I switched off the lamp and Janey Louise put the photograph back beneath the mattress. We went to sleep. Neither of us knew what else to say.

Childhood is a long season to be without a father.

4

At night before putting us to bed, August made hot cocoa and brought it to me and Tucker. He read stories until we finished sipping the whipped cream that melted into the chocolate. Tucker sipped his longer than I did, so when I finished mine and Tucker was still working away at his cup, I felt very alone. When August was through reading, he leaned down close to whisper a string of nonsense into our ears. He made us laugh.

And I could smell all the weathers on him—his thick, Vaseliney hair oil and the cheap cologne he wore. His arms smelled like bushes, because of the time he spent outside. But on that almost-spring night in 1949, I took his dry face into my hands and held it to look at him longer in the dark room. He smiled before he pulled away.

My father's face had many different weathers. A cold wind could blow in behind his eyes and keep its place for a whole season. Even on sunny days his mouth, or any playful expression, could not hide the cliff of wind that hung behind his eyes. My mother said he always wanted to be somewhere else. This had been true for years.

"Your father is a dreamer," my mother said.

We all knew he had one main dream: to go to the Sea of Cortez. So what happened on that night in 1949 was not a complete surprise. I even had a premonition about it.

A few days before August left our house, as I walked on the road beside the river, I felt a tingling in my arms. The day before that I had noticed how birds flew in crisscross patterns before me on the dirt road to the creek. So I knew something was about to happen. I was only ten years old and could not imagine yet what my own life was going to look like. For that reason, I worried a lot.

One night August tucked us into bed, then lingered at the doorway, standing awhile in the light from the hall. The sense of him stayed in my head—enlarged like the shadow of a person, not a real person at all. All his weathers stiffened and became a hard silhouette of a man, with no face. From that day he grew into a form that could disrupt dreams and make the dull boredom of my days chafe against the edge of something real.

Tucker had already turned over in bed and was going to sleep when August paused at the door. He didn't notice how August had read a story describing the Sea of Cortez, and he didn't notice either how August stopped in the middle of his reading—mind and voice halting, so that I knew he was telling us something important.

"Thousands of years ago," August said, "mountains collapsed and settled into the sea." He made everything sound big and faraway. "Now, when you swim underwater there, you can swirl around the tops of those mountains. And you can see hills underneath the water, like little secrets." He looked at me, and I felt fabulous. I sat up and asked him to take me there, as he had taken me to the pond and the river.

"There's a mysterious island," he said, "and a sea full of strange creatures. If I go there, I'll send you something from under the sea." His face grew full of light. When he left our room, he did not close the door all the way.

In the middle of the night Tucker moved over to my bed.

"I want to get in with you," he said. The clock showed 3 A.M., and he had been awakened by our mother talking loudly on the phone.

"Why?"

"I just do. I heard something."

"What'd you hear?"

"Mama was yelling at Daddy, and I think he's gone. She thinks so, too."

"Why does she think that? She tell you?"

"She said it on the phone to Miz Marsh. And she called Volusia, I think. She was crying. I heard her. She said she thinks he's gone."

"No, he isn't." But I believed Tucker's words more than my own. "He gave us cocoa, and read to us, and everything." I could not stop thinking about the way he paused at the door.

Tucker snuggled down under the covers as though he planned to stay. "Don't think you're sleeping here," I told him. "Not all night."

"I won't. I'm just getting warm." He pulled the covers onto his chest. "It's my fault."

"What is?"

"That he had to leave. The other day I got in trouble at school for fighting with Harold Percy, and I gave Harold a black eye."

"You gave him one last year."

"Uh-uh, that was his brother. Anyway, this time they called Daddy to come in. Mama too, but she came late. Daddy said he'd already taken care of it, but Mama wanted to say something to the principal, so that caused a big ruckus. Mama started yelling and she yelled at Daddy all the way home. I'm afraid I've been so bad they could send me to jail. Things happen in jail. Things too terrible to even think up."

"I heard, too." I turned to Tucker, because he wasn't looking at me and I thought he needed to. "Things like rats that get into your food and eat it before you do, and other things. Worse. What people do to other people, torturing—gouging eyeballs with a dirty spoon, or digging sticks under your fingernails. Things like that."

Tucker began to cry. "I don't want to. If they come to torture me, I'll run away." He began to cry harder. "I'll jump into the pond."

"They won't silly. You're not going to any jail. You haven't *done* anything. There's no way a jail would even *take* you."

"It wouldn't?"

"They won't even let you go in unless you hurt somebody real bad, like with a knife. Or else not pay your taxes."

"I don't have taxes."

"So, see?" I lay back down.

Tucker relaxed and let his side push up against me. He was warm, and the heat of his body made the covers warm. "You can stay a little while, I guess." That was the last thing I remembered saying before drifting off to sleep.

When we woke the next morning, August was gone. The day was March 18th, and though rain came early that morning (even before dawn), the light cleared off to a freshness that was unusual for March in Mercy, Georgia. The ground lay wet and muddy, warm like spring, but it was too early.

Everyone knew this was a false spring.

My mother did not make us go to school the next day. She infused the house with common sense by informing us at breakfast that our father had left in the night and that his departure was something she'd known might happen.

"Your father has dreams he thinks he has to follow and no one can do a thing about it." She turned to get out a clean dishrag, then put it back. Her face screwed itself up into a terrible form. "But he loves you," she said, turning around. "I can tell you that."

Tucker ate breakfast thinking his father would be back by suppertime, but I planned to write a letter, even if I had no place to send it. I would write numerous letters, so when the time came I would have them ready. And though I didn't say it, I began at that moment to think of calling him August. I thought this might please him.

"Why can't we go to school?" Tucker asked.

Volusia came in quickly through the back door holding up her umbrella as though she might hit somebody with it. She told Tucker to hush. But when she came in, she brought with her the hope that all of us needed.

"You hush!" Then she motioned for my mother to sit down. Her large body was hopeful, and Mama sat in the kitchen chair, relieved to have Volusia in the house. "Volusia's gonna take care of things now."

Volusia often spoke of herself in the third person. She knew how to move quickly into a rhythm around the house that felt like a natural geography.

The day turned hot bright, and Volusia washed all the sheets and hung them on the line. Mama worked along with her, doing whatever Volusia said, and at lunchtime they sat together at the kitchen table and looked out at the sheets drying in the sun. I had never seen my mother and Volusia sit at the kitchen table together, and I wondered if this was another sign of changes to come. I wondered what people would think if they came to our back door.

"Where's Janey Louise?" I asked Volusia. I wished for Janey Louise to be here, too.

"School. She has to go to school." Volusia did not turn to look at me as she spoke, but handed me a wet rag and told me to wipe off the counters. "She can't decide not to go to school like you folks can. She got to be there, else the truant officer come out and says, 'That girl of yours playing hooky, Volusia? You keeping her out for something? You making her work, or is she just footloosing around?'

"And I say, 'No, sir, I don't think Janey Louise ever footloosed a day in her life. She been sick with the chicken pox and I had to nurse her well.' That's last fall when he come out there to the house and accuse us like that. For nothing."

"I am so hungry," Tucker said.

"Whatchu want?"

"A ham sandwich, and some milk. I want four cookies."

"You don't need a thing." She gave him two cookies and some fruit cocktail. "Now when you finish that, you go out and bring in my grip."

Volusia had an old suitcase full of clothes that she called a grip. Tucker liked being bossed around by her.

Mama said nothing, but stood at the sink and looked out at the sheets. I could not stop staring at her. My mother's back looked like a dress on a hanger.

Janey Louise came in the late afternoon. Volusia had given her bus fare to come to our house, but hadn't offered any explanation. The note said: *Come over to the Bells' house. Bring clothes to stay.*

"What happened?" Janey Louise asked when she entered the kitchen, but Volusia shook her head, indicating that she should be silent. After dinner I took Janey Louise to the backyard, and told her that August was gone, though I pretended he had left to work on a research project.

"You and Volusia are gonna stay here tonight," I told her. "Maybe you can stay here lots of nights." I wanted to make it sound fun.

"Where'll we sleep?" Janey Louise pulled at her dress.

"In the room off the kitchen."

"They's just one bed in there."

"There's a cot for you."

"But you got *two* beds in your room. Ask your mama."

When I asked if Janey Louise could sleep in my room, Volusia broke in and said no.

"Now, don't start causing trouble and wanting everything for yourselves. You both being selfish and not thinking of your mama who won't need y'all asking for something you can't have."

My mother didn't say anything. She looked sad and lost, and she didn't know how to answer us. I knew we would ask again on another night.

"Where do *I* sleep?" Tucker said. He didn't want to be ousted from my room. He still thought our dad would be home before bedtime.

"Where you always do," Volusia said. "Now I don't want to hear another word about it." She gave a look to Janey Louise as though Janey Louise had caused trouble and was completely to blame.

5

March 20, 1949

Dear Daddy,

Where did you go? Why did you read to us and then go away? Did you know you were going to do that? I think you are mean, if you knew. People have asked about you. They ask how you are, but that is not what they want to know. They want to know *where* you are and *why* you went away, and I would like to know that too. When Tucker asks when you are coming home, what should I tell him? If you come back, Tucker will be good and not get into any more fights. I will be good too.

I told Tucker that I was going to write you a letter, and if he wanted to say something I would write it down for him. So far he has not thought of anything. He is a very stubborn person.

You will not guess what has happened in the last few days. Volusha moved into our house and Janey Louise along with her. Janey Louise is just a year older than I am, but she is about two years taller. They are our live-ins until you decide to come home, whenever that might be. Volusha sleeps in the room off the kitchen and Janey Louise sleeps in there too on a cot. I do not know how this will work out, because Janey Louise wants to sleep in my room, but Mama won't let her. Janey Louise is fun to be around. She thinks up good things to do.

I am wondering if the Sea of Cortez if a very long way off, because I do not know where to mail this letter, so I will save it until I hear from you. Don't wait too long.

From Your Daughter,
Genevieve Bell

P.S. I have taken some of your Nature books and put them beside my bed, and I look through them every night—the things you showed me. I hope I can understand these things by myself, because I was very, very interested when you explained them to me. If you call us, whenever you do, I will ask you about night crawlers and katydids (which is a name I love).

March 3 0, 1949

Dear Daddy,

The other night after supper Volusha talked about her husband who died. His name was Finney. He was Janey Louise's daddy, but Janey Louise says Volusha never talks about him much. So this was not usual. There are pictures of her daddy at their house on Latham Street, but Janey Louise has one she keeps under the mattress. I have seen this picture.

He is a handsome man, even though he is colored, and I am not ashamed to say it. He is very tall and has shoulders like a fighter. His skin is smooth on his face, but rough on his arms. You can see this because he has on a shirt with the sleeves cut off. He has worked outside and has a look on his face that is like a smirk, but not mean, more like he has a secret he can't tell—one he's just busting to say, but can't.

I did not say any of what I thought to Janey Louise. I just said, "He looks nice. Where's he from?" I asked this trying to be polite. But she did not want to talk, she just wanted to show me him. Sometimes Volusha and Janey Louise laugh at me when I say things that are polite, but don't mean anything. They think it is funny.

Another thing, Volusha wakes me and Tucker up every morning. She gets us ready for school. It is better than when Mama did it, because Volusha is what people call a Morning Person. She is in the best mood every morning, so we get in a good mood too. I have always been okay in the morning, but not Tucker. He is cross, though now, with Volusha he is not so bad and will even make a joke at the breakfast table. This is unbelievable. Mama is usually gone by the time we have breakfast.

She took on work in Kresses basement and leaves the house by seven.

Volusha does everything around the house like Mama used to do, and Mama comes home and sits down to supper like you used to do. It is the strangest thing, Mama says, and I agree. But I am not sure why it is strange. Janey Louise says it's because Mama Agnes (that is what she calls Mama) is not a wife anymore, but she is still a mother, and usually those things go together. Volusha says that Janey Louise is exactly right.

Your Loving Daughter,
Genevieve Bell

P.S. I hope you will call and give us your address soon. Mama says you will.

April 8, 1949

Dear Daddy,

We had Tucker's birthday supper last night, but you did not call us, and I was so mad I almost decided not to write to you ever again. I hope you do not forget my birthday, when it comes. Volusha and Mama made three desserts to make up for you not being here. If you had been here, you would have liked our meal, I can tell you that.

I wish you were here. Mama says she is surprised you have not called, but she is glad to get the checks that are coming in. She says you are always some place different. I think she is going to call a lawyer, and she seems mad all the time at you and at us.

I want you to know that I am writing down all I see at the pond, just like you told me to do. But even though I write it down, I cannot send anything to you. Get it, Dad? Do you *get* it? I mean, I am tired of writing letters that I cannot send anywhere. You see, it would seem like a conversation we were having. A long all-the-time conversation, and I would not feel so lonesome. I would know you were hearing me, but lately it seems like my words go out into thin air, like I am sending up a kite that never gets far from me. Sometimes I say to myself, say it out loud—Why even do this? But I do not get an answer.

Your Lonesome Daughter.
Evie Bell

April 18, 1949

Dear Daddy,

I was very happy to hear your voice on the phone, and I will look for the letter and picture postcards you have sent to me. I am also happy to have an address where I can send my letters to you. You will love hearing from me. Tucker drew four pictures for you. I drew one of a bird I saw and didn't know what it was.

I like hearing about what you are doing, and I'm glad you have a good job. But I do not understand why I cannot ask you when you will come back. Mama told me not to ask, and I try not to, but I can't see why. I picture you in my mind on that island looking for things people have never seen before. I wish I could be with you, because when you show me things, I learn them so good. You are the best teacher I have ever had.

Me and Tucker went to the creek a few days ago, and now we are all itchy. Doc Beryl came by and told us to stay away from the poison ivy and poison oak. He showed us pictures of what it looked like, but sometimes a picture won't make you know it. I asked him to show me outside, so he took me and Tucker into the woods and we walked until we found some. I was careful for the rest of the walk, but Tucker kept jumping over logs, showing off for Doc Beryl. He acted like he was about two years old. There are some people you can't do anything with.

I will send all my letters to you, and Tucker's pictures. I hope you have not gone on another trip, and that I will hear from you soon.

Lovingly Yours,
Evie

In April, Janey Louise came down with the flu. She wanted to be sick at her own home, so Volusia took her back to Latham Street, and Tucker and I had to do most of Volusia's work around the house.

My mother let me visit her after school at Kresses, and buy candy. I came home with several small white bags of candy corn, jelly beans, and malted-milk balls. I saved the candy corn for Janey Louise, so she would like me.

After a week of the flu, Janey Louise and Volusia came back. Volusia said she had received a letter from Albert. Albert was in the army, and getting a letter from him was Volusia's highest pleasure. Sometimes she brought the letter to our house, and read it to us. She was proud of her reading. She said her dead husband was not able to read, and most of his trouble she blamed on that fact. We had no reason not to believe her.

When school let out, I began to rise early and go to the pond. I missed August. I missed having him there to tell me what I'd discovered. I tried to be a teacher to myself. Sometimes I went to the river, almost a mile away; sometimes Janey Louise and I rode our bikes there.

We brought home scoops of water and placed them beneath the microscope. I tried to teach Janey Louise and Tucker as August had taught me, but they weren't interested. Still, I learned more that summer than if August had actually been there. That was my first experience as a teacher.

Sometimes I sneaked out to wander alone at the pond. I sat for long periods of time waiting to see something. If nothing rose to the surface of the water, I reached down to stir up the sand. Animals scattered and came back. They hardly ever collided.

My body grew nourished with studying, and I wrote down everything I saw—for August. I missed him. I missed his brows that could bring a soft rain, and his voice that could come in and dry things off. There were times when he still lived at home that he could move into the house like a wind. He might walk fast into a room, not shouting or speaking, but bringing in a sudden change like the excitement of a storm. I longed to feel his weather around me again.

August taught me to see, and then to see again, until I could build in my mind a structure of reality that was bound to patterns in the world. He wanted nature, and especially water, to be a window to the rest of my life.

When I went to Corny's Pond, I developed an eye for times of feeding, and I recognized creatures that could hang in the water without movement. These creatures achieved a stillness I could not imagine. Even when I looked at them, I couldn't imagine it.

6

One Saturday, after August had been gone for four months, I took Janey Louise downtown to Turnbull's department store. The store was new and had held a grand opening the week before. My mother told us that the bathrooms had pink-and-white tiles, and that the sinks were made of marble. I promised to take Janey Louise to see it.

No one noticed as we went through the doors, but as we walked down the aisle beside the perfume counter, a lady pointed to us and told Janey Louise that she couldn't come into the store, she had to wait outside. I nodded to let the lady know we heard, but we still went toward the back where I saw a sign that said: LADIES.

As we pushed through the large door, we bumped into Mrs. Casy, a friend of my mother's. When she saw Janey Louise, she waved her hand and said, "Shoo, now." She looked as if she had seen a goose. "Both of you. Shoo." She touched my head. "You know good and well you're not supposed to bring her in here, Genevieve Bell."

"Hello, Mrs. Casy," I said, hoping she might change her mind.

"You know better than this." She gave me a hard look that said she would speak to my mother. I knew that Janey Louise had turned around and was running out the side door. I knew her feelings were hurt, and that Mrs. Casy had embarrassed her. I thought maybe I should run outside with her, but decided to walk past Mrs. Casy into one of the large-tiled stalls. I would tell Janey Louise about it. I didn't have to go out just because she did. The toilet paper was pink with white roses. I tried not to use much of it.

When I came out, Janey Louise stood, without moving, in front of Turnbull's biggest window. She looked in at the merchandise. I stood beside her for a moment and pretended to look, too. Neither of us mentioned what had just happened.

"What can we do now?" I asked. Janey Louise didn't answer. I wanted her to ignore what had happened.

She began to walk along the edge of town into the woods. I

followed her as far as she wanted to go. Then she went behind a tree and squatted to relieve herself. I wanted to do this with her. I wished I'd waited.

"Don't let anybody see me," she said. The hem of her dress touched the ground in a circle.

That night, before bed, I told Janey Louise to come out in the backyard a minute, that I wanted to show her something.

"Don't you two run off anywhere. You got to go to bed soon," Volusia yelled. Janey Louise still slept in Volusia's room, though she stayed one or two nights a week in mine. We were wearing down my mother with our requests.

"What do you want to show me?" Janey Louise said.

"Nothing." I spoke very low. "It's just that Mrs. Casy is *stupid*. I just hate her, don't you?"

"Sometimes, when I hold my breath," Janey Louise spoke to the yard and trees, "I can hold it until I am *gone*. I can leave my body and not be in it."

When she said this, I knew what it meant to be "beside yourself."

"Next time," I said, "I won't go into Turnbull's bathroom. I won't go in at all. I'll wait and go in the woods with you." I wanted her to turn her face and look at me. "It'll be fun," I said.

"You are my best friend," Janey Louise said to the yard.

The next day Volusia received three letters from Albert. She made a big dinner and promised to read them out loud to us. She stayed in a good mood all day. She baked johnnycake and let us dip it into milk. When she read the letters, she let Tucker sit in her lap.

She never asked my mother to read anything for her. She was proud. We all sat in the light of the kitchen with trees growing dark outside and a large, hard circle drawn around us.

I hoped August would read my letters with such fervor.

June 6, 1949

Dear August,

I am calling you August now. I have been calling you that for a long time, but only in my mind. Now it is out loud. And I am calling Mama—Agnes. She hates this change. Tell me what you think of it.

My hair is so long. Agnes says it is as long as Aunt Myra's and the same color. Volusia calls it strawberry blond. She says it is what people will call me beautiful for someday. She says that women have one or two things that make people call them beautiful, and that mine is my hair. It goes down past my shoulders. Agnes says if you had been a girl, you would look like me. Tucker laughed when she said it. He got so tickled he fell off his chair laughing. Who knows what he was thinking about—you in a dress or you with hair down to your shoulders. It is a funny thing to think about.

I wish I could see you so I could show you some things. These are the things I would show you: my gerbil, the cat (you remember the cat, only he's bigger), my box of old jewelry collected from Mama and Myra, and Fanny Bledsoe's grandmama's brooch, the notebook I write in everyday, a shell collection from since I was seven, two goats on the Wompler's hill, and the new twins born to the Johnson family. That makes six kids they have.

Gotta go now.

Lovingly Yours,
Evie Bell

P.S. Tucker and me are making costumes for the summer festival at Corny's Pond on June 12th. I am going to be a Gypsy who tells people's fortunes. I will charge ten cents, and if you send ten cents I will tell yours. I have a crystal ball made out of wax paper. Tucker wants to be a pirate and ride in a canoe on the pond, but all he really wants to do is carry the sword Volusha made for him out of cardboard and tin.

July 10, 1949

Dear August,

I am sorry I have not been writing to you as much, but we go swimming everyday. On the Fourth of July we took a trip to the ocean. Janey Louise and Volusha could not go with us. Mama Agnes says they cannot go with us everywhere the way somebody white can. I wanted Janey Louise to go with me so much, but instead I took a friend of mine named Margaret Turnbull.

Margaret is rich, and sometimes when I spend the night at her house, I can see how rich she is. Her father owns the department store downtown, and she gets almost anything she wants. Sometimes, though, she is mean.

Justine Branch is my best friend. She goes swimming with me at the pond. She is not rich, but she knows a lot of boys. She is teaching me how to flirt. Justine says that she already has a Love Life.

Daddy, sometimes I imagine that I see you downtown or somewhere, and that you have come back and will see me in just a minute. Sometimes I imagine things so hard that I think they are true. And in a way they are—for a little while. I even tell my friends that I have heard from you and that you are coming back. I feel so happy when I say it, but then the world comes back in and I know you are not here.

I was wondering if maybe you could come back this fall. I was thinking about Thanksgiving, or Christmas. So if you could think about it too, then maybe it could come true.

Lots of Love,
Evie

August 26, 1949

Dear August,

In answer to your question about Tucker—Yes, he is giving Mama some trouble, but not too bad. He is giving *me* trouble though, in case you wish to know. He has turned sneaky, and he spies on people. He spies on me.

Tucker talks about you a lot, but he gets things wrong. He has a picture of you in his room. One (before he was born) of you and Mama and me. (I am just three.) Mama is big with him, so he thinks of himself as being in the picture too—like he is just under her skirt or something. I tell him I don't know if that counts, because he wasn't even born yet. But he says it does count, so I don't argue. He keeps the picture hid under his clock on the nightstand, and I don't know this for sure, but I bet he looks at it every night before bed. *I* would.

Anyway, we saw a snake at the creek. It was the prettiest thing—yellow and black, like some Indian had painted it. But Tucker killed it with a stick, beat it until it was dead. It was so scared. Do you think that is right? I thought it was straight-out mean, and I told him so. Scared or not, that snake wasn't going to chase us or anything. It was just sleeping there on the path to the creek, and Tucker killed it.

When I got back home I told Mama, but she didn't do a thing. She said maybe he should have killed it. I wish you would speak to Tucker in your next letter about the wilderness and how things should live. What I am afraid of is that he could end up as a mean killer-person. What do you think? And another thing—sometimes when I'm taking a bath, I see him open the door and peek in. At first, I didn't let on that I knew he was doing this, but now there is a lock on the door, and I use it.

I will close now. Jancy Louise says hey. I keep thinking you are coming home soon. Now I don't know. Sometimes when I think about you, my heart feels punched by a big hard fist and I have to stop and wait until it quits.

Your Most Loving Daughter,
Evie Bell

7

Janey Louise liked to cut pictures out of ladies magazines. She chose glamorous women with fantastic clothes. White women. She never chose a boat or a faraway place—to her, the women themselves seemed faraway.

She told me that when she grew up she planned to lie around all day with long fingernails, worrying about whether or not they would break. She imagined inviting people in for fancy dinners. We had seen these people in the movies talking on the telephone.

Every Saturday afternoon Mama Agnes drove us to the movies at the Riviera Theatre, but we couldn't sit together. The town had a strict code about colored people going in through a particular door and bringing their own drinks and popcorn. Janey Louise had to go up the steps to the balcony, and I was not allowed in the balcony, so we began to plot ways to sit together.

First, I snuck into the balcony with Janey Louise to watch a Loretta Young movie. But I didn't like it. I didn't like the way everyone around me talked to people on the screen, speaking in response to what someone was saying. No one actually believed the movie star could hear them, but still they spoke out loud.

Loretta Young would say, "Have Beulah bring it out to me on the porch. I'll wait out there."

Then someone near me said, "*I'll* bring something out to that porch. She don't know what *wait* is." And someone else said, "She don't know what *porch* is," and laughed.

The way they said it made me think I'd missed something about the story. I asked Janey Louise what they were talking about, but she wouldn't speak to me. Someone behind us made a remark about my presence in the balcony, but I couldn't make out what they said.

I never wanted to go to the balcony again, but Janey Louise couldn't wait to sneak in downstairs with me. All week she worried me about a plan.

The next Saturday when my mother dropped us off, I'd already decided that Janey Louise should sneak in through the exit door and sit on the floor near my seat.

"You'll have to stay low," I told her, "because if the usher sees you, I'll be in more trouble than you will. Anyway," I said, "they can tell by your hair what you are." Janey Louise touched her head. "I mean, they would *know* it was you."

I positioned her in the alleyway next to the exit. "Wait till the picture show starts," I said. "When they start the newsreel, I'll open the door and you crawl in. I'll act like I'm looking for somebody, or else like I might be deciding to leave, then changing my mind."

Janey Louise nodded, her hand still on her hair. "I'll crawl in *real* fast," she promised. "But don't let me miss the cartoon. I don't want to miss the cartoon."

"Stay *low*," I said, and went to buy our tickets.

The newsreel began and a man's voice told about a threat of war in North Korea. He spoke of the polio virus, and pronounced its whole name: poliomyelitis.

I knew about polio because teachers at school had discussed the symptoms. Every day after lunch they told us to rest our heads on our desks—so we wouldn't get polio. As the newsreel ended, I went to the exit. A curtain blocked the door, so no one noticed the small amount of light I let in.

"Hurry," I whispered. Janey Louise had scooted quickly by my legs, but I hadn't seen her. "Hurry up!" I said.

"I'm right here!" She tugged at my dress.

"Shhhh," someone said.

I sat down, but couldn't tell where Janey Louise was hiding. The usher walked once down the aisle. I sat very still through the cartoon, assuming Janey Louise was somewhere watching it, but I didn't know where she was.

A swell of music began the movie and everyone settled in to watch Rita Hayworth. I'd never cared much for Miss Hayworth, but Janey Louise thought her hair looked like a waterfall.

Then I saw Janey Louise crawl on her belly beneath the seats, coming toward my row. No one sat in front of me, so I let her proceed, but she caught her dress on the bottom of a seat and I heard it rip. Janey Louise said a bad word. Volusia would ask how her dress got torn, and we would have to lie.

As she reached the row directly in front of me, I held out my foot to make her stop. She poked her head up and strained to see above the seats.

"Stay as low as you can," I said.

"I will!"

She acted mad about something, and I decided never to sneak her in again. I felt sorry she had to sit on the floor, but I didn't see why she had to be so cross.

The theatre was almost empty, because the show had run for almost ten days, and in fact Janey Louise had already seen it once. She knew what was going to happen by what people said, or by the music, and she strained upward telling me, "I got to see this part," whenever she knew Rita Hayworth was going to dance, or cry.

She finally decided to pull herself again beneath the rows of seats, back down toward the front, where she could lie on her back and watch the show above her. When we got home she said it was the greatest experience of her life so far: to watch a picture show from that position. She said I should try it.

The next time we went to the Riviera Theatre, Janey Louise headed straight for the balcony. She had ruined her dress that day with me, and Volusia had been furious. So we sat apart. Sometimes, I sat with Margaret or Justine downstairs, but if the movie became especially sad, or funny, I turned to wave to the balcony. Then Janey Louise would throw a candy wrapper, rolled into a small hard ball, at my head—to let me know she saw.

After the Rita Hayworth escapade, Janey Louise began to tack movie pictures onto the walls of Volusia's room. Volusia hated those pictures.

"What kind of fool thing is this?" she said. "What you think I wanna look at that for?" She swept with one hand and grabbed a fistful of pictures off the wall.

"Mama, don't. I'll take them down." Janey Louise looked afraid that her pictures might tear.

"All you think about is movie stars and wild dresses."

"That's what I wanna be!" Janey Louise packed her movie-star pictures into a box, and when she began sleeping in my room, she kept them under the bed. Mama Agnes bought her a scrapbook at Kresses so she could paste the pictures in. Mama Agnes said she wanted Janey Louise to be ambitious.

The scrapbook was kept under the bed with the box, but on the day my mother said Janey Louise could move into my room for good, she brought it out and put it on the shelf. On that day Mama Agnes bought blue chenille bedspreads and a silver brush (which no one was supposed to use) and some plastic flowers in a vase. Our room looked like a magazine picture.

"I am on-my-way," Janey Louise said when she walked in. She danced around the room, holding her arms high like Miss Hayworth.

"Humph!" said Volusia, bringing in fresh towels from downstairs.

8

In Texas, I'd been teaching biology to seventh graders for six years. I taught them the way August taught me, by giving them hands-on experience. Yesterday, before leaving for Georgia, I took my students to the woods.

Our assignment was to find ladybugs and put them in matchboxes with some sour grass. All morning we carried them around like jewels, opening the box at times to bring them out and see them glitter on our hands and sleeves. Some got away. At noon we put them on the lunch table with some leaves and flower petals. I would not allow the students to assign a name, or feel ownership.

At the end of the day, I told everyone to release the *coccinella novemnotatas* (Nine-Spotted Ladybugs). The students liked the Latin name. They said it with Spanish accents. We let all the ladybugs go, and when we returned to the classroom everyone felt strangely bereft.

We sat quietly, and I endorsed their feeling of loss—as though it were real. This was part of my lesson. But before we left for home, I reminded them how we found such jewels just by looking around us.

I showed them pictures of hummingbirds that could not be caught, but could be watched. We inspected a cup of pond water beneath the microscope, and I told a wild story taken from Pliny's seventeenth-century *Naturalis Historia* about a creature with the body and tail of a lion and the head of a man. I showed them a drawing of such a creature and read another story about a man who sniffed an herb and died. When doctors opened his head they found a nest of scorpions there. I gave out sprigs of mint to chew. Everyone left for home with nice breath.

My students are twelve and thirteen, only a little older than I was when August left home, and when Volusia moved into our house with Janey Louise.

9

At times I tried to interest my own son in the natural world, but he was somewhere else. I couldn't excite him the way I could my students. Ty liked to build a fort or a tree house. He liked sleeping outside on summer nights in a tent, but he was never aware of sounds, or of any splendor around him.

He caught frogs and crawdads at the creek, but he didn't want to know anything about them. Sometimes, if I suggested we cut something open, he would find the suggestion gory enough to demand attention; but by the time I set up the outside table for the experiment Ty was nowhere to be found. Johnny made excuses for him, saying that he was too interested in athletics to be a young naturalist.

The only time I really cared was when I was aching to show someone a fantastic web or a spiky new leaf. If I showed the web to Ty, he tightened his lips and said, "That's good, Mom. Can I go now?"

I telephoned Johnny as soon as I landed at the Atlanta airport. I planned to rent a car and drive to Mercy, but Johnny wanted me to call him as soon as I landed. He had a fear of flying, but as far as I could tell it was his only fear.

"I'm still alive," I said.

"Good."

"Is Ty home from school yet?"

"No, but I took his uniform to him. I'll meet him at the game."

"Don't end up coaching them again, Johnny. You don't have time for that this summer."

"We'll see," he said. "I already miss you. I'm glad you're alive."

"Me, too. Tell Ty I'll call tonight."

"Your principal called," Johnny said. "He said not to worry about these last few days of school and that you can turn in your grades when you get back."

"I've already done them. They're in a folder on my desk. You could take them by the school."

"Okay."

"I love you," I said.

"I know," Johnny's voice grew husky. "I want us to get married, Evie." He'd said this before, and knew how I was still fighting the effects of my short marriage to Lowell Hardison.

"When you get back," he said, "we'll talk about it."

I met Johnny Kessler when he came to paint my house. I'd been divorced for two years, and was settled into my routine of teaching and taking Ty to nursery school. Lowell sent a child-support check sometimes, but it was nothing to count on.

I'd scraped up enough money to have two rooms of my house painted. My mother sent money to paint the outside. Johnny arrived on that first day in a Ford pickup truck and explained that housepainting was just his "temporary work," and that he was finishing a degree in engineering. He had dark hair and was handsome, in the nonchalant way of Italians.

He arrived at the house each morning at 7:30, so I offered a cup of coffee and sometimes sat and drank one with him before taking Ty to nursery school. Then I went to my own day of teaching. One morning I got the flu, took Ty to KinderCare, and returned home to find our dog grappling with a squirrel in the kitchen.

"Damn dog. C'mere, Buster." The squirrel got loose, but when Buster caught it again, I saw that it was bleeding from its shoulder and head. Blood dripped onto the kitchen floor. I tried to pull the animal from Buster's mouth.

"Damn! Let it go!" I slipped on the greasy blood as Johnny came in the back door. He led Buster out by the collar without trying to take away the squirrel.

I stood up and brushed myself off. Squirrel hair stuck in clumps on my sleeve. "I didn't think you'd be here today," I said.

"Why not?"

"It's supposed to rain." The sun was out and I could see no sign of rain, though the weatherman had predicted it.

"I can start on the inside." He handed me a color chart, and I felt a wave of nausea go over me.

"Anything," I said. "You choose." I told him I was sick.

Johnny pointed to the blood on my leg and got a wet rag. I felt suddenly shy to be alone with him in the house. He wiped my calves with long sweeps, and though I felt no intimacy in the gesture, I responded to the gentleness in his touch.

A May sun drew bars of light across his body and the floor. As he touched my leg with a wet rag, then a dry one, he kept a secret beneath his tongue. Then he made a clicking sound. I could not believe the empty bowl of my heart, the high ringing that could shatter into pieces.

"Thanks," I said, trembling. I asked if he wanted fresh coffee, and offered to make some.

"You go to sleep," he said. "I'll get to work." He went to his truck and carried in a ladder and a tarp to cover the floor and furniture.

Johnny worked all morning, playing a radio he brought with him each day. At noon, I came downstairs and offered to make him a sandwich.

A shower had come while I slept, and the sun made the trees and air sparkle. The whole world looked lovely, and my fever made me feel slightly in love.

When Lowell left after only two years of marriage, I was relieved and I stopped believing in a "one and only" kind of love. Whenever I saw a sappy love story on TV, or the movies, I laughed and felt superior to anyone who believed in love like that.

I made a sandwich and looked at the work he had done.

"You like going to the movies?" he asked me. He raised his arms above his head to stretch. Everything he did looked relaxed.

"Sure."

"Maybe we could go together some night."

I nodded.

I wondered what our first movie would be and if I would remember it romantically.

Two nights later, on a day when Johnny did not come to the house, he called to suggest we go to a movie. He invited Ty to come too, but I decided to hire a baby-sitter.

We sat in the world of movies. The large images and music made me feel dreamy. During a car-chase scene, while we feared for Sean Connery's life, Johnny reached for my hand. I knew 007's safety was guaranteed, but as Johnny's hand gripped my knee, my blood grew hot. Movies voices funneled through my head.

When he brought me home, I didn't want to go into the house. I could see a light on in my bedroom, and one in the kitchen. Ty's room was dark. The baby-sitter stood at the kitchen sink, looking out the window at the car. She wanted to leave.

I thought of how much I loved my bedroom—its white spread and the comforter folded at the foot of the bed. The china lamp that belonged to my grandmother. My dressing table with its flowered skirt, like the one I saw when I spent the night in Margaret Turnbull's rich house. My comfortable reading chair with stacks of books beside it: used books with other people's underlining, August's old books, new ones.

I'd made the room into a place of comfort, but tonight I hated the thought of going back to it. I didn't want to leave Johnny's car, and hoped he might try to kiss me. But as he opened the car door, his whole demeanor indicated that he wouldn't.

"I had a good time," Johnny said, but I couldn't tell if he was just being polite. He walked me to the back door.

"I did, too." I wanted him to ask me out again, and to ask quickly. I wanted him to need me.

"Well, I'll see you tomorrow. I'll finish that back wall, then start again on the outside."

"Okay," I said. "Thanks." Then, "See you tomorrow."

He turned to go down the narrow porch steps.

"Johnny?" I called. "Maybe you could stay for dinner tomorrow night. Ty would like that."

"Can't," he said. "Maybe another night."

I staggered visibly but he wasn't looking.

The next morning I could tell that Johnny had arrived because I heard groans from the pipes at the outside faucet. I looked at the clock and saw that he was twenty-five minutes early. I showered and dressed.

When I entered the kitchen, I was casual and my hair was still wet. Johnny sat at the table watching the door where I would come in.

We went out two more times before he finally kissed me. The waiting made me wild. He kissed me first in the car, then on the porch steps. He followed me inside, and I closed the door. He followed me to the bedroom, where books lay scattered on the white bedspread and the table. He lifted the books off the bed.

"We can do just as much as you want," he said. He knew how hard it was for me to trust anyone's love. "No more than what you want."

I made a sound low in my throat that revealed how much I wanted. He undressed me and laid me down. I hadn't had love like this, I hadn't known what I was missing.

After a few weeks, Johnny began to call me Dreamboat in public, or Sweet Damsel. He grew corny, and touched me affectionately. He reached out so easily, not like anyone I'd ever known. His touch was not desperate, or selfish.

"Come over here, Dreamboat," he said.

Each time I was with him my body grew absurd with love. He kissed me, and I was startled with the importance of his face, his lips. Everything I had dreamed of early in my life became possible. And I realized that the TV shows about love were completely true.

10

I drove along a back road in north Georgia as familiar to me as my own arm, and secret as a fever. The hills far-off, and even the ground nearby, trembled in the hot sun. I stopped at a store that used to be called Heck's, but now was FastFare. The large bin that held soda pop was gone, so was the church bench and chairs where farmers had gathered to talk at noontime.

The inside of the store was different, too. No more wooden floors, no more smell of tobacco and sawdust. One of the women behind the counter looked vaguely familiar, and I wondered if I'd gone to school with her.

As I drove into town, I saw a Marriott on the hill where a barn used to be. The landscape now was manicured, and the Marriott looked down on the town, like a snob.

A fancy Italian restaurant had replaced the ice-cream parlor, but the Riviera Theatre still had its marquee, and Turnbull's department store continued to dominate the downtown area. Janey Louise and I used to call this part of town Greater Mercy.

My mother had been married for several years to a man named Mr. Shallowford. They lived together most of the time, though Mr. Shallowford still had his house down the street, and would spend some of his time there. The arrangement seemed to suit them both.

The house I grew up in faced the corner of the block. Sidewalks, cracked and in disrepair, gave the neighborhood a dilapidated appearance, and some of the more run-down houses had been turned into duplexes.

Our big yard sat in front like an apron, and a long porch opened around large double doors. Another porch jutted off from the side, and made the house seem sheltered and serene, like someone certain of his place in the order of things.

On summer nights Janey Louise, Tucker, and I slept on the

screened-in side porch. Because the house faced the corner, and because of the wide yard, people tended to stop and look at the house. I
did so now, pretending I was a stranger in town.

I lifted the key from above the door sill and unlocked it.

Upon entering, I could smell dinner in the oven and the discreet
odor of cleansers. The smells were more familiar than the sight of furniture. Drapes covered the windows, but neither drapes nor windows
were closed.

When I was growing up here, we had curtains and blinds to keep
out the hot afternoon sun. The drapes now looked like the ones in
Margaret Turnbull's house, where everything matched. Whenever I
spent the night with Margaret, I envied her drapes and bedspreads cut
from the same material as the skirt around her dressing table. Her
dressing table held bottles of all sizes. I tried to conceal my fascination
with the celebrity of her room, but when I came home its images lingered. I wanted a version of that deliberateness for myself.

What I didn't want was the misery in Margaret's house. At night I
woke to hear her father yelling. I listened for, but could not hear, Mrs
Turnbull's replies. And though I knew Margaret could hear her father's loud voice, she pretended to be asleep.

In the morning we made no mention of the nighttime tumult, but
at breakfast I could not help staring at Mr. Turnbull. I imagined he
might be embarrassed, or ashamed. I noticed that he had bitten his
nails until they bled.

Our house still held Volusia's presence. I expected to see her at any
moment. I went upstairs and opened the door to her sewing room,
which hadn't been opened in a while. The room had been August's
study before it became the room where Volusia made her hats.

August's table and chair were pushed into the corner, and some of
his books lay stacked on the shelves. I stood by the window where I
had hoped for him to drive up and surprise us. I called my mother at
Joe Sugar's store. She had told me she would be there. Joe answered
and recognized my voice immediately.

"Hello, honey," he said, the way Volusia might have said it. Hearing
him made me sad and I couldn't speak. My mother came to the phone.

"Evie? Where are you?"

I said I was at the house.

She covered the phone and asked Joe Sugar something.

"Your bed's all made," she told me. "Take your things upstairs. I'm hoping Jane can stay with us for a few nights. She's so tired." My mother took a big breath.

"What's the matter?" I asked.

"You know how Volusia kept begging us to let her die?"

"Yeah."

"Well, her body was full of pills. The coroner says she took an overdose."

"How is Jane?"

"She's here at the store. Must be a hundred people here. This is where they have Volusia's body, you know."

"At the *store?*"

"Jane hates funeral homes, so Joe said he'd keep the body here. Anyway, people are used to seeing her at the store. Joe and Capp both wanted it that way."

Capp would be about nineteen now. Joe and Volusia had adopted him twelve years ago from a foster home in Jasper, Georgia. He'd never been able to speak, but played a flute beautifully. He was mute, but not deaf, a handsome boy with the blank expression of someone retarded. Volusia fell so in love with him as a little boy that she brought him to live with her at Joe's store.

"How are *you* doing?" I asked my mother. I heard in her voice the scratchy sound of tears.

"I'm glad you're here, Evie. Nobody knows how I miss this woman."

I imagined her touching Volusia as she spoke. My mind saw my mother surrounded by canned goods and crates of oranges, touching Volusia's strong dark arm, her flat hand.

I set the table and included a place for Jane, and another chair for Volusia's spirit. The whole house smelled like pot roast. My mother had left out a box of rice, so I measured two cups and put water on to boil, then I took some frozen lima beans from the freezer.

As I worked, I recognized kitchen habits forced by Volusia, and I tried to imagine something I could place into the grave with her, some token I could leave. What came to mind was one of Albert's letters.

I hung the dishrag neatly over the faucet and called Joe Sugar to ask if this was a good idea.

"Yes," he said quickly, so I knew he liked it. "I'll send a couple of letters with Jane when she comes over later."

"I don't know if she's coming or not, Joe." I wondered if he knew how Jane and I had separated ourselves from each other.

"She's coming," he said. Then, "I have something to tell you."

"What?"

"Your daddy's coming to this funeral."

I heard my mother's car pull into the driveway and watched as she got out with Mr. Shallowford, Tucker, and Becky—the girl Tucker would marry. And though I knew that Jane would come later, I was disappointed she wasn't with them now.

"Evie." My mother held me a long moment when she came in. Mr. Shallowford hugged me, too. He smelled just the way he used to smell.

Tucker ducked his head to enter the kitchen. He was taller than I remembered, or else the entrance to the kitchen was low. He wore steel-rimmed glasses and his hair was dusty blond. He introduced me to Becky, and though she was lovely, I could see that she did not like to talk. I imagined that she was smart, as smart as Tucker. Her face looked serious and shy.

Tucker was in the ninth grade the year we found out he was smart, that he had an IQ of 165. The principal called for my mother to come in for a parent conference. He said that Tucker was brilliant, and should take a chemistry course and physics. I was amazed when they told me, because I thought *I* was the smart one. I settled for being more sensitive, but Tucker turned out to be more sensitive, too.

For days after Tucker was declared brilliant, I made him more normal in my mind by remembering him on vacations when he had to ride in the front seat because of car sickness. My mother, or whoever was not driving, rode in the back with me. But even with all our maneuverings, Tucker still had to yell, "Pull over. Quick," and I watched him vomit. Then the car smelled sour. I held my nose and let wind blow in my face.

When we called August to tell him about Tucker, how smart he was, Tucker spoke into the phone like a celebrity. My mother kept repeating that we hadn't realized how smart he was, but Volusia claimed she knew it all along.

"I *knew* it." Volusia spoke to the sink and stove. "Nobody's telling me anything new. That boy's got some sense," she said to thin air.

Tucker had a good job at Westinghouse, and was going to be able to buy a house for Becky. As he sat down at the table though, he looked at me with old eyes, with his carsick eyes.

After supper Jane came in and brought with her two of Albert's letters. "Joe said you wanted to put these in the grave with Mama." She handed them to me, and my first impression, as I took them was that Albert's handwriting was strange, childlike.

"I wish I'd thought of it," Jane said. Her response seemed more friendly than polite.

I nodded. "Good." We were both aware that we hadn't yet hugged each other. Neither of us wanted to. I fixed a plate of food for her. I had no idea if we were still friends.

"Did you hear yet about the coroner's report?" Jane asked.

"Mama Agnes told me," I said. "What're they saying?"

"I'll tell you what *I'm* saying. I'm saying she saved up pills over a period of a week, then took them all at once. What *they're* saying is different." Jane's body looked coiled, ready to strike.

We sat for a long moment, the silence broken only by the sound of the clock.

"You already eaten?" my mother asked her.

I got up and cut two slices of cake. "Betty Early brought over one of her lemon-cheese cakes." I cut a hunk with my fork and offered it to Jane.

She closed her eyes with pleasure as she took the bite. "God, I haven't had cake like this in ten years."

"You want some milk?" I said.

"Yes, please."

"Do the police think somebody gave Volusia those pills?" I poured milk into tall glasses.

"I don't know. If she saved them up, then she had to live with a fair amount of pain before she died. They're saying maybe somebody gave her the peace she was asking for."

"They're not accusing *you*," I said, but it was a question.

Jane drank all of her milk. "Not yet," she said.

I couldn't tell if she was teasing.

If Volusia were here, she'd have us talk about something neutral. "You want to see a picture of Ty in his baseball uniform?" I asked.

I lifted my pocketbook. As I took out the pictures, and placed them on the table, I showed Jane another one kept hidden in my wallet. A picture of the moon. The celluloid was cracked and peeling.

Jane studied the picture a long moment. Then she brought from her own purse two photographs of Max and Sammy, and another picture of the moon—a small dot. I was glad to see she still carried it with her.

Then she took out a photo of two girls. A dark close-up taken at night. The camera was held at arm's length to show their faces, huge and laughing—hers and mine.

11

October 15, 1949
Dear August,

We are getting ready for Halloween, and Tucker gets so excited we have to tell him it is a long way off. We drew some
Halloween pictures for you, and I am sending pages from my
notebook so you can see. I have crushed some plants found near
the river. Janey Louise goes with me sometimes, and I teach her
like you taught me. Janey Louise has drawn some pictures too.
Her pictures are the best. We thought you could put them on
your kitchen wall, so when people come to your house they will
know you have children.

You asked about presents you could send us for Christmas. I
have made a list of things. I think you should buy Volusia and
Janey Louise something too, since they are part of our family
now.

My grades are good. I got A in Social Studies, but the
teacher is a witch. Math is my worse. I have a C- in it. English
is good though, because I love to read things. My teacher said
we could write a report from something in the library—either
Mark Twain or Jane Austen. Which would you choose?

I want to tell you something that has happened in my life.
Since school started, boys from the 7th grade have turned
up on my porch. Volusia says it's because I make Popsicles
for them. Mama says they hang around like hound dogs.
Tucker likes it. He comes out to talk to them until Mama calls
him in. Robert and Sammy and Billy Blue came over today.
I don't like Robert and try to show him, but he doesn't get it.
Sammy and Billy Blue are okay. Billy Blue is funny. He makes
me laugh.

Mama says you will not be here for Thanksgiving, as I was

hoping. Is that true? Our dinner will be real good, maybe the best we have ever had. Maybe you will surprise us by coming.

Lots of Love,

Evie

P.S. There is something I've been meaning to ask you, Daddy. Do you ever wonder why the person who loves you the most is me?

November 2, 1949

Daddy,

I had a fight with Justine. Usually that is nothing, but the fight this time is something I will not get over as long as I live. Justine is hateful in ways I never imagined, and I hesitate to even tell you about her.

It is this: this morning on the way to school I went by the corner where I always meet with Justine so we can walk together to school. As I got near I saw someone with her. At first I thought it was somebody hurting her, like they were fighting or something. But that was not it *at all*. He was kissing Justine *on the corner*. Kissing her like they do in the movie musicals, and Justine was doing it back. It was completely disgusting, because I had no idea who he was, and because they were in pure public view. He is older than Justine and I know I have seen him at the filling station.

Mama says that Justine has always been fast, and tells me not to be fast like that. I won't. If you could have seen them, it would have made you sick to see. I am not kidding. I know Justine better than anybody does, and I was shocked!

I walked right up (he was still kissing her hard) and said "What are you doing, Justine?" Justine just stopped and turned slowlike. Then she said, "This is Lyle. Lyle Gibbs." She acted like I hadn't caught them at anything, then she rolled her eyes and said "I gotta go, Lyle." She acted like I was stupid and not a friend at all. When we walked away together toward school, we did not say anything until we reached the schoolyard. Finally I couldn't stand it and said "Justine, who *was* that? What do you think you were doing?" And she said, "Shuud-uup." I was so hurt.

Your Hurting Daughter,
Evie Bell

November 22, 1949

Daddy,

I have something to tell you. It is like a secret. B. J. Forrest has changed. He is not the same as he used to be. He is so smart. He wears glasses now and is tall and extremely thin. He looks exactly like someone you think of as smart. He has been coming to the porch to get Popsicles every day. We sit on the swing. When he walks up the hill to the house, he does not walk on the driveway. He walks across the yard and straight to the front door. He does not swerve.

When I loved him a few years ago, I did not know what Love was. But B. J. is older now, Daddy. He is nearly 14, and I love him so much. I think he is the *one* that I love. The *one* that I have been waiting for. I have not told him this, but I have kissed him, or let him kiss me, and I knew then.

Daddy, he is so tall. He is my first kiss. Other boys have walked me home, but he is the first one to kiss me on the lips. It was embarrassing beyond belief. I am telling you. Our lips mashed flat and his teeth (which stick out just the slightest bit) hit my teeth, and we jerked back. Can I tell you this? Then he did it again, Daddy, and this time slow and not mashing, and our knees and chest touched. I cannot say how this was like, but if he was to kiss me again, I would let him.

From Your Daughter,
Evie Bell

December 8, 1949

Dear August,

A man moved in down the street. He is new, but he is old. I visited him yesterday with Mama and we took him a warm pound cake that Volusia made. He thanked us, but did not ask us in. I think Mama wanted to see what his house looked like. She said she couldn't imagine it—him being old and a man with no woman there. But we didn't get to go in and walking home Mama said she thought he was just shy and if we come back, we might be asked in. His name is Mr. Shallowford. He has a good face, but his teeth are bad.

My science teacher is wonderful, though at first I didn't think much of him. His name is Mr. Steele, and he teaches me about Nature the way you did. I am looking for a book called *Lakes, Streams and Ponds* by Caldwell. If you have it, will you send it to me? When I see you again, you will be amazed at all I know.

Daddy, D. J. has not come by the house in several weeks. Where is he? Can you tell me why a boy would kiss like that and then not come around? I do not understand boys, even though I have a brother and a father. Tell me why a boy would act like that?

Your Sad and Puzzled Girl,
Evie

December 10, 1949

Dear Father,

Sometimes I think you are not my father at all, not my real father, because you do not remember when to call when you say you will, and you did not remember that I was in the Christmas pageant at school, and all day I was so sure you would be here. Even though Mama said not to count on it. I thought, I will look up in the middle of the play and see you, or else maybe before the play you would come backstage and tell me that you would be sitting out front. Either way I knew how it would feel to see you. And all my friends would see that I *do* have a father and that we are together special to each other. All of this would have been seen, if you had only been here. But that is not how it was at all. You were not here and it is over and I will never again be the Christmas Angel, and I don't even care.

In case you didn't know, I was *wonderful.* Everybody said I was the best they had ever seen. Justine says you don't *deserve* to see me and she is right. Tucker says he hates you too.

I don't know if I will send this letter or not.

> From Your Very Wonderful
> Daughter,
> *Genevieve Jackson Bell*

December 19, 1949

Dear Daddy,

Yes, I do think that someone can be forgiven, if they promise to make amends. I like the amends that you have planned. Me and Tucker will gladly accept a ticket to the Sea of Cortez, finally, and it's about time. This is such a dream, I cannot believe it. I feel wavy in my mind. I have told everyone at school that I am going to this place and I have showed them pictures. But even though I tell all these people, still it feels like a secret. I wonder if this is the way a turtle feels. Do you know what I mean?

I have seen turtles you can ride, but I would never do such a thing. I have such respect. I will respect the Sea of Cortez in ways you won't believe. I have read about the man who was the explorer and I feel like I am going to discover something too. Tucker is excited so that he does not go to sleep at night, so we tell him that the trip is not for a long time. I mark the days on my calendar and keep it under my bed. It is three months and eighteen days from tomorrow. I have already marked off today, and Mama said you would send tickets in the spring.

Mama and I went again to visit with Mr. Shallowford down the street. This time we went into his house, and I must say it is very strange. Chairs are not in the right place to look at, but in the right place to sit. He does everything by comfort, but almost nothing by sight. Mama says this is the way a man will act when he is left alone to do for himself.

In a few months I will be in the place of your dreams. I cry when I think about it. I cry, too, when I think of my name, and wish I had a new one. Mama says your mother's name was Genevieve, and that you picked my name. I'm not saying I blame you. You probably thought it was a fine thing, but I must tell you that at some point I plan to change it—when I am old enough to do so.

> Love,
> *Evie*

12

On our first Christmas without August, Volusia's sister and two nieces from Florida decided to spend Christmas with them on Latham Street.

"But what about *us?*" I felt desperate to keep them at our house. Each of our families had a hole in the heart, and I wanted us to work together as one family in the same house—mine. Volusia refused, but promised to come by on Christmas morning and open gifts with us.

"We'll have a nice Christmas," my mother said. The Korean War was on everyone's mind.

I went to the attic and brought down our set of bubble lights. Janey Louise, Tucker, and I strung popcorn and cranberries. After the tree was decorated, we turned out all the lights in the house and sat before it. Gifts lay spread beneath the branches. Janey Louise had made me promise not to lift or shake the present she had for me, and I felt excited by the added restriction.

I had purchased a large box of Evening in Paris perfume for Janey Louise. The package included powder, fancy bottles of lotion, cologne, and one small bottle of *parfum*. I knew Janey Louise would like the small bottle best, because it was something real.

The whole box was silver, wrapped in blue cellophane. I put Christmas paper around it, and said even if she lifted or shook it, she still wouldn't know what it was. Volusia put presents under the tree for my mother, one for me, and another for Tucker. We felt vibrant with expectation, and our house smelled like a bake shop most days. I helped Volusia make two pies, and a large pound cake.

On Christmas morning Tucker wanted to open presents before Volusia arrived, but my mother insisted we wait. They would arrive at nine o'clock, she said, and at exactly nine they drove up to the house. My mother and Volusia brought coffee into the living room and we turned on the tree lights. Janey Louise opened her present first. She quickly tore off the Christmas paper, but I could tell she didn't want to tear the cellophane wrap. She poked her hand inside the wrap and pulled out each bottle.

"Put some *on* you," I said. I wanted her to smell the *parfum*.

She placed her finger at the end of the smallest bottle and dabbed a little onto her neck. Then she leaned to let Tucker smell her.

"Eeech!" He pushed her away and grabbed at the gifts trying to find one of his own. I thought he was turning into a brat, and said so. Everyone ignored me.

"That's nice, Janey Lou," my mother said, and leaned to sniff her neck.

Volusia tried on a long, hot-pink chenille robe that my mother had chosen for her. I gave Volusia a large round rhinestone pin. She stuck it onto her robe and strutted around like a rich person.

"Thank you, honey," she said and gave me a kiss. She handed me a small square package. I opened it and found the most beautiful notebook I had ever seen. Each page had a small drawing of a shell, or a twig, or a leaf in the top left-hand corner.

"It's so you can go out in the woods, like you do, and write down what you see." Volusia loved to hear me read to her what I had seen in the woods or at the pond. I read it to her while she was cooking. "And you can keep reading to me what you write about. I tell you, honey, hearing you talk has made me see things different."

Tucker had opened two of his toys—trains with tracks and a race car that was an imitation of something at the Indianapolis 500. But still he was acting bad. He kept whining until Mama Agnes lost patience with him, but Volusia calmed him down. Volusia allowed Tucker his bad moods, because he was "the boy."

Janey Louise and I had begun to realize the advantage in being a boy. We had tried to kiss our elbows, because we were told that kissing our elbows could turn us into boys. We didn't know if boys could turn into girls the same way.

We spent one whole Sunday afternoon trying to change our gender, then imagining what people would say when it happened. We had picked out boys' names. Janey Louise chose Clark (for Clark Kent) and I picked Roy Rogers—the whole name. For the longest time we believed we could change ourselves.

I lifted the largest gift under the tree, and Janey Louise made sure I didn't shake it. She took it from me to keep it steady, and untied the bow herself.

"Let me do it," I said. The box was the size and shape of a hatbox, so I thought she might have given me a hat, but when I opened it what I found was a thousand buttons. They were all sizes and shapes and colors, and I put my hands into them up to my elbows.

Janey Louise had seen me go into Kresses and dive my hands into the bin of loose buttons. I loved the way they felt on my fingers, and the clicking noise they made as they hit against each other. The buttons sounded like water running, or like tiny insects. I couldn't believe it. I loved the hatbox they came in and everything.

My mother had opened her presents, but one she was raring to use was a set of six glasses she had admired in Turnbull's china department. She went to put them on the table at everybody's place. She had made breakfast and hoped Volusia and Janey Louise would eat with us. As we ate, I thought this was the best Christmas we had ever had, but I felt guilty thinking it.

The day wasn't cold, so after Volusia and Janey Louise left I took a walk to Corny's Pond with my notebook. Tucker went next door to play with Arnold Pepper, his new best friend. Later in the day I wrote to August.

Dear Daddy,

I hope you had a good Christmas. Ours was different, but good. We had Christmas dinner without Volusia and Janey Louise, but they came to open presents and eat breakfast with us. Volusia's sister and two nieces were visiting with her, and we could not go over there to be with them. I do not know why.

I missed going with you on our Christmas walk to the pond, but I went by myself and saw a rabbit and some new fish. I swear I think I know all the fish in the pond, then I see something new.

Me and Tucker loved your presents you sent. Mama let me open one on Christmas Eve to make it seem like you were here, then we opened the other ones this morning. My favorite was the one on Christmas Eve, because that was the Brownie camera. I have taken about a million pictures and Mama had to go out and get more film at the only place that was open, which was Bowdin's Drug Store, because of people who might get sick on Christmas Day.

At breakfast I tried to take a picture of Volusia in her rooster apron, but she said no. Janey Louise told me she thinks a camera can take away part of yourself. Do you think that is true about a camera? I also want to thank you for my bracelet and the book about bees. It is so interesting. I took it when I went to the pond. I pretended you were teaching me about bees. In a way you were.

I hope you got the bathrobe I sent you and the bedroom slippers from Tuck. Mama says you will call us tonight. Anyway, the Brownie camera is my favorite present, and another favorite is what Janey Louise gave me—a box filled with a Thousand Buttons. I keep it beside my bed. When I dig my hands down in it it feels like soft pebbles in water.

> Merry Christmas From Your Loving Daughter,
> *Evie*

P.S. Tucker is writing to thank you too. Mama is making him, but she did not have to make me.

13

I did not get to meet Volusia's sister or Janey Louise's cousins, but after they left Janey Louise became a different person. She smoked cigarettes and invited me to join her. We said cruel things about people we saw. We said they were fat or ugly, that they had pimples. Sometimes we said it loud enough for them to hear. To say these things meant we were outside the loop of fat or ugly, and I found our meanness extremely satisfying.

We smoked at a place in the woods, or in our bedroom, when Volusia was out of the house. Our hate of ugliness provided a bond, made us friends in a way we hadn't been before. We wrote hate letters to people in the government, and mailed them. We sent one to Edward R. Murrow, but I didn't feel that he deserved it. We stayed inside our hate until it flung itself out, then we began to play the Queen Game.

Janey Louise got her idea about queens from the movies and magazines. Whenever we played, she got to be Queen and I was her Attendant. She told me what to bring her, then arranged the items on the bed. She imagined that many people were around her and she talked to these other people, though I could tell by the way she spoke that I remained highest in rank.

"You are," she told me in an affected voice, "my favorite one."

I played this game because Janey Louise could imagine good scenarios. She bestowed fantastic names that I believe she thought up as she said them.

"Far-en-tina," she said, or "Bu-ushie" (pronounced Boosheh), or "Al-a-nora." The names sounded foreign and mysterious. She told a story to go along with each name. "You were born on a small island that was just now discovered. And *you* are the reason they discover it."

She told the story of my capture, how I was taken away, how desperately I wanted to return. The story usually included villains who chased us, then someone else who arrived in the nick of time. A man who loved us—though who mostly loved her. When this man came to the door, she sent him away. She told *me* to send him away.

"Say I can't come out right now. Say I'm sick."

She spent much of her time on the bed or in a chair, while I ran back and forth to other rooms answering the door. The few times I suggested we swap roles, Janey Louise said she was tired and wanted to quit.

"Say, 'yes ma'am,' when you come into the room," Janey Louise instructed me. "Say, 'yes ma'am?' like you asking somebody something."

"Yes ma'am?" I said, entering with a deference to my shoulders and arms that Janey Louise did not know she had taught me.

In Georgia daffodils began blooming in February. In 1950, two days after Valentine's Day, the daffodils in our yard bloomed and on our outside thermometer the day measured sixty-five degrees.

I had received a letter from August that morning telling me that Tucker and I could visit the Sea of Cortez in June, and I could talk of nothing else. Janey Louise wanted to go with me. My mother and Volusia could not console her, and finally Volusia took her into the room off the kitchen. When Janey Louise came out she didn't mention going with us anymore. She didn't mention much of anything the rest of the evening.

That night, after we had gone to sleep, I woke to find Janey Louise gone from her bed. I had heard of people sleepwalking and thought she might be wandering through the house with her arms out straight in front of her, as they did in the horror movies.

I looked in the bathroom and down the hall. I went downstairs, calling in a whisper. Then I saw her descend the porch steps. She wore a man's shirt, Albert's shirt, which she liked to wear most nights. The moon was full, and I saw that she carried something in her left hand. I ran to catch up with her, and made sure the screen door didn't slam. She heard me coming across the grass.

"Thatchu?" she said, startled.

"Yeah. I thought you were asleep. I thought you were walking in your sleep."

"I could see the moon from my bed, and it look so pretty I want to come out and take a picture of it."

"Is that *my* camera?" I asked.

"Yeah. So what?"

"I don't think you can take a picture of the moon," I told her.

"Why not?"

"Because it's 252,000 miles away."

"But I can still *see* it," she said. "How you know how far away it is?"

"My science teacher told us. Anyhow I didn't say you could use my camera. My daddy gave that to me."

"I'm just using it for this one little thing. Don't be so stingy. I never used it before." She held the camera up to her eye and looked at the moon. She snapped a picture, then gave it to me. "How far is that Sea of Cortez you and Tucker going to?"

"It's all the way across the country."

"It's not as far as the moon though. And I can see that. How far is the Cortez Sea?"

"I don't know. I wish you could go. I really wish you could. I asked my mama."

"Mine said no, too. She said it would not be fun for me, and she said she would take me to see the ocean that is closer than that sea. She said it is all the same water, and that the water you would be at would be the same water that I was seeing."

"Gah."

We sat in the yard's moonlight. I wore a nightgown with pockets, and big tulips on the front. The night was unseasonably warm and we lay down in the grass. The ground made us cold.

Janey Louise stood up and stretched out her arms and legs. "Don't you feel like something magic could happen out here?" she said. "I mean in the moonlight like this and it being so warm in the dead of winter?"

"It's like it *already* is magic."

"I know. It's like we are watching us, instead of *being* us."

"Sometimes," I said, wanting to confess something, "sometimes, you know what I do? I pretend there are people watching me, like with a camera. Watching everything I do."

"Everything?" she said. "What if you have to go to the bathroom and stuff? What about when you get nekked in the tub?"

"Then I say, 'Can't-see-me-now, can't-see-me-now,' I say it three times, and it goes off."

Janey Louise thought for a moment.

"It's not a *real* camera," I said.

"How many is they watching you?"

"About fourteen," I guessed.

Janey Louise held up the Brownie camera, getting the moon in full focus. She spread her legs apart like a tripod, and snapped pictures, dancing around as though she would get all the different angles of the moon's surface.

"Don't use up all my film," I said.

"Here. You wanna try it?"

I focused and clicked until only one picture was left.

"C'mere," I said. "There's one left."

I put my face next to hers and held the camera at arm's length. Janey Louise thought this was hilarious. I held my arm stretched as far from our faces as I could reach, high, as though the moon might be taking a picture of us.

The picture came out too dark, and showed only the outline of our faces, but the moonlight showed on the ground behind us and gave our faces a background. The features of our eyes and nose and mouth could be seen, and our smiles. Our pictures of the moon turned out to be just a tiny swell of brightness in a black sky.

"Is that *it*?" Janey Louise asked. "That tiny dot of something?"

The moon was so much smaller than what we had actually seen. In real life the night had been magnificent, but we kept our pictures of the moon in the drawer of our bedside table and vowed never to give them up.

"I bet we're the only people in the world who have something like this," Janey Louise said.

"I bet people would pay good money for these pictures," I told her.

"They *would*?"

"But we would say no. We would not give them up."

"I don't even want to think about it," Janey Louise said.

14

Tucker drove Becky home, but came back to the house to spend the night. I asked Jane if she wanted to stay over. I knew we wouldn't sleep in our old room, but I liked the thought of staying together in the same house. Jane agreed, and my mother went upstairs to make sure the guest room was ready.

I took out the two letters from Albert and started to open them. "You might want to wait," Jane said. She didn't want me to read them in front of her. Then I saw another letter, one in my own handwriting. I held it up.

"Joe thought you might like to see that one, too," she told me. "It's one you wrote to Mama when you went to the Sea of Cortez. It's the only letter you ever wrote to her, and she saved it. Joe thought you should know she saved it, and he thought you might like to have it now."

I fingered the flimsy paper the letter was written on. When I was eleven I thought that onionskin paper was beautiful and liked to write letters on it. Jane told me good night and went upstairs, leaving me to read the letters alone.

"I'll see you in the morning," she said. Jane's expression softened. The moons in her eyes looked small like in our pictures, but I imagined each dot might be bigger than it seemed, and farther away than I thought.

June 5, 1950
From The Sea of Cortez

Dear Volusia,

I have already written to Mama Agnes, but wanted to write to you. I could not tell Mama exactly how wonderful it is here, and I could not tell her that Daddy is with another woman. I do not think she knows, do you? The woman's name is Melina, and though Tucker likes her, I do not. She has skin that is very dark, almost as dark as Janey Louise, but she is not colored. This is amazing to me! But Melina will come later. What I must tell you about is this:

The Sea of Cortez is not what I imagined. It is not a real sea, they say, but it looks the same as a real sea. None of this matters for I must say that nothing in the experience of my life has been so amazing as the one I am in now. THE WATER IS THE COLOR OF BLUE PEARLS, if there is such a thing. It has blue washed over with white. Also, Daddy took us out in a boat and we put on masks and could see all the coral and sea grass, that is wavy and soft. It looks like it is always in wind. Sponges grow on the ocean bed, and the sponges are just like in our kitchen. It is like somebody dropped them on the ocean floor, and do you know they are GROWING there. I am amazed.

Tell Janey Louise that August took us on an all day boat trip, and that I am bringing her a surprise that she will love. Tell her not to be mad at me because she couldn't come. Tell her I miss her and will send her a postcard with a picture of the big turtle she wanted to see.

Melina did not come along on the boat trip with us, which I was VERY glad of. We went into the lagoons and part of the river that feeds into The Cortez—that is what people call it. We went into the marshy places and saw birds like ibis and osprey and night herons and blue herons and pelicans and storks. We saw trees brushed off at the top by wind or by hurricanes, so their mangly limbs tangled around each other. And when we got out of the boat, we had to crawl through some places because the limbs were so low. It was scratchy to do this, but I felt like I was crawling around in a mind—like this was the forest's mind and we were going through the place in the mind where it dreams, where a forest would have dreams. And the dreams might be bad ones, because it was scary to step down sometimes where the mud was so black, and my foot might sink into a deep hole.

The reason we crawled through the limbs was to get to an old Indian burial ground. And this is the part I couldn't believe. These Indians had been buried in their graves for over a hundred years, and there was a huge tree that had grown up through the graves, but the roots—get this—the roots had pulled up bones to the top of the ground. So there were pieces of shin and one small shoulder socket—like it was a child or a small woman, Daddy said. There are people coming to study these bones in the next few weeks, but we got to see it before anyone else. Daddy discovered it, so now he has got another job as a person who works as a guide *and* a scientist in this area.

Daddy knows a lot about plants and animals and stuff, so this is good work for him. He loves it and says to me and Tucker that he has followed his dream and that he hopes we too will follow our dreams, but I say what about us? What if somebody's dream takes them away, so that they do not have a father or a mother? And he says, You still have a father, Evie. I did not say anything to this, because he thinks it counts that he is a father just because he is *alive*, and I do not see it that way at all.

I will not leave my responsibilities behind when I grow up to be a person. I will be like the Sea of Cortez which is faithful to its streams and lagoons, and if it was not here what would happen to all the bird life? If the Sea of Cortez got up and went somewhere else, what would happen then, huh?

I did not say this to my Daddy, because he would not understand what I meant by it, neither does Tucker who thinks his Dad is great. But maybe everything worked out good, because if Daddy had stayed then you and Janey Louise would not be living with us. Now, I have to find what my Life Dream is, but I don't want it to hurt other people. Maybe I cannot help this. Tucker will never have a Life Dream, because he is so stubborn. I am afraid Mama will not have one either. I hope I am wrong about this.

Volusia, the Sea of Cortez really is like a dream. I believe this when I step through the sloggy eelgrass, or turn over a rock to find the ground crazy with life. I have some coral to bring for

you and Mama. I think I know where you will want to put it—
on the mantle next to the bowl that Tucker made.

Love and Kisses,
Evie Bell

I read the letter twice, then I read Albert's letters, and realized that
though Volusia had read many of Albert's letters aloud to us, she
hadn't read us these.

July 2, 1951

Dear Mama,

Im learning alot at the school they send me to. I go everyday
to classes and can get my diploma certificate before long. Dont
worry about America and the War in Korea. That is not something you should worry about right now. I like the cakes you
send me, and so do the other guys in my squad. I have heard
that I might be promoted to Sergeant soon, but it is just a
rumur. I will let you know.

I want to say that Im treated different here in the Army. Im
learning alot. I feel smart here and want to bring my ideas back
to Georgia. The Bells sound nice, Mama, and I know you like
them. But do not get too close to those people. You know how
you get.

Love,
Albert

And:

June 2, 1953

Dear Mama and Janey Louise,

Ill be back in Mercy on the 13th and that is not a unlucky
number. It is lucky because I will be given the Distinguished

Service Cross—which is a honor, if you don't already know. I do not have it with me now, but will go—and you will go too—to the White House where President Truman can pin the medal onto me at a ceremony there. Colored people hardly ever get this honor.

When I come back to Georgia Ill have respect. People will respect me. Another thing, I dont want you anymore to live in the Bells house. To live at the Bells and take care of them goes against everything I have learned. I will talk to you about this, and want you to know I believe I can make some difference by acting this way.

Get some new clothes for our trip to see the President, but do not ask the Bells to come. I know you, and I am saying this is for *me*. Do *not* ask them to come.

Love,
Albert

When I went upstairs, I saw a light under the door in Jane's room. I knocked, and she told me to come in.

"Thanks for these letters," I said.

Jane nodded. "You want to ride over to Joe's with me tomorrow," she asked, "or do you need your car?"

"I'll ride with you," I said.

Jane said how hard it was to look at Volusia, because she was so thin.

"What dress did you put on her?" I asked. I hoped it was one I would recognize.

Jane made a clicking sound with her tongue. "Her blue silk with roses on the sleeves."

I smiled at the choice of her favorite dress. For a moment Jane and I had one memory, and it was the same.

I went to my room and put away the letters. My fingers felt sore where I had gnawed the cuticles, and one was blue from mashing it in the kitchen drawer last week. My thumb bled where I had peeled off too much skin again.

When I switched off the light, the room filled immediately with moonlight. The moon tonight was full, complete. Not even one edge was dark. But I was thirty-eight, too old to find my old boxy camera, wake up my friend—too old to sneak out and take more pictures of the moon.

15

By noon Joe Sugar's store was full of people.

Chairs had been brought in from the church next door, and people stood beside the stacks of canned goods and boxes of cereal. Rows and rows of Volusia's homemade hats hung on the walls. People had brought their hats in tribute to her. She had designed something for almost every man and woman in town. Even after she went blind, she continued to make hats. The store looked like a museum.

When Jane and I came in together, the people standing around Volusia's body moved back. The coffin was open, propped along a row of sawhorses. Volusia's chest looked slack, so that the blue dress with roses on the sleeves fell loosely around her. Her arms, though, still appeared strong, and her face remained recognizable because of her wide forehead. I imagined she might open her eyes.

Jane whispered a complaint about how the funeral home rolled Volusia's hair into a French twist, which Volusia would never have done herself. A hat lay propped in her hands, one she had made years ago, her favorite.

I reached to pry the hat from Volusia's hands and could hear whispers behind me. A woman with a huge purse poked me in the back. She didn't want me to touch the body. I didn't turn around, but struggled to release the hat from Volusia's grip. Finally, I was able to loosen her fingers from around the brim, and placed the hat firmly on her head. I wanted to hide the unnatural-looking hair.

When I did this, Volusia suddenly looked like herself. Everybody saw it, and noises of approval came from around the room. People felt the pleasure of seeing her again.

Her shoulders and arms seemed more her own with the hat in place. "She looks younger," the woman with the big purse said, and I imagined that Volusia wore this hat when she was young, and they were remembering her face from that time.

Joe Sugar brought a plate of food to me and one to Jane. Neither of us was hungry, but we thanked him. Then Joe pulled me to the other side of the room, his face urgent.

"Your daddy's coming in." Joe touched the crook of my arm. He knew he had already told me this. "Your mama wants you to pick him up at the plane station. She told me to ask."

My first thought was that I didn't want to pick him up. All those years I wrote letters to provide a string to him, to keep him alive in my head, but during the last decade that string had sagged.

"He gets in this afternoon," Joe said.

I felt my body jerk with an old wish to see him. "My mother thinks I won't say no to you, Joe. She counts on it."

"Mostly she's right."

"Will you go with me?" I asked.

"Can't," he said. "Too much to do here." He patted my shoulder and I spilled some food. "You be all right," he said. "Plane gets in at 3:45." He kept his hand on my arm. His face, without Volusia, looked lost.

A young man came into the store from a back room. I didn't recognize him. He turned around as though he'd forgotten something. I could see him move about in the storeroom, then he emerged with what looked like a long flute. It was a piccolo. He played a few notes that resembled bird calls, played them perfectly—the store seemed suddenly like a pleasure garden.

I hadn't seen Cappadocia in several years, but he recognized me and waved. He was quite handsome. His face had a blankness that was appealing, and his playing of piccolo, flute, and harmonica was, I learned, legendary around Mercy.

"Cap-a-do-sha!" Volusia had said the word for the first time when she called out spelling words for my geography lesson.

"That the prettiest name I ever heard. Be a nice name for a man, or a little boy."

"It's a *place*," I said. "It's a place in Turkey."

"Mr. Cappadocia Carter, come right in," she said, ignoring me.

"Stop it, Volusia! Finish calling out these words to me."

"You know 'em good enough. You don't have to make a 100 every *time*."

"Call them out!"

"Lord, you would worry a wart. I am tired of this." She looked furious, the way she looked when she told me and Janey Louise to pick a switch from the forsythia bush, which she then used to swipe our legs.

"You just want to go to your room and smoke your Old Golds. Your room stinks! It smells like a pool hall in there."

"I don't remember anybody asking you to come into my room, do you?" She threw my geography book and hit the wall. The book fell behind the radio. When I went to get it, she motioned for me to get out.

"I catch you in my room," she said, "I switch you twice."

Capp had been in Joe's store playing four long, mournful notes all day, like a train sound. His shoes were scuffed, and when he wasn't playing the piccolo he kept nodding and shaking his head.

"He's real sad," Joe said. "Night before last he didn't know what to do with himself, kept running off into the woods, and we had to go find him. Jane and I got almost no sleep at all."

Capp reached out to shake my hand. I wondered if Volusia had ever told anyone how she picked his name.

Capp ambled off into the crowd and Joe took me by the arm into the storeroom.

"Now, I've got one more thing I want to say. I know it's none a my business, but Volusia thought you ought to go on and get married, and wherever she is now, she still think it. She say for me to tell you to marry that man you living with, and if she was here, she'd tell you herself."

"I know it," I said. "She told me. I told her I'd get married."

"You *say* you will, but *when* is what I'd like to know. Volusia was thinking about that boy you got."

"Listen, Joe, we live just like a real family. Ty thinks of Johnny like he's his own daddy. We're married in every way, except on paper."

"Paper counts."

Joe got up and walked to where Capp was sitting. When Capp wasn't working, he liked to sit and do his arithmetic problems. He'd filled boxes of notebooks with his arithmetic, and some of them were done right. Volusia called it "his ciphering," and we could see he felt important doing it.

Joe told Capp to put down his notebook and bring out the hatbox. Capp handed me the box and Joe said, "She made this hat for your wedding day. She said it won't need a veil. She said it'll be too late for veils. But this is a wedding day hat just the same."

Joe opened the box slowly, making me wait to see it, a ceremony of looking. The hat was small around the crown, but had a wide crocheted brim, and a tiny wreath of yellow and green flowers. The flowers were not as large as the ones she had for the weddings of her own relatives, or for the hats she sent to weddings in Ohio or Alabama. They were small delicate flowers, and they looked completely real.

"She said tell you you could have it for when the time come."

"It's coming," I said. I wanted to lift it out, wear it tomorrow for her funeral.

"Well, take it then," Joe said. "And don't forget to pick up your daddy."

"I will."

More people were coming in to see Volusia, and the crowd had filled the store. Joe took Capp outside, but before the door closed all the way Capp turned and lifted one hand to say good-bye.

After the store had cleared out, I asked someone where Tucker was. I wanted to tell him August was coming back, and I wanted him to be here when I placed Albert's letters in the coffin.

I sat alone on a chair and leaned over the body to smell Volusia's arms through the rosy sleeves. Her dress kept a smell stronger than her body. Tucker came up behind me. He saw me lean over and asked if I was kissing her. I said no.

"I'm putting two of Albert's letters in here with her," I slipped one beneath her back. Her body felt like lead. I gave Tucker the other letter to put in, and he pushed it beneath her head, carefully, so that he wouldn't disturb her hat.

"The reason I thought you were kissing her is because that's what I did," he said. "I waited until nobody was around, then kissed her on the lips. I thought that's what you were doing." He laughed as though he'd told something funny, so I laughed, too. Then it *was* funny. We laughed out loud, and Capp came back in to see if something was wrong.

Tucker and I held each other, rocking back and forth.

"August is coming," I told him.

"I know it. You're picking him up."

"You want to come with me?"

"I haven't talked to him in two years," Tucker said. "He's never seemed very interested in what I do. I'll be nice to him, but I won't pick him up."

We were still rocking each other, so Capp joined us, uninvited, putting his long arms around us both. He liked standing between people, and he wanted us to keep on laughing. Volusia's laugh had always been raucous and impudent.

Whenever we had gone away from Volusia, when we were going on a long trip or for any length of time, she rocked us back and forth—like this—before we left. We did the same thing now, rocking ourselves in the arc of her hard love.

16

One day in the mail we got a check from August that changed everything. I was about twelve, but didn't realize until years later that my mother had asked him for the money. However it happened, everything from then on (at least financially) began to improve. Mama Agnes and Volusia had decided to start a hat shop—a business that happened almost by accident.

The first hat Volusia ever made was for her Aunt Sylvie in Cleveland. Volusia was then sixteen years old. She formed a sort of cup out of stiff material and wove in dried flowers and netting, along with a little dot or two of lace from one of her mother's old slips. She put a perfect feather from a blue jay in the back, and the effect was elegant—even though no single part had an elegance of its own. Aunt Sylvie loved the hat, and wore it to church meetings and funerals. She received so many compliments that other women began to ask Volusia to make something for them, and offered to pay her. Volusia made a hat for almost every woman in church. She made a hundred dollars that summer.

Volusia told this story so often that I said, "Why don't you make a hat for Mama Agnes? Or me?"

Volusia made two hats. Mine was small and caplike with a spray of different colored veils. One veil was black and came down over my eyes. I wore it to church where my friends grew envious and said they wanted a hat like that for themselves. Margaret Turnbull said she would pay anything for such a hat, and where did I get it.

"I can get you one," I told her, "but it won't be exactly the same."

I told Volusia to make five hats and said I'd sell them for her. The same thing happened when Mama Agnes wore her hat to church. Her hat had a spray of dark feathers that swooped around to one side. Hers had no veils, just feathers that hugged her head and pointed to places on her face. All the ladies wanted hats with dark feathers, and those unexpected swatches of color and lace.

We didn't tell anyone who created these hats. We told them we had ordered them from a place in Ecuador. We offered to order hats for all of them, if they wanted. Volusia made thirty hats over a period of five weeks, and we cleared a hundred and twenty-five dollars. That's when Mama Agnes got the idea for a hat store.

"We'll start a business," she told Volusia. Volusia was skeptical, but agreed to try it.

My mother found a place downtown and wrote to August requesting money for the down payment. Volusia began to create hats to put around the shop, but she refused to make a hat unless she could see the face of the person who would wear it. She said she had to make a hat for a particular face, and that's why they turned out so well.

We told people at church to give us a snapshot of themselves, and if they weren't satisfied with the hat they wouldn't have to pay. Satisfaction Guaranteed! was the sign in the window—just like the advertisements I had seen in the back of comic books.

Mama Agnes made an appointment at the First National Bank. She dressed up and put on perfume when she went in. She wore a hat and gloves. She went to the courthouse to get a license that entitled her to run a business. She told Volusia that she would handle all the business aspects, if Volusia would work with the snapshots and make hats.

From the beginning The Hat Shop was a success. After a year, Volusia could make six to eight hats a day. She drew a sketch of the hat on a large sheet of paper; then she cut out material. Her orders came at first from people at church; later requests came from nearby communities.

"I'm making white people's hats today," Volusia said, and she brought out a flat, head-hugging, caplike hat that had a veil, or a band of tiny flowers around the crown. The hat she made for her own Aunt Sylvie had a large brim that swept upward. Huge floppy flowers hung around the edge.

"Looks like a basket." I lifted Aunt Sylvie's hat from the box.

"Supposed to," Volusia said. "Supposed to look like it's about to spill over, because Sylvie herself spills over. You ever seen her?"

"No." I tried to picture this very hat on somebody's head and told Volusia to put it on. The hat, far too small for her head, appeared to lift her up. When Volusia stood, I thought the flowers might take her off the floor. I told her she looked like a big fish coming up from the water.

"That's right." She laughed.

"Why don't you make white people's hats like that?" I asked.

"They don't want 'em." She turned to see herself in the long hall mirror, and reconsidered. "You think they'd like this?"

"They might."

"Well," she said. Her body filled the whole mirror. "Maybe I will."

Everyone in town knew that I had a father who'd left on a daring adventure and hadn't returned. Sometimes I bragged about August. I made the Sea of Cortez seem extraordinary, and the fact that I had the kind of father who would go there and send back trinkets created a special daring about my own life. I spoke about my father's adventure in a way that suggested a person would not want to come back after visiting such a place.

Whenever I brought to school an object from the Sea of Cortez, I imagined my friends' apparent indifference stemmed from jealousy or envy. They couldn't understand how my father's gifts affected me, or how I had to forgive him every day for not being there.

Once August sent a photograph of his face, a close-up. Someone else had snapped the picture, but he didn't say who took it for him. I put the picture beside my bed and asked Janey Louise to snap a close-up of me, so I could send one back to him. Then I took my Brownie camera to school and arranged people for photographs. I wanted August to know my friends.

While I snapped pictures of my classmates, one boy accused me of taking pictures for Volusia so she could make more hats. That's when I knew Volusia's hatmaking was common knowledge, and that no one believed we ordered them from South America.

17

When Volusia wasn't in her sewing room, she was in the kitchen telling stories. She could start talking in the kitchen when she baked a cake or cooked up some big dinner for a holiday, and she didn't seem to care if we understood what she was saying, though she cared if we listened. One day we sat at the kitchen table playing cards. Volusia kneaded the pie dough and rolled it out onto the counter.

"Albert love my pie shells," she said. She cut and fluted three pie shells, then started her ritual for cooking apples.

Mama Agnes had asked some women to come in for lunch. Now that she had a business, she had become more social in the town. Volusia had baked a ham to slice cold, and made a lime Jell-O salad. She rolled out two piecrusts, and talked about Finney, the father of Albert and Janey Louise. Finney had left a few months before Janey Louise was born.

"He was tall, so big and handsome. Girls could not stop looking at Finney when he walked by. When I walked along beside him, I felt more beautiful than I was."

"Did you love him more than anybody?" I asked. I could ask Volusia anything. If she didn't want to answer she'd tell me to hush up.

She didn't answer my question directly, but said, "I almost left him, but couldn't. He done everything to me. He left me alone for days without no money. He didn't show up when Albert was born, though he so proud it was a son, when he came back home, he went out bragging about his son born that day."

I looked at Janey Louise, but she had heard this before.

"Then when Janey Louise come along he said he'd get me to the hospital, but he didn't. I never fussed at him, because it didn't do no good." Volusia's expression changed to a dreamy one. "Sometimes though, he'd come in late and bring me something, some flowers or a box of candy, or some little trinket I had to pretend I liked. Once he bought me a dress, and I tried to picture Finney going into a store and picking it out. He got the right size, and the price tag was still hanging on the sleeve."

Volusia brought us a bowl, with a generous amount of batter left in it and two spoons. "He said for me to try it on," she told us. "'Try it on right now,' he said. Well, I pulled off my clothes and slipped on the prettiest, softest cotton dress you ever saw. Tiny little flowers all over it. Little flecks of yellow in the middle of every blue flower. There was long sleeves reaching all the way to my wrists." She touched her wrists to show what she meant.

Janey Louise and I had stopped our card playing and listened, our attention divided between the batter and Volusia's description of the dress.

"Had little lace cuffs at the end, and around the neck. I didn't know what to do when he bought me that dress. I thought 'Now this'll be a man I can stay with forever.' But I always thought that, so why I was thinking it so definite was due to that dress.

"Now during the night I lay awake and could hear Finney breathing. His hairy arm thrown across my waist. That was before Janey Louise was born, but I knew I was pregnant when he gave me that dress. I just hadn't tole him yet. When I tole him he started burning things down and stealing, but, come to find out he'd been stealing all along.

"He burned down a store outside town. That was the first time, but it was just a old abandon store, not anything in it, though I think he thought there was. He did this with some of his no-good friends. Finney could never pick friends to amount to anything. He came home and tole me he did it, bragging, just bragging about how he and Ned Pooler walked slowlike to a place he knew this store was and they brought kerosene and matches. 'We wanted to see something burn,' he said, explaining to me.

"I wanted to touch him when he said it. I think of him now and my mind curls up like a dry leaf and breaks in pieces. There never was a person like Finney. He was a sorry, no-count man, but it softened a soul to look at him and to listen to him talk."

Volusia turned to take the bowl from us and said, "We would wrestle. Whoo. Wrestle on the kitchen floor till we was tired." She pointed to our kitchen floor as though she meant they had wrestled there. "He got heavy though. I guess I did, too. But we'd wrestle in those young, thinner days until we couldn't move no more. Then Finney, he would pat me like I was a baby or a pet and then he'd fall asleep, nuzzling his head in my arms and making me stay there on the hard floor till he woke. I never minded this. I never minded when he did those things.

"What I minded was his absence and his quiet times that seemed worse than absence. I minded his moving inside me before dawn, thrashing and pushing till he was through, not caring what I felt like."

I looked at Janey Louise, and we giggled as if we had heard some little piece we weren't supposed to hear. "Then one day he stopped moving to me before dawn, then he stopped coming home at all, and I was thinking he had another woman, but that won't it. He just went off in the woods and cut his sweet throat, or else somebody cut it for him." I had never heard this part, and when I looked at Janey Louise she did not look back at me. I wondered why she never told me how he died.

"Him doing that, knowing how Volusia care so much," Volusia spoke now with disgust, "And Janey Louise not yet born." She turned to face us. "It was his stealing that done it. I come to know he stole those trinkets and that candy he used to bring, and he stole the dress with the little blue cornflowers, and a ashtray I loved more than him almost—though neither one of us smoked. But this ashtray had colors like a rainbow in a glass. He knew I would like that.

"He would say, 'Volusia, baby, I ain't no robber,' and I believed him." She turned to look at us. "You think I am some kind of *fool?*"

She did not want an answer, but still we said, "No, ma'am."

"You think Volusia was a fool to believe him when he say that? 'I know you not,' I tole him. And it was true. No matter how much he stole, still he was not that kind of person. It was something else in him made him do it. I believed that, and that is why he loved me more than most people love other people, because I believed him."

She came to the table and picked up our cards. She was going to send us out now. "And if there is a moral to this story, as we know the Lord would like every story to have, the moral would be this: Believes in the people who you love, because if you don't, there's just no use in it."

18

I left Joe Sugar's store with Tucker and came back to the house. Jane stayed with Joe and Capp. I would pick up August in the afternoon, but I wanted to call Johnny first. I needed to hear his voice. I wanted to tell him I had a wedding hat.

Johnny worked with construction companies now, all over Texas. He had completed his engineering degree and was hired for large-scale projects. He had an office in downtown Houston.

"You know what I want to do to you, don't you?" I said into the phone. "Can you guess what I would do, if I were there right now?"

"Who *is* this?" he said.

"I'm going to spoil you for other women," I continued.

"That's fine." He sounded formal. "And I'll look forward to it."

"You have somebody there with you?" I asked.

"Yes."

"You want me to talk dirty?"

"No. I don't think so."

"Johnny?"

"I'll call you tonight."

As we hung up, I heard him tell someone that that was his wife.

Johnny called me back in fifteen minutes. I mentioned the wedding hat, and that I would be home in a few days.

"How is Jane?" he asked. He wanted to know how we were getting along.

"Better than I expected," I told him. "Listen, tell Ty I wish him good luck in his game. Isn't he pitching?"

"Not until next week. Call him tonight. He thinks you're mad because he didn't want to come to the funeral."

"Tell him I'm not mad. Tell him Volusia herself would've wanted him to stay for his game. I'll tell him when I call tonight. Johnny, I'm picking up August at the airport this afternoon. He's coming back for the funeral."

"I wondered about that." Johnny said.

"Another thing," I told him, "when you hung up the phone a little while ago, I heard what you said."

"What?"

"You told someone that I was your wife."

"Was that *you*?" he asked.

The last doll I ever got for Christmas wore a skater's costume with fur trim on the cuffs of her sleeves and the edge of her skirt. Perfectly shaped legs and arms extended gracefully from her torso. Her minuscule waist and large breasts reminded me of Katy Keene in the comic books, or Archie's girl, Veronica. Long dark hair fell in coarse strands down her back, but could be pulled up into a ponytail. I named the doll Gloria, but kept her with me only when no one could see. I was getting too old for dolls, and felt more mature than girls who still played with them.

Sometimes I liked to pretend that Gloria was going out on a date. She wore her skating costume and smoked cigarettes. When the man came to pick her up, he kissed her immediately—overwhelmed by her beauty. I named this man Ormando.

Margaret Turnbull already had breasts and sometimes put her hair into a ponytail. My own breasts were getting a slow start. Janey Louise liked to stand (without a shirt) in front of our long mirror on the back of the bedroom door. Her breasts were brown, but the nipples stuck out pink. She poked at her chest, pointing to them.

"Here they come!" she said.

I never stood before the mirror when she was there, but when I was alone I wondered why nothing was happening to me. I tried to imagine a whole life without breasts.

I asked my mother if I could buy a training brassiere. I hated the word "brassiere," but felt more embarrassed to say "bra"—as if I were pretending to know more than I did. I felt embarrassed about anything that had to do with breasts. Volusia called them "bosoms"—which was worse. I prayed to the moon that mine would grow huge.

During the summer Mama Agnes gave me a Toni Home Permanent to make my hair curl. I looked older with short curly hair and
older boys began to follow me to the drug store after school. Sometimes they whistled at me. I believed that in some way the Toni Home
Permanent had made my breasts larger. My training bra filled to its
pointy little ends, and I could stand before the mirror with Janey
Louise and watch them come.

Around the time of brassieres and home permanents, I began to bother
Volusia with questions about love and sex, about men. Lowell Hardison
had already kissed me in the fields behind the cemetery. He had touched
my breasts, and I felt we could do everything together. In school we had
a day on Reproduction, (the boys went to one room and the girls to another), and no one could look at each other at lunchtime. After that day
I followed Volusia around the house and asked her questions.

"Stop bothering me. I got to shell these peas before supper."

"I want to ask *one* thing."

"You been hanging around me all day. What's the matter with you?
Go ahead and ask. Get it over with." She shucked peas into a big glass
bowl, her hands working like a machine.

"I'm wondering what it's like to love somebody." I remembered seeing love between my mother and daddy, and said so. Volusia said that
Janey Louise never saw that kind of love. "Not anywhere in her life,"
she said. But she wouldn't answer my question. She kept on dropping
peas into her bowl.

"We gonna have anything besides peas for supper?" I asked. Volusia
used to cook a pot of lady peas with a little bacon grease. My mouth
watered to think about it.

She let the back of her hand brush hair from her eyes. "First," she
said, deciding to answer me, "a man's got to know *how* to love. Because
if he don't know how, there won't be a thing you can do to make him.
But now, you find a man who can love, you can tap into that love like a
well inside yourself. All you been saving up, all you been holding onto
because you so scared—it just come gushing out." She smiled a huge
grin. "When a man loves you, honey, go after that. Won't be so many
who know how."

"And what else?" I said. She wasn't really answering the specifics of what I had asked.

"What you want? A list?"

"Yeah." While she was thinking, I got up to get a pencil and some tablet paper.

"Five things," she said, and held up one finger. "Has to be some laughing. You get through anything if you can be laughing. Two," she said, "you got to think he's handsome. Won't matter if anybody else thinks so, but you got to think he's the best-looking man around, and got to tell him so. Same for him. He got to tell you the same."

She held up her third finger. "Three, he has to like children, and be willing to look after them when they come—as they will. Four, you got to like the way he smells. Love the smell of your own man, love it so you can pick him out of a crowd with a blindfold on."

She smiled into her lap of peas, remembering something. Volusia had been going out with Joe Sugar on her days off, and I believed she was thinking about him.

"And five," she thought hard. "I can't remember what five is."

"But don't you have to *love* him?" I asked. "Is that the fifth one?"

"Naw," she said. "If all these other things are true, you're loving him already, so the question of love won't even have to be asked."

The wind blew a soft breeze across the porch, and Volusia got up. I decided to stay and help her with supper. I wanted to stay near her in the kitchen, because she had told me about love.

Later that same day, Janey Louise and I walked to the pond, and I found a chrysalis. Janey Louise told me to keep it away from her, that I could get a disease.

I kept the chrysalis in a jar and observed it for changes. I didn't know if it would be a butterfly or a moth. I hoped I wouldn't be asleep when it came out. I hoped I wouldn't be at school, or at Margaret's house.

Margaret's period had started. She showed me the pad she used, a dirty pad with brownish blood caked inside its folds. I wished she hadn't shown me. She said that blood came from inside her vagina, and that now she could have babies if she wanted to. I had heard the word vagina and knew it was the most private part of a woman. Janey Louise said it was like a hole. My doll Gloria did not have a vagina.

At night I touched myself and pushed until a wild feeling came. I loved doing this. I loved what I thought about while doing it. Sometimes I made myself sore, and Mama Agnes had to run water in the bathtub. She let me soak until the hurting went away. She told me not to push at myself so much, so I promised, but the promise was hard to keep. Finally, I stopped calling my mother and ran the bathwater myself. I soaked until I felt soothed.

The chrysalis opened on a Tuesday evening before supper. I was talking on the phone to Bobby Batson, one of the boys who had begun calling me. I saw the husk open.

I screamed into the phone, as I saw the long body, with bright glistening wings, pull out. It looked like an emperor. Every part of it was wet.

I dropped the phone and ran outside with the jar. I opened the lid and let it go. For a moment it hovered on the lip of the jar, and I studied its decision to fly.

"Go on," I said. "It'll be easy." I watched with a string around my heart until it was gone.

19

Early in 1951 we heard rumors that the United States might invade North Korea. We looked up North Korea on the map. Albert called to say he had furlough time in October. He thought he would be sent somewhere after that, but he didn't say where.

Volusia's happiness about seeing Albert was clouded by her dread of war. I kept hoping that when Albert came back, he would visit our house. His presence in my life was huge, because of how much Janey Louise talked of him, and because of the way our conversations at supper always seemed to come back to his name. I wanted more than ever to see a picture of him.

"He's gonna be here for eight days," Volusia said for the umpteenth time. "So we won't be coming in during those days." She spoke these words directly to my mother, and repeated them, so my mother couldn't object. "I'm gonna make all his foods. I hope I still know what he like."

I helped Volusia make two coconut cakes. They were large, but she would not allow me to cut even one small piece for myself.

On the day before Albert arrived, I reminded Janey Louise of her promise to take me to her house and show me her pictures of him. She had forgotten the promise, and when I mentioned it she didn't want to take me. I had never been inside her house on Latham Street.

Finally, I persuaded her. Albert would arrive on Saturday, so we had only one more day. We caught one bus, then another before we reached Latham Street.

On the first bus I sat in back with Janey Louise, but the driver got upset. "Move up front, sugar," he said. "Let that little nigger-girl stay in back." He didn't turn around, but watched me change seats in his rearview mirror. I moved up just one seat, so I could still be close. Neither of us mentioned what the driver had said, and I wondered if Janey Louise heard him.

After riding the last bus, we walked two blocks to Latham Street, and I told Janey Louise how a friend of mine at school had gotten sick and how they said it might be polio.

"If it *is* polio," I told her, "our whole school might close down because of it."

"Lu-u-cky," sang Janey Louise.

Her house sat stuck back in a row of other houses. People looked out their windows to stare at us. The street went through a section of town I had heard my mother describe as "the poor section."

"Gosh!" I said, trying to sound impressed.

The house looked dark, like a shoe box, settled back into a run of scraggly trees with small patches of scattered grass that covered the yard. Janey Louise reached for a key they kept below the second porch step, and let us in. The house had four rooms, counting the bathroom.

The living room had a couch with an old bedspread draped over it. The kitchen was behind this room and had a small stove and refrigerator, round at the corners. The kitchen table was set with a jar of honey, salt, pepper, and sugar in the middle. A picture of Finney hung above the stove, but photographs of Albert were everywhere.

"Who took all these pictures of Albert?" I asked, curious, because Volusia refused to let me photograph her.

"He sends them from wherever he is in the army," Janey Louise said.

Pictures of Albert in uniform, in civilian clothes, pictures with women (different women), pictures with friends (white men as well as colored), and one picture of Albert alone with his gun in front of him and his feet apart. Beneath the picture Albert had written: Parade Rest.

"Why'd you want to see his pictures?" Janey Louise asked.

"I don't know. I thought I would learn something about him from seeing them. I thought if I saw his pictures I would know what to say to him."

"Well, you're not gonna have that chance."

"Why not?" I couldn't believe that Albert would not come by our house and be introduced. "He *has* to come by our house."

"Uh-uh. He won't even come *near*. He hates for us to be in y'all's house. He says we got to get out. He says it all the time."

"But *why*?"

"He gets real mad at white people. Long as I remember he's been mad at y'all."

"But I thought I'd get to see him. I helped make his coconut cake with Volusia and everything. Will you *tell* him I made that cake?"

"Yeah, I'll tell him. But won't make any difference."

"Why not?"

"*Cake* can't make him not be mad."

On the day Albert arrived, Volusia cooked a ham with a crust of brown sugar, orange juice, and mustard. She cooked vegetables she never made for us: white beans with hocks of ham, collard greens, corn scraped off the cob and stewed in thick cream and butter. She made cornbread sticks. As she cooked she seemed fidgety. Janey Louise seemed of a different mind, too.

Albert spent his eight days at home, and our house felt empty without Volusia and Janey Louise. I kept looking for them when I came home from school, even though I knew they would be gone.

"I want them to bring Albert over here," I told my mother. "Why can't they bring him here?"

"Maybe he doesn't want to come," my mother said. I could tell she missed them too, and Tucker whined almost constantly.

For the first few days, Volusia called us at night before our bedtime, but then she stopped calling. Janey Louise told me later that Albert made her stop.

"Why is he so *mad*?" I couldn't think of what I had ever done to Albert, and wondered if he was mad because I had come to their house and seen his pictures.

"He's mad because of the army," Janey Louise explained, and I guessed that was true.

When the week of Albert was over, Volusia came back to our house with a small fresh coconut cake for me and Tucker. She sat in the kitchen all that first day, humming songs that sounded mournful and not recognizable.

"Go out and play now," she said to me.

"I want to stay in here."

"Do what I tell you." Her dress showed soil, and her eyes appeared red, swollen with crying. She let Tucker sit on her lap without fussing at him. She let him ask her for things. She let him do anything, because he was the boy.

20

At first Tucker complained of being tired and spent a few days resting in bed. No one mentioned polio, but we thought about it. School was already out, and the community center and all the public swimming pools were closed. My mother made us take naps in the afternoon, to prevent polio from taking hold. So when Tucker came down with polio symptoms, I wondered if he'd been cheating on his naps.

Doc Beryl came to our house to examine Tucker. He brought us all into the dining room.

"Now, I don't want you to be alarmed," he said in the most alarming way, "but we'll need to take Tuck to the hospital for some tests. I'm thinking it might be polio, but if I'm right, we've caught this in the earliest stages and I believe he'll be all right." We moved like zombies, getting things ready. Tucker liked all the attention.

Mama Agnes slept on a cot in Tucker's hospital room for the first two nights while we waited to hear the test results. Doc Beryl said the test indicated polio, and that we had some rough months ahead of us. My mother called for August to come immediately.

Tucker grew sicker by the day. His fever spiked to 106 degrees, and made him too confused to recognize us. August stayed in a motel near the hospital, but he took over my mother's job most nights in Tucker's room. Doc Beryl said that Tucker might have to be put into an iron lung.

I'd seen pictures in *Life* magazine of a machine that breathed for a person when that person could not breathe for himself. Tucker's iron lung looked and sounded like a large animal that had swallowed him up, though not completely. His head stuck out, and we teased him about being a turtle. He stayed in good spirits, better than I would have imagined.

I checked out books from the library about Kit Carson, and Custer, Little Big Horn. We read the books, looking into the mirror above Tucker's head. August bought him an Indian hatchet and cowboy boots. They talked about what he would do when he got well. Each afternoon before my mother left the hospital, she took August into a private room, either to pray or talk about money.

Volusia came to the hospital every morning and afternoon. She and Tucker played games. Volusia could make him laugh, but once we got home no one laughed about anything.

"That child all closed up in his big lung just break my heart," Volusia said. "Every time I see him I want to pull him out. Janey Louise, you ought to go in there and see him, 'stead of just sending him notes and cookies."

"I don't want to. I don't want to go."

I was afraid for Tucker, but I was never afraid he would die. Two months went by and we had a ritual of visiting him. Then one day I walked in expecting to hear the whu-ush-thump of the lung's working, but the room was quiet. Tucker was sitting propped up on some pillows.

"Tuck!" I cried. He was out of the iron lung.

"Yeah, I know," he said, looking somewhat heroic. I noticed how one arm moved more slowly, was more awkward than the other. It looked floppy.

Doc Beryl told us that Tucker would be slightly paralyzed on his left side, and that he needed physical therapy to help him walk and use his left hand.

"His face might be paralyzed," the doctor said. Tucker's mouth did pull down on his left side, but I could not believe he would always look like that. His right side looked fine.

Volusia refused to baby Tucker. She treated him as she always had. She fussed at him, though it was clear she loved him best. She spanked him just the way she had spanked me and Janey Louise.

Usually she spanked us all at the same time, the way she gave out treats. But with Tucker, she never used a switch. Even if he was as guilty as we were, she didn't make him pick a long switch from the forsythia bush.

"Why don't you make *him*?" Janey Louise asked. She resented Tucker more than I did. "He did it just as much as we did."

"I know what he did," Volusia told her. "You not the one in charge here. When you be the one in charge you can do what you want."

August had been around for most of three months, and I was used to seeing him again. When he left, he called every night.

We carried Tucker to the phone, but during the rest of the day we made him walk to exercise his legs. He got very tired. Sometimes he cried and begged us to carry him.

Before Tucker was even old enough to walk or talk, I went into the nursery and found him sitting in bed playing with the stomach of his blue teddy bear. The sun fell through the slats of blinds and drew lines across his face and arms. His legs stuck out straight in front of him. I was the first to see him sit up.

I went to get my mother, because I wanted her to know that I'd been the first. But as I turned to leave the room, Tucker fell forward and hit his face on the rungs of the crib. He began to scream, and my mother ran into the room.

"Oh, Evie! You woke him up."

"I did not! He was already awake. He bumped his head."

"What's the matter?" my father came into the room.

"Evie woke up Tucker," she said.

August lifted me, throwing me high into the air and catching me, as if I were the baby. He laughed and put me down. "I need to take this girl to the pond," he said. "That's what I need to do."

I didn't mention that I'd seen Tucker sit up, but the next morning they discovered it for themselves. Still, I didn't admit to seeing it first. I felt that Tucker and I had a secret knowledge about what he could do, and I still felt that way, as I helped him practice his walking.

"I snuck into your room one time when you were real little," I told him. "I saw you sitting up in bed playing with your bear. It was the first time you ever sat up."

"I remember that." He lifted his brace and clamped it onto his smallest leg. I helped him close it down tight.

"No you don't, stupid. You were too little. You couldn't walk or talk, but I remember the exact day, because the next day Mama saw you sit up, but I saw it first."

"Really?" he said, understanding the importance of what I was saying.

"It was like we had a secret before you could even say anything," I told him.

"Yeah." He pushed himself up, stiff-legged, and balanced with one hand on my shoulder. I took his arm and we planned to walk the length of the room twelve times. After nine lengths, he wanted to quit.

"You did ten yesterday. Doc Beryl said we had to increase it every day." We walked one more, then another. He was about to sit down.

"If you do three more, I'll play crazy eights with you for an hour."

That night Tucker's legs were sore, and he had to soak in the tub longer than usual. We played thirty-four games of crazy eights. Whenever he won, he smiled and his mouth pulled down on one side. But each day his smile looked less droopy, and we knew that one day he would wake up and be fine.

"I did good today, didn't I?" he said.

Tucker had missed half a year of school, and would have to start again in the fifth grade. He was not looking forward to going back to school and not being with his friends.

"You did great."

"My legs hurt, but I *like* it. I think when they hurt that I'll be able to run soon."

"You *will*," I told him, and felt the power of our secret knowledge. "You will run *so* fast."

21

When school began after Christmas, Tucker went for only a half a day at first. The school nurse, Miss Rice (who looked like a movie star), called my mother to talk about Tucker. Then as Tucker started attending full days, she called me to her office.

"I want to talk about your brother," she said. "I mean, if you don't mind." I amazed myself by telling this nurse more than I meant to tell. The moment I saw her face, I knew she could help us. I told her how sometimes boys made fun of Tucker, and how I got into fights when that happened.

Miss Rice came to our school twice a week. She explained that she had been hired to work with children affected by polio, and that I could help her do this. I asked her not to tell anyone that I talked to her. If people knew, they might think I had a problem, too.

"I won't tell a soul," Miss Rice said.

Whenever we talked, I felt a dark line drawn around us, enclosing a place where I could talk about Tucker.

"What's that lady ask you about?" Janey Louise wiped her nose on her sleeve. We stopped at the drug store and I went in to buy a cherry smash, and to bring one out to Janey Louise, who wasn't allowed in the drug store.

"Who? You mean Miss Rice?"

Janey Louise wore Volusia's blouse, which was miles too big. She thought it looked good. She had on an old skirt of mine and purple shoes bought at a thrift shop.

"You look *awful*," I said. "Did you wear that to your school today?"

"It's *your* skirt," she said, trying to bring me into the awfulness. When she got haughty, she acted like someone who had just won a prize. "What does that lady talk to you about?"

"Who told *you*?"

"Mama Agnes. She said you'd be late today because you were talking again to the lady at school about Tuck."

"We just talk." I wanted to change the subject. "That's all."

"What she say?"

"Nothing. Mostly I do the talking. One thing though—I think she can help him."

"You think she can make him not be cripple anymore?"

"No. I don't think that," I said. "Anyway, he's not so cripple now. He can run fast. I *like* the way he runs."

"Me, too. I hope they don't change a thing about him."

I opened a bag of candy that I kept in my red leather pocketbook and offered some to Janey Louise. I'd spent my entire allowance on jelly beans and candy corn. Janey Louise took a handful of the candy corn.

"Our brothers both fighting some kind of war," she said. "I hope they gonna win."

When we got to the back door, Volusia waited at the sink. "We heard from Albert today. He's gonna be at Inshon. He be stationed there and I think it'll be better than most places. Don't you?"

Later that night, Mama Agnes got out a map to search for the place where Albert was. We drew a circle around Inshon. We put the map on the refrigerator door and everytime we got food we thought about Albert.

At night we listened to Edward R. Murrow and every morning we read Mercy's *Morning Herald*. Tucker's grades began to improve and so did his social life. Whenever Miss Rice came on Thursdays to take Tucker out of class, she was so bright-eyed and pretty that conferences with her made Tucker seem special. When Tucker returned to the classroom, all the other boys wanted to know what she talked about.

They treated Tucker as if Miss Rice were his girlfriend. They nudged him, and didn't tease him anymore about his braces. They wanted to be part of his world, so Tucker settled into a routine that allowed him to hold up his head.

At school I was known as the daughter of a woman who had started a hat business, whose father had run off, who had a brother with polio, and a colored family living in the house with them. Everyone suspected that Volusia and Janey Louise were more than just servants. Margaret Turnbull had spread a rumor that Janey Louise slept in my room.

My mother had started to play bridge with a group of ladies on the third Wednesday afternoon of each month. Volusia prepared finger sandwiches, and sometimes I helped cut off the crusts before putting them on the platter. Some sandwiches were spread with cream cheese and olives, but others had cucumbers and weren't as good. The best were Volusia's own pimento cheese. During the summer months Janey Louise and I would help ourselves to several pimento-cheese fingers before putting them onto the platter.

My mother placed small bowls of candies on the card table and a scorecard with tassels. She bought special bridge napkins, not for regular use, with hearts, diamonds, spades, and clubs engraved in each corner.

Margaret's mother, Adele Turnbull, was one of the bridge players. She wore dresses made of linen or silk, or wool, depending on the weather. She wore over her shoulders a sweater that was dyed to match her dress, or skirt. And her shoes sometimes had jewelry on them.

All the ladies liked to see Volusia when they came to our house. They always went to visit her hat room, to see what she was working on. Volusia served them coffee or tea, then brought in the tray of sandwiches. She never wore her uniform on the days they played bridge.

Volusia didn't wear her uniform on most days, but usually my mother didn't care. On Bridge Days she asked Volusia to wear it, and Volusia said her uniform needed washing. No one ever asked about her uniform, except Mrs. Turnbull.

If I came home while they were playing bridge, Mrs. Turnbull would motion me to come speak to her. She would hug me and say I should come over to see Margaret sometime soon. Everything she did was an act, but I knew she was glad I had never told what went on in their house.

The last time I spent the night at Margaret's house, we slept in the basement. Mr. Turnbull liked me and allowed us to do daring things. He suggested we sleep in the basement, and even put a radio and a mattress on the floor, saying that sleeping bags would not be comfortable.

The night we slept in the basement, Margaret told me that her mother had lost a baby, and when I asked what she meant, she explained that a baby came out of her mother's stomach too soon. I hadn't noticed that her mother looked pregnant, but Margaret claimed that she "wasn't showing yet." Margaret was wise to know about these things in the seventh grade.

I asked was it a boy or a girl, the way people ask about new babies. She said a boy. I didn't ask why the baby came out too soon, or if her mother would have another one.

22

Volusia's back began to hurt all the time, and her bad moods extended to everyone except Tucker. She blamed her back pain on the roll-away bed she had to sleep on. She complained every morning, then one day after school I saw a large truck in front of the house, with two men lifting out a bed with a new Beauty Rest mattress and box springs. My mother acted very excited.

The men carried the bed into the house and my mother told them to put it in the room off the kitchen. She urged them to hurry, because Volusia had gone to the grocery store and we wanted it to be in place when she got back. Tucker and I brought clean sheets and a bedspread from upstairs. We made up the bed, and my mother folded a blanket at the end. Janey Louise watched us, without smiling.

When Volusia returned, the men were gone and we helped her bring in the groceries. Tucker couldn't wait to tell her, but we kept punching him to make him shut up. Volusia seemed tired and wanted to start supper. She told Janey Louise to boil some water for macaroni, and she hung up her sweater by the door. My mother waited for her to open the door to her room.

Volusia froze when she saw it, and a tiny smile came to her mouth. "Now what do you suppose happened in here?" she said. A pleased fussiness came to her voice whenever she didn't know how to be grateful.

"We just thought you'd like something that wouldn't be so hard on your back," my mother told her.

"Well." Volusia reached to touch the smooth oak headboard. "I never saw anything so pretty." She sat on the edge of the mattress slowly, as if she thought the whole bed might collapse.

Mama Agnes closed the door and let her be alone. "I'll make supper tonight, Volusia." The water had begun to boil and we threw in the macaroni and warmed up some grated cheese and milk. I liked the idea of Volusia in the next room on her new bed, her feet up. And us cooking dinner.

When we asked Janey Louise to set the table, her face formed itself into a scowl. She said she had something to do, and besides she didn't feel very good. Her head hurt and so did her back.

That night Janey Louise and I snuck Tucker into our room. He wanted to hear what we talked about at night. He wanted to be in on our night talk. We carried him to our room and laid him on a mat between our beds. We left his braces beside his bed in case my mother looked in on him.

He listened to us talk for a while without saying anything, then from between the beds his voice came up. "Why do colored people sing so much?" Our lights were out and his voice sounded slightly sleepy, as though maybe he had been dozing.

"What do you mean?" I said, because Janey Louise hadn't answered him.

Tucker sat up. "Mama said it had to do with their souls and how much they love God."

"That's bound to be right," I told him. We spoke as though Janey Louise wasn't there. "Because what's sung is mostly church songs." I said this even though I had heard other kinds of songs. I'd heard blues and rock, but even those sounded like church.

"They sing for the fun of it," Janey Louise said, as though she wasn't one of them.

"*You* don't sing," I said, accusing.

"*Some*time I do. Sometime I *hum*."

"I don't ever hear you," said Tucker. "Why don't you sing now?"

"I don't feel like it. If I don't feel like it, I can't do it."

"But I want you to sing now," I said. "For me. I want to hear if you *can* sing." My tone became a demand.

"Well, I cain't. Not if I don't feel like it."

"This is *my* house and you have to do what I say, just like Volusia has to do what Mama Agnes says."

Tucker grew very still between us.

"Not al-ways. Not *ev*-ery time."

"Name one time."

"They are times. You just cain't see."

"Well, it's behind the back then. That won't count."

Janey Louise didn't answer, then she said, "It is *your* house, but it is *my* song. You cain't make me sing if I don't want to."

Volusia heard us arguing and came hurrying up the stairs.

"If you girls don't stop, I'm gonna switch both of you. You think I am *born* to climb these steps everytime you start your fussing?"

Janey Louise turned from her mother.

"Now what's this about?" She directed the question to Janey Louise's back.

"Nothin'."

"Good Lord! What is my Tucker doing in here on the floor?" She didn't want an answer, but lifted Tucker and carried him back to his room. When she returned, she spoke only to Janey Louise.

"Maybe you just better come downstairs with me. You two can be apart for a while."

I heard Volusia whisper-fussing at Janey Louise, and I got out my Tangee lipstick hidden in the springs of my bed. I put it on my lips—a thick coat. While I was doing this, the shadow of a bird flew across my room and a glimpse of light came in at the side of my eye. I imagined it came from the movement of an angel.

23

I arrived at the airport early, but so did August's flight.

I felt nervous looking for him, then I saw a man come off the plane and though the hair was different, I recognized him immediately. His tall lankiness was noticeable anywhere. The shape of his head, his smile, slightly sad. What surprised me most was the briefcase he carried, and the fact that he didn't recognize me.

Then I realized that the man I saw was the August of years ago—a younger man who couldn't possibly be August now. When I looked around, I saw another man with glasses, shorter, stooped, with a paunch, and not much hair. He bore only a slight resemblance to the father I'd known, and I was shocked to think that I could've passed him on the street and not recognized him.

He approached me with open arms, but his gait was tentative, as if he had to work to coordinate the movements of his legs and back. The man with the briefcase was embracing his family.

"Did your mother tell you I was coming?" he asked.

I nodded. I couldn't get over his appearance. I wondered if he had looked this way five years ago, and if my memory had kept him young.

"Where's Tucker?" he asked. "I was hoping he'd come with you."

"Tuck has a girl he wants you to meet. He's engaged, you know."

"Your mother told me, and Tucker called to let me speak to her. He'll be married before *you* are."

"My first one doesn't count?"

"Only because of Ty." He put his suitcase into the car and didn't ask to drive.

"It counts," I said, and felt defensive. "It counts because the failure of it keeps me from trying again."

"Poor Evie. You think you can protect your heart from being broken?"

"I was hoping so."

"Forget it."

I looked at my father with new eyes. I had not thought of his heart ever being broken.

The first time August returned to Mercy, he had been gone for a year and a half. Tucker and I had been to see him at the Sea of Cortez, but our second summer without him was ending, and I was no longer expecting him to show up.

The air had been quiet and final all day. Janey Louise had gone wandering off toward the river again. She liked to fish, and I hadn't seen her since lunchtime.

A car drove up the road. I didn't recognize the car, but could see two people inside—a man and a woman. I imagined for a moment that the people were my mother and father, and I sat down on the porch steps, waiting for—I didn't know what.

A dog that wasn't mine lay in the yard and barked when the strange car drove in. I could see as it drew closer the outline and shape of my father's face. I could see through the windshield the shadow figure I still carried in my mind from the night when he paused at the door. I remembered that moment in the same way someone feels a shout in the face. As the car pulled into the driveway, I knew who the man was, and I knew the woman was Melina.

August saw me. He opened the car door slowly, as if he were afraid of being shot. I'd seen men get out of cars like this in the movies, and always they were afraid of something the person seeing them might do. But I was already running toward him so he didn't need to be afraid. I ran and put my arms around his neck, jumping up to wrap my legs around his waist. I was too big to do this, and he staggered with my weight. I held on and he kept saying "Evie-girl, Evie. You are so big, honey. I didn't know you would get so tall."

He swung me around in circles and for a moment we were the only two people in the world, the ones who mattered the most to each other, then I saw the woman, still sitting in the car. She got out and stood by the car with the door open. I had met her when I visited the Sea of Cortez, but I never expected to see her here at the house. She was prettier than I remembered. Her dark hair was shiny on her shoulders, and she wore a long red skirt. I didn't like anything about her.

"You remember Melina?" August said. "She's never been to Georgia before."

I nodded, trying to be polite, but I didn't say anything. I didn't know what to say.

"We'll visit here a few days and then go back. Do you think that'll be all right?"

"You gonna stay *here*?" The dog began to bark again.

"Not in this house. I mean, we'll be around for a few days." He looked into the doorway of the house. "Is your mother here? Where's Tuck?"

"He went with Volusia to get Mama. She has two jobs now."

"Well, I have a check to help things out. Maybe she won't have to work so hard."

"Volusia stays with us all the time. She and Janey Louise live here now."

"Good."

Melina walked toward us and began to speak to my father. She spoke with an accent.

"You want to come in?" I asked. I didn't want her to say yes.

"We can just sit here on the porch," August said, but he didn't sit in the place where he used to sit. I sat on the steps, and Melina stood. Her red skirt hung full and long around her ankles. I wondered what Mama would think, or Volusia.

"She's so pree-ty," Melina said about me. She pronounced pretty as though it were something true. "And Too-ker, he ees smarrt, no?" I hated how hard she was trying.

"Tucker made bad grades this time," I said. "He got a C- in spelling."

We could see a car coming up the road. Volusia was driving and she leaned forward to see who was on the porch. Tucker and Mama sat scrunched together in the front seat. Janey Louise had not come back from the river. If she didn't come soon, she would miss everything.

"I think that's them coming now," I said.

August stood up, and squinted.

Tucker got out of the car and I could tell Volusia had already told him who was on the porch. He ran and jumped into August's arms.

August swung him up high. I wanted to repeat the fact about his bad grades.

When Mama got out of the car, her face looked as hard as a table. The thought of August being here was registering on her mind. Volusia went into the house, but her eyes looked like the eyes of a dog when it doesn't know what is about to happen.

My mother walked straight to the porch where Melina stood in her long red skirt.

"And what do you think you're doing?" she asked my father, not even looking at Melina.

August took out a check and handed it to my mother. "I wanted to give you this." Mama didn't take it, but turned to go into the house. Tucker was asking a million questions, so Volusia called for him to bring in a sack or two of groceries, "Because" she spoke emphatically, "Mr. Bell will still be here when we finish bringing everything in."

August followed my mother into the house, leaving Melina on the porch. I felt sorry for her, and asked her to sit down.

I could hear low talking in the next room, but Volusia kept telling us things to do until their talking was over. My dad came into the kitchen where we were putting groceries away. He lifted Tucker, holding him high, then close to himself.

"Tell me what a silkworm is in its first stage of life," he yelled. I wanted to answer. I knew the answer, but I knew he would have a more difficult question for me.

"A moth! A moth!" Tucker said, laughing as though he had been tickled. I felt we were back again into something we knew how to do.

August turned to me, not lifting me as he had done before, but putting his hands level on my shoulders. "Do you remember the story of the French prisoner?" he asked.

"Yes! Yes! He made friends with a little spider in his cell. He wasn't lonely there, because he played a flute and trained it to come and go as he told it to."

"He beguiled it," said August.

"He *beguiled* it," I repeated.

"And he studied how it was different in different kinds of weather."

I remembered this story, and even the name of the Frenchman.
I said the name, but did not pronounce it right.

"Quatremère Disjonval," August said, without seeming to be
corrective.

He pulled me to him, my face into his warm shirt, and I could
smell him, his skin, and I remembered exactly who he was.

"Can you stay?" I asked stupidly, and without fear.

"Oh, honey," he said, which I knew was no.

I used to believe that the brain had a separate section to hold dreams,
and that a dream came in full-blown, turning on like a movie when we
slept. Then when we woke up, I believed we could tap into the dream
again, without even closing our eyes. I don't know if I learned this
from August or not, but we used to tell our dreams to each other. And
we believed in their reality.

The secret was to pay attention in a different way—to listen to a
bird, waiting for particular notes, or decipher the detail of a sparrow's
wing—its flexible, hollow bone, the barbules in each feather.

This kind of precision made me feel unencumbered by the useless
burden of chores. I felt free to let cobwebs grow and to observe the
habits of ants along kitchen counters. My mother and Volusia complained, but August had taught me the freedom that comes from such
sight. August the dreamer, the open-eyed wonderer.

We drove to August's motel. We'd always called it August's motel, because he stayed there each time he came to Mercy. He had stayed there
during Tucker's polio.

We stopped the car and he asked me about Volusia. I told him
about the weeks of pain and the overdose of pills. I said that Volusia's
body was in Joe Sugar's store.

"Did you know Volusia was blind for almost two years before she
had her cataract operation?" I asked. August shook his head. "She
wouldn't admit it though. She wouldn't wear her glasses and we
thought she was just being stubborn. She kept bumping into things."

We stopped in front of the motel, but neither of us got out of the car.

"Was she still making her hats?"

"Yes, but she had to devise a different way to see people. Once when we were in the dining room, Mama Agnes gave Volusia some pictures to look over. We put the pictures on the table and Volusia said, "You know, I'm blind as a bat. Can't see a thing.""

"I asked if she could see us, and she said, 'Can't see the table, can't see you.' That's when she got the idea of letting people come by the house so she could see them with her hands—feel their faces."

"She touched them?"

"People made appointments and came by to let Volusia discover their heads and faces. I think it must have felt like magic for someone to touch them like that." I reached to touch August's face to let him see how it felt.

"She just touched their eye sockets and ears and hair and chin—like this," I said. My fingers roamed lightly over his skin, and I thought of Volusia's hands running over a face and head and shoulders, like a piece of thread.

August smiled with pleasure. "That *is* magic."

"Her touch was light as a scarf," I said.

I left my hand resting on my father's shoulder and looked into his rheumy eyes. I wanted to say something about the French prisoner: his determination to make things right, his spider, and the ability to beguile.

II

BACKWATERS

A close childhood friend once came to visit Joseph.
They had shared the secrets that children tell each other
when they're lying on their pillows at night
before they go to sleep. These two
were completely truthful
with each other.

The friend asked, "What was it like when you realized
your brothers were jealous and what they planned to do?"

"I felt like a lion with a chain around its neck.
Not degraded by the chain, and not complaining,
but just waiting for my power to be recognized."

"How about down in the well, and in prison?
How was it then?"
"Like the moon when it's getting
smaller, yet knowing the fullness to come.
Like a seed pearl ground in the mortar for medicine
that knows it will now be the light in a human eye."

RUMI
"Childhood Friends"
translated by Coleman Barks

24

Joe Sugar began to come around our house during the fall of 1952. He had the blackest skin of any man I'd ever seen. He was the color of veins, and stood two inches shorter than Volusia. He looked square, like a chair, and his voice boomed when he spoke. But his tone was cheerful. He teased me and Janey Louise about everything.

"Look like you girls trying to outdo each other with your fine dresses. Boys won't have a chance when they see you." We giggled, because we knew his teasing was meant to make us feel beautiful.

His head looked bald, though upon closer inspection I saw a stubble of hair. He smiled broadly when he saw someone he liked. His face kept the appearance of a circle, immediately pleasant, and his arms fell beside him, thick and arched like those of a prize fighter.

We had heard that he was married as a young man. No one knew who the woman was, but we believed she had died and broken his heart. For a while Joe Sugar's grief made him drink, but when he inherited his father's land and built a store the drinking stopped.

He stocked the store's shelves with fresh produce from his summer garden—produce so fine that even white people came in to buy it. He increased his garden to include lettuce and butter beans, crowder peas. He stocked peaches from a neighbor's orchard.

After a few years Joe began to sell staples, so when people came in they could pick up salt or rice or macaroni, or washing powder and soap. Within five years, the store had a reputation (even in neighboring towns) for its produce. People came from as far as the Alabama line to buy his tomatoes and butter beans and new leaf lettuce.

Joe hired Tucker, Arnold Pepper, and three other boys to help him with the work in his garden. They added corn, squash, and blueberry bushes. Joe grew tomatoes that people bought and left the store eating like apples—juice running down their fronts, as they leaned over trying not to get tomato seeds on their clothes. In the fall he grew pumpkins and sold them for pies and Halloween jack-o'-lanterns. People paid more for one of Joe Sugar's pumpkins.

Volusia bought her produce from Joe Sugar's store. She drove over in the 1948 Dodge my mother gave to her when we got our new Studebaker. She bought Joe's tomatoes before he grew famous for them. But he didn't start coming by our house until after Albert left for Korea.

One Sunday afternoon a truck drove up and Joe Sugar walked to the front door to ask if Volusia Davis was there. My mother invited him in.

"Volusia's in the kitchen," she said. I stood beside the door, so he handed me a sack of tomatoes he had brought. He barely acknowledged my thank-you before turning to walk down the hallway toward the kitchen. He looked huge in our hall, like a bulldozer—that much out of place. He still carried an armful of fresh picked corn.

We heard Volusia humming to herself, and waited for Joe Sugar to reach the kitchen. My mother had never told a colored person, or anyone else selling something, to go to the back door. The first time I saw that done was at Margaret Turnbull's house. I couldn't figure the reason for it, though I'd seen most coloreds go to the back door anyway. Joe Sugar had never gone to anyone's back door, but people liked him and let him get by with it.

We listened for Volusia to be surprised by Joe, and felt like eavesdroppers. We could tell he already knew her pretty well by the greeting she gave him. Then we heard him give her the corn. Volusia said, "Why, thank you, Joe. We'll cook this for supper tonight."

"I guess you're busy," he said, being polite.

"No, I can fix you something, if you want. Sit down now."

My mother turned to me, "Let's go upstairs."

Before long Joe Sugar came over most Sunday afternoons and on Thursdays, Volusia's day off. They went off together in his truck. Volusia wore hose and high heels. Not like church, snazzier than church. I could tell she thought she looked pretty. Joe could not stop looking at her.

Sometimes Joe would come early in the morning to eat breakfast with us. On those days Volusia made hotcakes. She asked Joe questions without looking up from the batter sizzling in the pan. She told me to get the blueberries from the icebox.

"Y'all want some blueberries in this?" Volusia asked.

I said I did, and Volusia reached for a handful and threw them in. Janey Louise said she didn't want any in hers. She said she didn't like for one thing to touch another thing. She said she wanted her hotcakes and blueberries on separate plates.

Volusia laughed. Her laugh could put anybody in a good mood. When she laughed at you, it never felt like derision.

Sometimes on Fridays when I got home from school, I'd find Joe Sugar sitting at the kitchen table, eating fresh peach pie or something else I'd have a piece of. I'd hear his strong, deep voice even before I opened the back door.

"How you coming along in school?" he would ask. Volusia would stand up, embarrassed and restless. Joe never got embarrassed. Wherever he was, he felt at home.

The air was heavy with summer when we heard that Albert would soon be home and that he was a hero. He had single-handedly saved a battalion of soldiers, and though Negro soldiers were rarely awarded the important medals, President Truman had insisted that Albert B. Davis be given the Distinguished Service Cross. The newspapers were full of Albert's name. The medal ceremony would be in Washington and his family was invited to be there with him.

Our yard sprouted tips of June vegetables by the side of the house. Joe had helped us plant them, and I worked with Janey Louise to keep out bugs and weeds.

"He is a war hero," Volusia said. She was preparing to pick him up at the train depot. "He has gotten himself the Distingish Cross." She had received an invitation from President Truman, inviting her family to come to Washington and be honored. Mama Agnes and I helped them pack.

I wanted to go with them, and kept asking my mother why I couldn't go. I was sure Volusia wanted us to be there. As Volusia tried on new dresses and Janey Louise fussed about her hair, I said, again, that I didn't see why I couldn't go, and Mama Agnes too, and Tucker. We could all go, I told them. But Volusia did not ask us to join them.

"You're just acting *prejudice*," I told her.

"And you think you know the meaning of that word?" Volusia asked.

"Yes, I do. We talk about it at school and it's like being jealous, but different, because jealousy means you want what the other person's got, and prejudice means you don't want any part of it, no matter what."

"I think you got some a your meanings crossed up." Volusia smiled at my mother, but my mother was not smiling. She looked at me with a chill on her whole body.

"No, I don't have anything crossed up," I said. "And I think you *are* prejudice. I think you don't want any part of me or Mama Agnes with y'all in Washington. And that's *mean*."

My mother turned on me like a snake and said, "Shut, Evie. You just shut up, now." That was the first time she'd ever told me to shut up.

When Joe Sugar came over later, I was pouting in the backyard. I went to the backyard whenever I felt hated. Volusia must have told Joe what happened, because he came out to find me.

"Where you?" he yelled.

"I'm here." I tried to sound pitiful.

He came and sat on the ground beside me. We faced the fence. I turned my back to him.

"You sulking, arncha?"

"No."

"You is too."

"My mama told me to shut up."

"There's been worse things said to people." I wanted to ask him what worse things, but didn't. Then Joe asked, "You ain't sick, is you?"

"No."

"You ain't scared of living?"

"No."

"Well, then, you just hurting. How bad can that be?"

I turned slightly toward him.

"Why you wanting to go up to Washington anyway?" he asked.

"Don't *you* want to? Don't you want to go see the President of the United States and be honored?"

"Not me that's being honored. Not you either. Just Albert. He did a brave thing over in that war and now he can be honored and we ought to let him, and let his mama and sister go be with him. Anyhow, what I wanna go up to Washington for? I been there once."

"You have?"

"Yeah, and it's not all that much. I'd rather stay here. I'm planting a whole new section of the garden while they gone. It's gonna be tomatoes and corn. You ever had fresh corn? I mean stalks of white corn taken and cooked right after they's picked? You ever had that?"

"No. I had corn though."

"You ain't ever had corn like this. It so sweet you don't need dessert."

"Can I plant it with you?"

"On one condition."

"What?"

"Don't tell Janey Louise what we're planting. When she come back, *maybe* we tell, but maybe we *don't*. Not till the stalks start to show."

"It's a deal!"

"Okay. Now come on back in the house, and don't say anything about why you can't go to Washington. Now, I'm afraid they gonna ask you to go with them, and you gonna have to say no."

"Hope they don't ask," I said.

"Me, too. I won't mention it. You don't either."

"I won't." We walked back with our arms around each other, like pals.

He said, "I hope they have a good time though, don't you?"

25

When Albert returned from Washington with his medal, everyone in Mercy was proud. People complimented Volusia when they saw her on the street. They asked about Albert's trip to the White House, and said how unusual he was. How brave. One day Albert walked into Mr. Sweet's barber shop. Mr. Sweet waved a welcome hand. "How you doin' Albert? You tired a being a hero yet?" As a boy, Albert had worked for Mr. Sweet, sweeping out his shop for a quarter.

"Not yet," Albert said. All the men in the barber shop laughed, but their laughter halted when Albert sat down in the row of people waiting for a haircut.

"You gonna wait till kingdom come if you think you're gonna get a haircut in here, Albert." Mr. Sweet thought Albert was teasing them.

"Why's that, Mr. Sweet? Why can't I get a haircut?"

"'Cause this ain't no colored barber shop." Mr. Sweet's tone had changed. "You know this's not for coloreds."

"Well," Albert's voice grew deliberate, "in some places that might be called discrimination."

After that remark, everybody in Mercy knew that Albert would have to be watched closely, that he was dangerous now.

"You talking back to me, boy? You can't talk smart just because you been in the army and won you a medal."

"Maybe I got *some* rights," Albert said. He stood, and so did everyone else.

"We like your mama, boy," Sully Cantor spoke now. Tom Hill and a few others left the barber shop. "And that sister of yours is getting to be a real looker, so don't go ruining the lives of colored folks in this town, just because you got a bug up your ass." Tom Hill returned with three new men.

"You're hurting my business, Albert. I don't want trouble. You go on home now." Mr. Sweet resumed cutting the hair of the only man in the shop who hadn't stood up.

Albert left, but as he pushed open the door, Mr. Sweet spoke loud enough for him to hear. "Can't believe he wanted me to cut his nappy head. What'm I supposed to do with his hair?" Laughter followed Albert out the door.

Albert left town for a few weeks, and people talked about the incident, treating it like a joke. They said it the same way every time, so that one version became the truth. But when Albert returned, he brought back men in suits, black men from the National Association for the Advancement of Colored People. They called meetings in churches and private homes in the colored part of town. One man's car was set on fire, but the meetings continued. We heard wild talk about a movement to integrate Mercy High School, but no one believed it would ever happen. The year was 1953.

During the summer of 1953, Margaret Turnbull's father bought a Motorola television set, so I went over to their house almost every Saturday night to watch the Milton Berle show.

Janey Louise wanted to go with me, but my mother explained that she couldn't go, because the Turnbulls hadn't invited her. Janey Louise asked how she could get invited, and my mother said that one day we would get a television set of our own. But she didn't say when. I knew they were too expensive.

When I returned from nights at the Turnbulls', Janey Louise wanted to know what I saw. I told her everything I could remember, and tried to recreate the program so she could laugh. Sometimes I spent the night with Margaret so I wouldn't have to go home and say the whole thing to Janey Louise.

The Turnbulls went to church on Sunday and they liked for me to go with them. The Episcopal church had all the rich people of Fulton County, and a stained-glass window in the front of the church with a picture of Jesus almost naked and dying. I cried when I looked at it, and I didn't know how everyone could act so normal standing under that church window and Jesus' torment.

When I got home Janey Louise and I would go to Corny's Pond to look for frogs perched on lily pads, and tiny fish.

"Is the reason I can't go with you to see Milton Berle because I am colored?" Janey Louise asked, and I said I thought it was. "I am the same inside as you are," she said.

I'd always known she was the same as I was, but I'd heard that the blood of colored people was different from white people's blood, though I didn't know how different, exactly. I told her this, and she wanted to test it.

Neither of us wanted to cut our fingers to draw blood, so I suggested we each take a booger from our noses instead, to see how different they were.

We planned this experiment for after supper. Volusia would go out with Joe Sugar, and my mother was playing bridge at Mr. Shallowford's house. Janey Louise and I would baby-sit Tucker.

Mama Agnes heard us whispering beneath the kitchen window, but she heard only one word. "Don't say snot," she told us. "It isn't ladylike."

Janey Louise raised her eyebrows, and I believed she enjoyed the admonition to be ladylike. She straightened her back and walked away from the window like a wealthy person.

At eight o'clock we put a white linen napkin on the coffee table, and I told Janey Louise to dig a booger from her nose. I said I'd do the same. We turned away from each other to perform our task. Tucker came in and wanted to know what we were doing, so I invited him to participate. We could learn something about how boys were different from girls. We felt as though we were performing an important scientific experiment. Tucker said that sometimes he and Arnold Pepper swapped boogers and ate them. I told him that that was disgusting.

We pulled boogers from our fingers and laid them onto the white napkin. We observed closely. They looked alike, except for shape. Janey Louise's had a shape like Florida, but mostly each one, even Tucker's, was indistinguishable one from the other. They were exactly the same color.

When we were through, Janey Louise and I were convinced that we had indisputable proof of her worth, and that now she must be allowed to watch television in the Turnbulls' living room.

By the end of the summer *Impeach Earl Warren* signs stalked the Georgia highways, and all over the country people spoke of integration and the trouble it could bring.

The summer of 1954 produced freedom marches in Alabama and Mississippi. Colored folks in Birmingham had their Rosa Parks story, and two colored children were said to be about to enter the Mercy school system. Albert and the men from NAACP mentioned Janey Louise and R. C. Brownlee as the two who would integrate the Mercy schools.

"Albert's gonna make me famous," Janey Louise said. I had my own fantasy of Janey Louise becoming famous, and reporters coming to the house to interview me.

When that happened, I wanted to be sure to say something that would make people listen, but Albert had caused so much trouble I was afraid nothing I said would matter. People in town thought Albert was somehow my family's responsibility, but they blamed the army for his uppity attitude.

"They gave him that Distinguish Cross. You can't give a nigger a Distinguish Cross like that. He never will get over it." They spoke this way all over town, all over Georgia, because Albert's fame was blossoming throughout the state.

26

Mama Agnes bought our blue Studebaker on the day I stayed home sick in bed. She drove it into the driveway and told me to look out the window. I hated Studebakers, but pretended it was pretty. I had told Margaret Turnbull we were buying a new Chevrolet, and I dreaded what she'd say when she saw the Studebaker.

Margaret turned mean when she grew breasts and got her period. For a while I didn't spend the night with her, then Justine moved to another town, and I began to be friendly with Margaret again. I missed Justine though. We wrote letters every week, and I told her about the Studebaker.

I wrote to Justine while I lay sick in bed, dreaming of boys. I told her about Lowell Hardison—how tall he was and what it was like to kiss him. Lowell was teaching me things that not even Justine had done. I felt guilty, but kept doing it anyway.

"Lowell," I wrote, "has legs as thick as posts." I liked staying home sick, and relished being wrapped in the romantic fog of my fevers.

"Your hair looks funny," Margaret said, the first day I came back to school. "It looks like your *hair* was sick." She laughed, so Phyllis Scofield laughed too. Phyllis laughed at anything Margaret said, because she was scared of her.

The Saturday after I got well, Margaret called the house to say she and Phyllis had a big basket of food and planned to walk to the river, and did I want to come? Her voice sounded cheerful and I thought a trip to the river might be fun. Then Margaret mentioned that Janey Louise could come, too. I heard Phyllis in the background second the invitation to Janey Louise.

"Phyllis *likes* Janey Louise," said Margaret, which was news to me, but good news. The first time Margaret came to my house, she called Janey Louise "a black person," as though Janey Louise herself had not realized it. "You are *black*," Margaret said, trying to emphasize the fact that she was more than just colored, worse. "Black as the ace of spades."

Sometimes when Margaret said things, her words sounded like facsimiles of words she had heard somewhere else.

"Why are you saying that, Margaret?"

"Because she *is*."

"So?" I wanted to threaten her with something. "Maybe you'd like for me to say what *you* are."

Janey Louise laughed—a quick bark. We both knew what Margaret was. After that, Margaret refrained from speaking rudely to Janey Louise, though I knew she talked about us behind our backs.

The best part of Margaret was that she could think up good things to do, and I really wanted to take Janey Louise with us on the picnic. No one had ever before included her.

"If we don't like it, we can just come home," I told Mama Agnes. I turned to Janey Louise. "She says she *wants* you to come, Janey Lou. She says Phyllis *likes* you."

Janey Louise looked pleased. Whenever my friends came over, she had to stay by herself at the back of the house. Once when she asked to be included, I ignored her question, so she didn't ask again. I didn't know how she might act with my friends, but I wondered if the situation might be similar to the way it was with Mama Agnes and Volusia.

Whenever ladies came to our house, Mama Agnes pretended not to like Volusia, and Volusia acted as if she didn't really have free run of our house. She asked my mother (in front of the ladies) if she could run the garden hose to water the daylilies and the ferns. Mama said, "Certainly, Volusia." But if the women weren't in our house, Volusia never asked my mother a thing. She just did whatever she wanted to do.

I hoped Janey Louise knew about that game, but she gave no signs of knowing it, or of being willing to play, so on the walk to the woods I began to bite my nails.

"I'm so *glad* you came," said Phyllis, spreading out the word glad until it had no meaning. She walked on one side of Janey Louise, and I walked on the other. Margaret stayed a little ahead of us. Janey Louise lifted her face to smile at Phyllis, and I noticed how Phyllis didn't smile back.

"I have food and everything. We can stay by the river all day, if we want," Margaret told us. "Later, they're having some fireworks out by my daddy's store, and he says we should come see them. It's a kind of *promotion* thing."

Janey Louise clearly loved the idea of coming back to see fireworks. "Like the Fourth of July?" she asked.

"Well," Margaret said in her adult-condescending voice, "not *that* many."

"*Any* fireworks is like the Fourth of July," I said.

We walked for a long time in the woods. Margaret spoke about school and how she thought she'd *die* if she didn't get into the Academy next fall.

Sunlight speckled the woods and the day gave us a perfect temperature. Pretty soon Phyllis began to ask Janey Louise about the colored school she went to—where it was and what it was like. Janey Louise answered her questions, but offered nothing more. As we walked, Phyllis asked more questions and our mood grew tense. But when we entered the pathway to the river, I broke into a more convivial state of mind.

"They say two men's bodies are down here." Margaret spoke in a whisper. "They sunk the bodies in the river and never found them." She was telling us something intimate.

"What men?" I asked.

"And *I* heard that if we come down here at night their spirits'll rise up out of the river and we might even *see* them."

"*What* men?"

"Those two drifters that got killed out here." Margaret said, irritably.

"I don't remember."

"It was *years* ago. It was in the paper and everything. They dragged the river for a week without a trace. You don't have to worry though." She turned to see Janey Louise's face, to study it and speak to her specifically, "Because we'll be back home before it gets dark. It's only dangerous after dark."

"I'm not scared," Janey Louise looked straight at Margaret, then Phyllis.

"*I'm* not either," I said.

"Not *yet*," Margaret said. "Anyway, colored folks are always afraid of the dead." She smiled at me. "Everybody knows that black folks are superstitious be*yond* be*lief*."

Margaret's father owned more than one store in Mercy. Her family was so wealthy that Margaret bought clothes in Atlanta. Her mother drove there to buy Margaret a dress or a pair of shoes to match a coat. They had always hated colored people, though they had many Negroes working for them.

Phyllis saw a big willow that leaned over the river's bank. "There it is," she said. "The dead men are down there."

The path was rocky, and Margaret made us climb out to a big rock where we would have our picnic. She opened a basket and brought out fried chicken, potato salad, date-nut bread, chocolate cake, small pieces of apple sprinkled with lemon juice, and lemonade to drink.

We ran out of forks, so they told me to share one with Janey Louise. Janey Louise claimed she didn't need a fork, but she picked up a spoon from the basket and made that spoon her own. I poured lemonade, and Margaret began to talk about boys.

"I don't think I've ever been in love before now." She shook her hair in an ecstatic gesture.

"Before now?" I asked, interested.

"*Jerome*." She sprawled out onto the rock. "He is the *best* athlete." She sat up quickly. "Janey Louise?" she asked, pretending, just that moment to think of the question. "What are the boys like at your school? Do you have a boyfriend?"

"No."

"Evie does. Evie has Lowell Hardison. If she doesn't watch it, she'll get a reputation. Haven't you ever had a boyfriend, too?"

"I don't guess so."

"Well, if you had, you would've remembered it." Margaret grew confiding, personal. She leaned toward Janey Louise, and seemed to simulate a confidence. "But *really*." Phyllis leaned, too. "I've heard that coloreds are *famous* for being sexy. Is that true?"

"I don't know."

"Now, listen Janey Louise, tell me this. You have a brother, don't you?"

"Yes." Janey Louise knew that everyone in town knew about her brother.

"Albert was a war hero." I spoke these words with patriotic pride.

"Oooo." Margaret's mouth looked like a doll-baby's mouth. "Didn't he ever tell you about girls he'd been with?"

"No."

"Didn't he ever bring somebody home?"

"Albert's always been real shy with girls," Janey Louise said, and lifted another sandwich from the basket.

Margaret's brown hair had a streak of orange-blond. She had painted her nails a bright pink that Phyllis kept saying she wanted to try. They both wore expensive clothes and if Mama Agnes could see them right now she'd tell them not to hunch over. I wished not to be here, I wanted to be with Justine, instead of Margaret. Justine would not be in on this meanness.

"I'll bet he's not shy anymore. From what I hear about those *army* men, they are never shy."

I grew tired of Margaret's needling voice. "Quit trying to get Janey Lou to say things." I spoke to both of them. "I thought we were going to do something out here. I thought we were gonna play a game."

Phyllis brightened. "Cops and robbers," she said, "a new version."

She proceeded to explain a complicated version of cops and robbers, which was actually a mixture of several games—one of them hide-and-go-seek. Janey Louise understood the rules the first time through. Margaret added more rules, and I said okay, but it was too much to remember. We finished eating everything but the chocolate cake, which we decided to save for later.

The tree stump beside the river served as base, and whoever was tagged had to run back to the base along a specific route designated by Phyllis. Along the route were objects to be picked up. Anyone failing to pick up the objects and run back to base had to be It.

Each of us had a turn at being It, except Janey Louise. No one could catch her, and she never missed a step in what she was supposed to do.

"You've got to be It now," said Margaret, who had already been It twice.

"Why? I wasn't caught."

"Because this isn't fair, for you not to *ever* be *It*." She looked as if she might cry, and I winked at Janey Louise.

"Count to a *hundred*," Margaret told her.

"A hundred?"

"That's what everybody has to do."

Phyllis motioned for me to hide first and pointed the direction I should go. Janey Louise started counting.

"To a hundred," Margaret called back.

Phyllis and Margaret caught up with me. "Let's *go*."

I could barely see their faces, because the forest was getting dark now, and I wondered how late it was.

"Hurry."

I followed them. "We'll never make it back to base from way out here," I said.

"Won't matter." They ran ahead of me.

"What do you mean?" We ran at full speed.

"Won't matter," Phyllis said, parroting Margaret.

I was running out of breath, "Where are we *going*?"

"Home."

I stopped, so they stopped with me. "I don't want to leave Janey Loulse out here alone, Margaret."

"Come *on*. It'll be fun."

They began to run again, but I didn't join them.

"Evie's not coming," said Phyllis, then she ran, but not at full speed. I turned to go back to the river.

"Look, Evie's not coming with us." They yelled in a lilting-mean voice, "Evie likes Janey Louise more than she likes us." I thought how true that was, and the thought surprised even me.

Margaret stopped again. She yelled from a long distance away. I could see the orange streak in her hair. "Come on, Evie. She'll be all right. She can find her way out. Daddy says these people, some of them, were *born* outside." The remark sounded like part of a joke, but Margaret repeated it as fact.

"That's mean, Margaret. You are *mean*. She's never been out this far. I'm not going to make her go back home by herself."

"You are *no fun*, Genevieve Bell." Phyllis jerked around on her heels, and walked off. She knew Margaret admired gestures of superiority.

"You know what?" Margaret said. "You sound like she's your *real* friend, like she's not just somebody you're nice to. What would everybody at school think if we told them *that*? You sound like she's your *best* friend." The words stood both as accusation and threat.

I didn't answer, but kept walking toward the river. The darkness was settling in very fast.

"Watch out for the dead men's spirits," Phyllis yelled.

"You'll miss the fireworks," was Margaret's last try.

I ran through the forest and hoped I could remember the way back. I'd never been this far downriver either. I had to find the path. I imagined Janey Louise panicked beside the rock, though I'd never seen her even remotely close to panic.

"*Nigger-lover*," Margaret yelled from a far distance, the words came without source into the woods. "*Nigger-lover*," Phyllis yelled with her.

The path that led to the river appeared shadowy and deep. I saw the frame of the willow tree and heard a nearby waterfall. Janey Louise sat on a stump beside the basket. She wasn't crying, but her hands covered her face. She looked very small on the rock, not taller than me anymore.

"What did you *do*, I mean when you saw that we were gone?"

Janey Louise pointed to the basket left by Margaret. "I ate all four pieces of chocolate cake."

I lurched forward with a truehearted laugh, at Margaret and Phyllis and all their dead men's spirits, and at Janey Louise sitting on a stump eating chocolate cake from the Turnbull kitchen.

Janey Louise had been sharing a room with me for almost a year. At night our conversations moved back and forth between our beds like bird calls.

"Tell me, *tell* me."

"I *can't*."

"You can tell *me*." We told each other all our family secrets.

"I got *another* brother somewhere."

"How?" This was better than anything I could tell.

"Mama and somebody. Long time ago."

"I don't believe it." I did.

"She was real young, like right when she got her men-stru-ation. You can have babies when you get that."

"Have you got yours?" I asked.

"A little bit."

"You can't have it 'a little bit.' You've either got it or you don't."

"I saw a little blood once," Janey Louise said.

"Oh, that was probably a cut or something."

"Did you get yours?" she asked, wary.

"No. But I think it'll come any day now. Mama Agnes says she started when she was fourteen and that's what I am almost."

"That won't mean nothing."

"That's what she *said*." I wanted her to believe me. "You know what though?"

"What?"

"Margaret's got *hers*."

"How you know?"

"She talks about it. She says, 'My cra-amps are terrible today. I almost stayed at ho-ome.'" I sat up to imitate and exaggerate the prissiness of Margaret. Janey Louise laughed.

"She's the worst I've ever seen," I said, thinking about our day in the woods.

"She is terrible!" We laughed again, then went to sleep.

Janey Louise never got sick from eating all the chocolate cake that day. Which is proof that a person won't get sick if they eat too much cake.

But we couldn't tell anybody this.

27

Over the past two years Albert's work with the NAACP had forced
the idea of school integration, though the idea was being forced everywhere. A preacher named Martin Luther King, Jr. had been to Atlanta
and to the bus strike in Selma, Alabama, but he came to Mercy to help
Albert plan his strategy to integrate. They would use Janey Louise and
R. C. Brownlee as the first two Negroes to enter a Georgia high
school. Both Janey Louise and R. C. had high test scores and could be
counted on to succeed.

Albert and Reverend King procured the help of several prominent
citizens: Mary Willingham and her family of politicians and wealth,
Judge Wilson who provided Albert with legal information and advice
about laws in Georgia, and Summerfield Jackson who was a member
of the board of education. These three people were the white Civil
Rights leaders in our town. My mother began to align herself with
their forces, though not in obvious ways.

Janey Louise began the school year of 1956 at Mercy High. She and
R. C. Brownlee were both in the tenth grade. That same year I began
the ninth grade, and I entered that year like a bad dream.

Mercy made the national news almost every night for the first few
weeks in September. CBS and NBC came to Georgia, along with the
National Guard.

Dear August,

CBS came to our high school today to watch Janey Louise
and R. C. Brownlee become the first colored students at Mercy
High. They filmed us in classes. Janey Lou was followed around
all day by a huge white policeman, who carried a gun. She won't
say how she feels about this. I don't even think she told Volusia
anything.

After the first day, when we came home, Volusia sat at the

table having her afternoon cocoa, and I asked Janey Lou what it was like to have that big policeman follow her around. She wouldn't answer, but the next morning when the policeman showed up at our door, Janey Lou said, "Again?" She must have thought he would be with her for just one day. Now she's afraid he's going to be there her whole life.

Volusia told her to let the policemen stay until folks got used to the idea. (Like Janey Louise could get rid of him if she wanted to.) Volusia believes this is a big chance for Janey Louise, but she's always praying. Her lips move all the time.

I don't know if people will ever get used to the idea of coloreds in our school, because Janey Lou has lived in Mercy all her life, and still they treat her like a foreigner. We have Civics class together, but Janey Louise never raises her hand to answer a question. She knows the answer. I know she does, because when we study at night, she says the answer before I do. So I ask her, "Why don't you answer? I know you know it."

She says they tell her not to. She says they tell her it will make people mad if she gives the right answer, and if she gets it wrong they'll make fun of her. They say to act like she's listening and to be glad of the chance she's been given. I don't know who she means by "they." I tell her to answer if she knows.

She said to me, "I *know* what you're doing, Evie." And when she said this, I felt like maybe there was a side to Janey Louise that I don't know at all. She sounded mad. She sounded fat with anger.

Love,
Evie

October 18, 1956

Dear August,

Janey Louise is doing fine in school, though people are trying to get her out. Mr. Turnbull comes to school everyday and talks to the principal, Miss Bright. Miss Bright is old, but smart, and proud to let integration happen in Mercy. Mr. Turnbull cannot make her do anything. Miss Bright wears long stiff linen dresses and low heels. She's thin and not tall, and has a voice that no one talks back to.

One time I went to her office wanting to go home. I told her I was sick, but wasn't. She knew I was faking, but called Mama Agnes anyway. Then she gave me a large glass of hot salt water to drink while I waited. She made me drink it all. By the time Mama Agnes arrived, I really *was* sick, because of the hot salt water. I will not complain again about wanting to go home. The next day when she saw me in the hall, she winked. I think she should give Mr. Turnbull some hot salt water.

Last week, when I was caught writing in a library book, Miss Bright made me erase all my marks, and all the marks other people had made too. She asked me why I'd written in a book that was not my own. I said that I'd found a passage so pretty I wanted to write my thoughts beside it. So she said, What was it? And I said the lines. I knew them by heart because they were so pretty. Here they are, they were written by a man named William Butler Yeats.

O Love is a crooked thing,
There is nobody wise enough
To find out all that is in it,
For he would be thinking of love
Till the stars run away
And the shadows eat the moon.

And when I said it, she gave me the book. Handed it right to me. "You may mark all you want," she told me. "It is yours."

This is all to say that things are confusing. I read the papers and what they say about Mercy. The thing that worries me is when people ask if I'm still friends with Janey Louise. Margaret Turnbull started a rumor that Janey Lou had been sleeping in my room for many years. When someone asks me, I deny this, even though it's true. What do you think? What can I say to these questions that people are going to ask me and Mama Agnes and Tucker?

Why aren't you here? I think it's your fault that we are in this fix.

Love,
Evie

One day at school Janey Louise wrote a note telling me Albert had called a meeting at the house on Latham Street, tomorrow at 4 P.M. Men from Washington would be there, and did I want to go?

That night we told Mama Agnes we wanted to get a blouse that Volusia had been asking for. That part was true.

"She's been wanting her blouse, so I thought we'd ride over after school." Janey Louise said. I offered to go with her.

"You get it and come right back," Mama Agnes said.

When the bus pulled within sight of the Latham Street house, we saw cars parked everywhere. Because of all the cars, I imagined Albert was having a party, and felt excited about the possibility of seeing dancing and wild goings-on.

As we came closer we could see the front room full of men in chairs, and one woman writing down what anyone said. The woman was white and sometimes asked a person to repeat something. Albert sat beside the man who led the meeting. Albert did not take notes, but looked as though he knew it all by heart.

"What's the meeting about?" I asked.

"They're trying to get us the Vote."

"Who y'all wanna vote for?"

"Won't matter. Albert just wants us to do it."

"I voted once. A long time ago, with August."

"You can't vote unless you're registered. Nobody can."

"I wasn't registered, but I was real little."

"Well, Albert said we had to get registered."

"Albert's gonna get in trouble for that," I said. I still had not actually met him, though I'd seen him enough times. I wanted to meet him, to know who he was, because I was afraid he was going to be famous, or dead.

We stood outside the window and looked in when Janey Louise said, "Mama thinks somebody's gonna end all this for him."

My heart pounded as I heard chairs scrape and people stood up to leave. I could see Joe Sugar through the window. We didn't want anybody to see us, so we ran toward the woods. We were stopped by a large black woman, apparently a neighbor, who motioned for us to come into her house. In her kitchen we saw another group of men talking and eating from a big bowl of stew.

No one saw us come in, and the woman sneaked us into another room. I could see and hear the men in the kitchen. One man, who was a friend of Joe Sugar's, leaned back on two legs of his chair, pushed the table straight with his arms and said, "How do you think we'll do?"

"We need a signal, something to start us off," another said.

"We need some fire starters," a young man said.

"You do, Sheriff'll get you. He'll get you for sure."

"Comes a time when a man won't care about that," the young man said.

"Has that time come yet?"

"Maybe, maybe not."

"Don't, Calvin." The neighbor woman's voice broke into the man-talk. "You're talking crazy, all of you."

Janey Louise pulled me toward the door. "We got to get Volusia's blouse," she said. We ran back to her house and heard Joe Sugar's voice in the living room. We snuck in the back door and hid in the hall closet. If I cracked the door, I could see part of the room where they were talking. I could see Albert turn toward the window, where the sun was going down. Joe asked him something, but I couldn't hear because Janey Louise was telling me to get off her foot.

"Shhhh," I said. "I want to hear."

"I got rights," Albert said. "I got rights like anybody else."

"I'm not saying you don't," Joe told him. "Other people might be saying you don't, but that's not what I said. You hear me saying you don't have rights?"

"You act like it. You act like you're afraid to make a move."

"I been in movements before, boy. This your first one. I been there, and know people are hell to move. Sometimes you can't even make 'em listen. I know about that."

"They'll listen now. Now they're ready. The white man though, he better *be* ready." Albert turned around and we ducked down. "If it were up to me, I'd get a gun and shoot 'em all—every last white one of 'em."

Joe stood and moved into our view. "Now what you wanna say a fool thing like that for?"

Albert didn't answer.

"You just mad," Joe said. "I know how that is. You think your life's your own, but it ain't. That army you were in and gave you a medal— they didn't think your life was your own. They thought it was *theirs*. But I'm telling you now: It ain't yours and it ain't anybody else's. And if I ever figure out whose it is, I'm gonna tell you, but right now we just listening to each other talk, trying to figure out something to do. We gone help each other get on that road to freedom we both want so much."

Albert removed his glasses and rubbed his eyes. "I'm aching to break the law, Joe. I am busting out of myself. You know what I mean?"

Joe went into the kitchen and walked by the closet where we were hiding. He came back with two cans of Vienna sausages and soda crackers. I heard them open the cans, and saw Albert sit down straddling his chair backwards. His eyelids dropped, but he didn't look sleepy.

"I tell you," Joe Sugar said, "freedom's a tough bird."

The sun went all the way down and Albert's image was caught in the dark glass of the window behind him. When Janey Louise spoke, I felt startled by her presence.

"We got to go," she said. "Nobody else's out there. We can go out. It's just Joe and Albert." But as we opened the closet door, we heard a car pull up outside. We heard a siren and saw the light from a police car popping around the walls of the room.

Joe Sugar saw us. "What the hell you two doing here?" he said. "Get back in there. Hide!"

"Don't come out!" Albert ordered. It was the first time he'd ever spoken directly to me.

Two policemen busted open the back door. Janey Louise and I stood behind the clothes.

"Your name Albert B. Davis?" they said.

"My name is *Jim Crow*," said Albert. "Call me Jim Crow."

He said very little after that. From the closet we heard sharp blows. Janey Louise scooted down into the corner and cried. We heard Albert make grunting sounds. We heard Joe scuffling, trying to stop them, then we heard somebody get hit with a blunt instrument. After a while the policemen left.

I pushed open the closet door, ran to the front window, and yelled to the policemen. "I *saw* that," I yelled. "I *saw* what you did." I was white and felt safe enough to say anything.

But one of the policemen walked back into the house. He came slowly up the steps toward me, took my shirt by the collar, and bunched up his fist under my chin. He squeezed my arm hard, and let his voice growl into my face.

"You ain't seen nothing, little girl. You say what you seen and it'll be worse than what you saw."

Everything around me was shaking. Even my eyeballs felt scared.

The policeman left and I ran back to the closet to get Janey Louise. We found some towels and washrags and wiped blood off Albert and Joe. Albert would not look at me. He told me not to touch him. Joe kept saying, "Thank you, honey. Y'all shouldn't a seen this. Thank ya."

Janey Louise washed Albert's head. His eyes were bloody, and Joe asked if he wanted to be taken to the hospital. Albert said no.

I went upstairs and searched around until I found Volusia's blouse. We caught the next bus home.

"Why'd you do that?" Janey Louise asked as we rode home. I sat on the seat in front of her. She had tucked the blouse neatly into a paper bag.

"I don't know, I just did. I didn't think those men should hit Albert and Joe like that."

Joe had told us not to mention what happened to Volusia or to Mama Agnes. He said he would call and say we'd been playing cards.

We got home a little past nine o'clock.

"We were worried about you two," my mother said. "Joe called and said you were playing cards."

"Yeah," I said. "It was fun."

"Well, the next time you decide to do something like that, give us a call." Volusia spoke sharply.

"I'm not so sure I want you over there anyway," my mother said, "with all the trouble going on now." She didn't look at Volusia when she said this.

"You get my blouse?" Volusia asked.

"Yes ma'am."

"Tell me how Albert is," she said. "You see him? I hadn't seen him in a week."

"He's fine," said Janey Louise.

"Is he happy about you being in that school?"

"I don't know. I think he is."

"Well, *you* don't seem *glad* about anything," Mama Agnes said.

"I'm real glad," said Janey Louise.

"She's just overwhelmed," I said. "That's what it is."

"It's late." Volusia wiped the kitchen table. "You two go on to bed."

As we undressed Janey Louise asked, "Was that torture? What they were doing to Joe and Albert? Did we see *torture* tonight?"

"I think so." I put on pajamas while Janey Louise brushed her teeth. Neither of us wanted to say more about it. We stayed silent until we got into bed.

"Remember when we tortured Tucker?" Janey Louise asked.

"Which time?"

"The time we tied beetles to his fingers and told him he could fly?"

"That wadn't torture. He *loved* that. He begged for it."

"Mama Agnes said it was mean," she reminded me.

"It wadn't though. I think he liked it."

"But we got switched for it. We got switched, and Tucker got to go to the kitchen and eat a piece of warm peach pie."

"Tucker got to do everything after his polio." I waited until Janey Louise had slipped under the covers before I turned out the light.

I was almost asleep when she said, "You sure did yell at those policemen, didn't you?"

"Yeah," I laughed.

"That was a brave thing, Evie. I wished I'd done it."

"But I can do more because I'm white."

"So, are you on *our* side now?"

"No!" I said. Then, "Sometimes I am."

"I'm not *ever* on your side," she said.

"You *might* be. Someday you might."

"Uh-uh. Not ever."

28

Someone in the bridge club suggested that Volusia could make hats for men. But Volusia had never made a man's hat. She didn't like the idea, until Mama Agnes found some gray felt that had the perfect stiffness for a nice brim. She brought home dark grosgrain ribbon strips to use as a band.

Volusia made her first man's hat with a one-and-a-half-inch brim and a dark ribbon with a tiny feather peeking barely above the band. She had seen a hat like this in a magazine. She made several just alike, because men never cared if their hats looked the same.

Volusia enjoyed making these hats in secret ways.

Inside the banker's hat, just below the ribbon, she put a row of BBs from Tucker's Daisy rifle. And for Mr. Turnbull's hat she put chicken feathers in the lining. She did not tell my mother, but she told me. I loved the thought of the banker and Mr. Turnbull wearing BBs and chicken feathers to work.

Mercy, Georgia became an army of men wearing identical hats, so Mama Agnes found some brown material almost as good as the gray, and a soft black material, so that Volusia could make an occasional beret.

My mother had found a location downtown where The Hat Shop could become a legitimate business: a space between the Krystal and Mr. Turnbull's department store. A narrow entrance and a display window were visible from the street, and the large front room had a dressing table with a three-way mirror and chair.

Hats were displayed so that a customer could wander around the shop, and come back to the dressing table to try something on. Volusia didn't approve of this particular kind of hat buying, she preferred that the hat be made specifically for the person's face. But my mother convinced her to be more flexible.

A smaller room in the back had a table set up for Volusia, with lamps at either end and a desk in the corner where Mama Agnes worked on the books and kept records of what was sold. The next step, my mother told Volusia, was to create a catalogue so people could order their hats.

Both women and men came in and told Volusia what they wanted. Volusia studied and sketched out something close to what they described. Then she went into the back room and said, "That woman won't need a hat to make her look wide, she need to look *tall*. I can make her look *tall*."

"Maybe you should give her what she asks for, Volusia," my mother said.

"She's too fat to want something like she said."

Volusia could make a hat that took ten pounds off a woman. There were no complaints.

But Volusia complained about being downtown. She preferred to work at home in August's study, and to use snapshots. She like to be in the house, because sometimes Albert would drop by to see her and they would have a cup of coffee.

One day I stayed home sick with the flu, and what I saw made me sicker than the flu. There was madness in Mercy. Everybody in town seemed angry at everybody else, but I hadn't imagined it would reach my own house. Heated arguments were springing up everywhere, and the presence of the National Guard made tempers worse.

On the day I stayed home, I was in bed listening to the radio when I saw my mother come up the walkway. She'd been working all morning at The Hat Shop, and was coming home at noon to eat lunch and pick up the hat order Volusia had finished. But I'd never seen her face so angry. She entered the back door and yelled for Volusia to come downstairs right now.

I heard them speaking loudly in the kitchen: Mama Agnes was accusing Volusia of selling hats on her own and keeping the profits.

At first, Volusia denied the accusation, but finally she admitted to selling a few hats to ladies in her church. "Because," she said, "none of those women are gonna be allowed to come into that hat shop and try on hats that white ladies try on. Now, Miz Agnes, you know that's not gonna happen. How they gonna try on hats they want? How they gonna see?"

"Volusia!" My mother's voice punctuated itself. "It is the principle of the thing! We have a business here. I've taken you into the business in a way that makes other people around town very critical of me." She was walking around the kitchen, pacing. I could hear her shoes on the linoleum floor. "You have no idea what I suffer because of what I've done for you and for Janey Louse. I think you're forgetting that."

I stood at the top of the stairs, but could hear everything plainly, until Volusia mumbled something to herself, as she often did, saying things people could never quite make out.

My mother's tirade continued. I imagined she was following Volusia around the kitchen, with Volusia keeping her back turned as much as possible. I had seen them talk this way before, whenever Volusia was mad or felt trapped. I came halfway down the stairs, so I could see into the kitchen.

"Now, Volusia, I want you to tell me how much money you got from these people, so we can see how much you owe me. Do you have any idea what it costs to run a store? The overhead? Of course, you don't. But I've tried to explain to you how much has to be turned back into the business. Because of the overhead."

Volusia mumbled words about head and over head. Two words. She was mad. Finally, she spoke. "I sole nine hats, and they was three to four dollar apiece. I know I sole 'em cheap, but these folks can't pay more'n that, so I sole 'em for what they could afford. I make about thirty-two dollar. Now you saying I have to give you all that thirty-two dollar, even though I made 'em and I sole 'em?"

"Not all of it, Volusia. Just a third. That's ten dollars."

"I know what it is. You think I can't figure what it is?" She still had her back turned. "I never use any of the good material. I made those hats outa scraps we had left over. We would thowed those scraps away. Anyway, I'm the one who have all the good ideas, and you don't pay me diddly-squat, and you don't pay me nothing for extra work I do sometimes. So I just take care of it myself."

Mama Agnes grew exasperated and left the room walking into the hallway. She saw me on the stairs. "What're you doing home, Evie?"

"I'm sick. I got the flu. Volusia said I could stay home."

She put her hand on my forehead. "You don't have a fever. You're not too sick to go to school. You get dressed now, and I'll take you after lunch. No need your missing the whole day."

"But Volusia said . . ."

"I don't care what she said."

I hated my mother, but went upstairs to get dressed. Volusia brought lunch up for me. She said she was sorry and that she knew I didn't feel good. She said, "Miz Agnes is on a tear."

"I don't think you ought to have to give Mama Agnes any of that money," I said. "I don't think it's fair."

"You get yourself dressed and don't worry about that money now. I make it back. I make it back and this time she won't know. Because it don't seem right to make a hat you know belong to somebody and not to be able to give it to them for the amount they can pay."

I had no idea what she had just said, but nodded anyway.

Mama Agnes drove me to school and tried to explain about her argument with Volusia.

"But what did Volusia *do* that was so bad?"

"It's like stealing, Evie, to keep that money."

"But sometimes *you* keep money," I said. "Like when Daddy sent extra money for the store. You didn't give Volusia any of that, did you?"

"That was different. That was for the shop."

"But Volusia's part of that business, too. Why didn't you ask her if she wanted some of it?"

"Evie, you are too young to understand about the business world." I could see her debating within herself about whether or not to say the next thing. "You also know what people say about us in Mercy, don't you? How we are almost 'friendly' with Volusia and Janey Louise. They talk behind our backs all the time."

"Yeah, but I don't care."

"You *will*. I predict that someday you will care. It's getting bad, and we have to protect ourselves."

From what? I wanted to say, but instead I mumbled a denial under my breath the way Volusia taught me to do when I couldn't talk back or defend myself.

That night the whole house felt mad. I walked around and turned on lamps trying to make rooms cheery. At dinner nothing was said about the day's interruption or even that I had stayed home from school all morning. But after Janey Louise and I climbed into bed, we talked about our mothers.

"I've never seen them mad like that at each other," I said.

"*I* have."

"When?"

"When I wanted to move into this room." She no longer called it "your" room, but she hadn't learned yet to call it "our" room.

"Really? Was Mama Agnes mad about that?"

"No. *My* mama. She didn't want me up here. Said I shouldn't be up here with you and that people wouldn't like it. That's when Mama Agnes said nobody should know, and that we'd keep a cot downstairs so that it'd look like I slept there. She said it'd be good for both of us."

"It *is*. Is she still mad about it?"

"Naw, but she tells me not to think I'm white. She says not to get any grand ideas just because I'm up here with you."

"But you *do* have grand ideas. Your ideas about everything are grand."

"I know it." Janey Louise laughed. "I just can't help it. Albert has grand ideas, too. Maybe I got 'em from him. My mama had all the grand taken out of her a long time ago."

"I think she ought to make hats and sell 'em anytime she wants to. I don't think my mother is right about that."

"Won't matter if anybody's right."

Volusia got so busy with women's and men's hats and the catalogue orders that my mother had to ask Janey Louise to come straight home from school and begin cooking dinner for all of us. She said that Janey Louise was old enough now to take over some of the cleaning chores. I was shocked when she said it. Janey Louise did not want to clean the house. Then my mother offered to pay her good wages, and she liked the idea of having her own money.

When Janey Louise took over Volusia's chores, everything changed between us. We couldn't play cards before supper, or walk to the pond after school. I stayed in town with Margaret and went to the drug store with Lowell Hardison, who had been my boyfriend now—off and on—for nearly a year.

I tried to get home late, so I wouldn't walk in on Janey Louise cooking dinner or cleaning bathrooms. When Mama Agnes gave her compliments on the supper, I pretended not to hear.

Janey Louise began to have money. She had more money in her pockets than I did, but Volusia kept most of what she earned. Volusia wanted the money to go for school clothes and supplies.

During the fifth week of Janey Louise's preparing meals and shopping, and of my trying to think of ways to stay out of the house until late, I grew tired of the charade. On a cold March day I decided to go home immediately after school. I came in the back door and saw Janey Louise: her tall figure at the stove frying chicken in a dark skillet of grease. She had potatoes already boiled and cut. She looked like somebody's maid, and the house smelled like Volusia's cooking. The potatoes were ready to be mashed, so I asked what she used to mash them. She showed me the potato ricer and said after I mashed them to add milk and butter. "Then use the Mixmaster to make 'em creamy," she said.

"If I help," I said, putting on an apron so that we looked alike, "then we'll have time to play cards."

When Mama Agnes returned from The Hat Shop and Volusia came downstairs from her sewing room, Janey Louise and I were sitting in the living room listening to the radio and playing gin rummy. Volusia and Mama Agnes quietly put everything on the table, and when they called us in to dinner, it was as if the supper had been made by them and we were waiting to be called in. They had to call us twice.

29

In April the All-Churches Revival came to town.

The revival came every year and set up a tent on the fairgrounds outside Mercy's city limits. People came from all over Georgia, some as far as Jefferson or Athens, to hear the preacher who had led these meetings for nineteen years. But this year a young man replaced the older one. His name was Warner James, and when I saw his picture on the posters, I knew I wanted to go. He was handsome, even his name was handsome. People who knew him called him Warn, and he said that's what he was here to do: Warn us.

His face on the poster enchanted me, and at fifteen I wanted to be enchanted by men. I had already been courted for a year by Lowell Hardison. Lowell took me into the fields and gave me long hard kisses. He said he loved me and meant it. I said I loved him, but he was not deceived. I could not deceive him any more than someone could deceive a tree.

Lowell Hardison had shown me how to carry myself. He taught me how to walk around naked in the shadows. But when he touched me, he was always in a hurry. Lowell was two years older than me, and he never took his slow sweet time.

My mother and Mr. Shallowford went with me to the first night's revival meeting. The tent was huge. The top swayed down in loops, like a circus tent, and a million chairs must have been set side by side, facing the preacher.

Warner James stood at the podium, talking to people and waving everybody in. He urged them, through the microphone to sit down front, and whatever he said sounded personal. His voice was like a movie star's voice, and I felt caught by its timbre.

When the invitation came to give yourself to Christ, he loosened his tie and a shock of hair fell down onto his forehead. His voice boomed with the fact of God's love, and people began to walk up front. I felt moved to follow them. I wanted to have God's love in my heart.

Warner James noticed me immediately and came over to hand me a small, white pamphlet. He took me to some chairs away from the other saved people, and suggested we sit down. He looked at me the way men look when they think I'm pretty. He took my hand, and I could see a wedge of hair that stuck above the top button of his shirt. He asked if I wanted to stay and help them prepare for the next night's meeting. I said yes.

After everyone left and the tent was empty, Warner James asked if I had ever been saved before.

"No. I never even came to a revival before. But I do go to church sometimes."

He moved his chair up close to mine, and I could smell his after-shave. He talked to me softly about Eternal Life and the soul. He said that he could see my spirit and that my spirit was strong and full of the Lord. I felt like bursting open when he talked, and could not take my eyes off his face and the small tuft that poked from his shirt. His hand brushed lightly on my arm, and he touched my hair once to push it out of my eyes.

"You're a very pretty young lady," he said to me. "Did anybody ever tell you that?" I could not remember at the moment if anyone had ever said such a thing.

"I don't think so," I said. He was thin, lanky in the way of August, so I told him that August had gone to the Sea of Cortez. I made it sound privileged, and then I said that I'd been there. He listened to all my words with a quiet attention that made me feel interesting and important to him. I couldn't believe the excitement I felt. Finally, he asked if I could come back the following night.

"I'll be preaching here for a week," he said. "I'd like to see you again." He acted as if he had asked me for a date.

"I can come tomorrow night." I said. "I planned to come anyway."

"Well, plan to stay a little later." My heart leapt up. "Wait until everyone has left and we'll have some refreshment in my trailer. It's parked over there in the woods." He pointed to a spray of trees, and though I couldn't see the trailer, I said, "Okay."

He stood and as we left each other I kept thinking about the word "refreshment."

When I told Janey Louise, she said, "You better be careful of that man. He's a preacher."

"But he is so handsome. He looks like Jeff Chandler."

"So what?"

Then she told me about a boy named Dake who lived near Latham Street. Seeing him, she said, made her feel excited and tired at the same time. She wondered what it would be like to kiss him.

"Do it!" I said.

The next night I put on some high-heeled shoes and a dress I'd been saving to wear for Lowell. I sat between my mother and Mr. Shallowford. I sang the hymns and felt saved. When Reverend James called people to come forward, when he made the invitation to dedicate our lives, I could watch others struggling with their souls. I felt proud and full of the Lord's love.

When the call was issued, Warner James looked at me with his bright, blue eyes and I nodded only slightly to let him know that I had remembered to come back. I'd thought of nothing else all day. I washed my hair and soaped my body twice. I bought a new slip at Kresses, because my own best slip was looking ragged.

I told my mother, "The preacher asked me to help hand out tracts for him tonight. I'll walk home when I'm through."

"Well, isn't that nice," my mother said turning to Mr. Shallowford. "Evie's going to help Reverend James." She was proud. I had never been interested in God before. "Don't be late," she said.

After the service, after the saved had gone home, Mr. James walked me to his trailer in a stand of trees behind the tent. He opened the door for me, and I was surprised to find how big the trailer looked on the inside. He had a table and chair where he ate, and a sofa with a green velvet cover. He turned on the radio and music came out from the walls. I felt like I was in a picture show, and said it.

Mr. James laughed and went toward the refrigerator. "I'm going to have something to drink," he said. "Would you like something, Evie?" He had a deep laugh that made everything sound fun.

"I would like a Coke-cola, thank you," I said, trying to sound older.

He took out two glasses and some ice that he kept in a small, fancy bucket in the freezer. He removed his sport coat and threw it carelessly across a chair.

I didn't want to sit down where he threw his coat, so I moved toward the sofa and sat on the edge of the velvet as he handed me a glass of ice. He poured my drink into the glass without speaking, and everything seemed crazy and from another world. He smelled like cigarettes and cinnamon. He sat beside me and gently reached for my hand.

"I'm glad you were willing to wait and come back here with me." He touched my arm to show how he appreciated me.

I nodded.

"I'm happy to see you. Your dress is so pretty."

I had put on lipstick, applied after the meeting, after my mother and Mr. Shallowford had gone. I did not use my regular Tangee Natural from Kresses, but a new Revlon color called Red, Red Rose. He leaned to touch my lips with his lips, just slightly, and I could not speak or breathe.

"I hope that was all right," he said. "I can hardly help myself, you are so lovely."

"Yes," I told him. Lovely. He said I was lovely.

He stood up to open a window and we could hear the new spring sounds. As I listened, I knew I could identify each one, so I named the sounds for him: the chirping sounds of baby birds, a loud bullfrog, wing sounds of a bat. A nightingale sang. We both heard it.

"That's a nightingale," I said, proudly. We heard an owl.

"You're smart as well as pretty. I'm lucky to be with such a delightful young lady."

Delightful. The words he used were strong medicine to my heart. I wanted him to kiss me again, and tried to send a silent message from my mind to his that would make him wild to touch me. He stood up to get another drink for himself.

"Does it bother you that I'm so much older?"

"No. Not at all," I said. "I hardly even notice it."

He laughed and when he leaned down again, he lifted me up with his arms, holding me like a baby. "I want to be close to you, if that's all right. I'm wanting so much to touch you and be close."

"Sure," I said. This was nothing at all like Lowell. Lowell would never take the time to talk this much, and he would definitely not carry me in his arms. I could not believe Mr. James had lifted me. I felt his breath on my ear.

"Mr. James," I said, "I must be heavy for you."

He stopped and let my body slide down, holding me close to him from my head to my toes.

"Now, Evie," he said, "if we're going to hold each other, you'll have to call me Warn. Not Mr. James."

"Warn," I said, but it felt like I'd said Warm. I *did* feel warm. Hot. I felt my body about to turn into flame. My dress came undone at the waist, and my breasts grew heavy with desire.

He took me into a small closet of a room, with only a bed and a rod where he hung his clothes. He laid me down and looked at me. I could not think of anything to say. He touched my breasts, turning his fingers around on my nipples. They were hard like little pebbles. He kissed me through my dress, and before I knew it, my dress was unbuttoned and he was pulling it off around my knees. He paused at my knees and looked at my slip, its newness. His hand went under my slip and he touched very lightly the crotch of my panties.

"Evie," he said. Just saying my name, then saying it again. "Evie, Evie." He sounded like he was singing. I closed my eyes and let him wander over me with his mouth and hands. I felt so loved. I had never felt so loved. This is what I had wanted all my life, I thought. This is what I've been waiting for. I never wanted to see Lowell again.

The next night I sat again between Mr. Shallowford and my mother. I could hardly wait to end the hymns and the sermon, the invitation, the call of the soul to Eternal Life, then again to follow Reverend James to his place in the trees where he touched me again and our bodies traced each other without speaking, just the language that made me feel alive.

He taught me to kiss his back and arms and legs. He taught me to nibble with my lips like a little fish. Caressing him tiny tiny times, over and over. He showed me how to use my hands and make him come. But on the third night he said that he would go into me, and I said okay. He knew by then that I was not a virgin, because I had told him about Lowell. He said nothing when I told him. I was afraid he thought I was cheap.

But he decided that night to go into me, and I could hear myself making small cries, as though this wasn't even me. "I love you, Warn," I told him that night. "I love you, I love you." He did not say anything.

My mother was still up when I got in. She sat in the kitchen talking to Volusia. They looked serious, and I was afraid they knew all about me. But when I came in the door, their mood changed quickly and their voices shifted to a new tone. Finally, my mother spoke.

"Evie, I don't think that preacher should keep you out so late. What are you doing over there?"

"We give out material, and he talks with people who come up front. There were lots of people tonight. I help him clean up a little bit afterwards, and he gives me a Coke-cola."

"Well, I don't think you need to help him anymore." She stood up, but Volusia watched as I went to the refrigerator and cut a hunk of cheese to take upstairs.

Janey Louise was waiting with the bedroom door open.

"Come *tell* me."

"I love him," I said.

"No, you don't."

"Yes, really. It is so *sad.*"

"What're you gonna do?" she asked. "He'll have to leave in a few days."

"*May*be."

"What'd you mean 'maybe'?" She closed the door to the bathroom so that we were completely closed in. We had wallpapered the doors to match the room, so the doors when closed were not distinguishable except for the knobs and the molding. We felt like we were inside a box.

"Well," I said.

"You're gonna have to forget about that man. What'd he do anyway?"

I lay back on the bed feeling sexy and older. "He touches me everywhere. He kisses me all over my body, and I kiss him like that, too."

"You do?"

"Yes. It's great. I feel shivery just thinking on it. He says it's okay because we are in the lap of God."

"The *lap* of God? What does that mean?"

"It's just God's lap, that's all. You're in it, too. And he says he's never seen anybody so full of love as I am. He says he is *glad* to know me."

"Well, maybe he *does* love you, girl. Maybe he gonna take you away from here. From me. I don't want you to go away."

"I'm not going anywhere. Maybe he could stay here," I told her. "Maybe he could get a church here and he could wait for me. Just live in Mercy till I grow up."

"Whoo."

On the last night of the revival I didn't go to the meeting, but waited until my mother had gone to bed, then snuck out to see him. I wanted to tell him my thoughts.

"Warn," I said, still thinking of him as Mr. James, but calling him Warn. "I've been thinking how you might stay in Mercy and get a church around here. Maybe not in Mercy, but close by, so we could keep on seeing each other." I looked straight at him when I said this.

Warner James did not say anything for a full minute. I was afraid he hadn't heard me. Then he said, "Evie, you are a wonderful girl. You should not waste yourself on the likes of me."

"No. I *want* to. I *want* to waste myself."

He took my head and held it like a vise. "Evie, I'm wanting you to do something for me tonight. I'll probably have to leave tomorrow after the service, so I want this last night to be very special for us."

I tried to figure out what he meant. "What do you mean?" I asked.

"I want you to put your mouth on me."

I had heard about this kind of thing, but I was frightened and didn't want to do it. He begged me, and asked if I wouldn't do this one thing for him since he had brought the Word to me and saved my soul, wouldn't I do this one small thing for him?

"Evie. Evie." His hands ran up and down my legs and I let him dismantle me. His fingers went everywhere, and for a while he kept his own clothes on. Then he asked me to undress him. He instructed me, slowly, and when I'd taken the last piece of clothing off, I knelt beside him on the bed.

He pulled my head down onto him and I closed my eyes feeling him rise toward my mouth. He held my hands and I put my lips over him, moving off the bed to slide down between his legs. I was surprised at how good he felt in my mouth, his pulse against my lips and tongue. I felt the power of how good I could make him feel. He moaned and moaned again. I did not want to stop. I moved with him until a new taste surprised me. I sat up and he smiled, but his eyes did not focus, and the way he smiled seemed to have nothing to do with me. I knew that he would be leaving and that not even this last act could make him stay.

"Baby, oh baby." He pulled me back down against him. "Now let me do you." But I moved away. I stood up and moved to the other side of the trailer against the sink. I picked up my clothes and began to put them on. He did not love me. I knew that now, as clearly as if he had said it harshly to me, as if he had yelled it. I dressed and went home, sneaking into the back door of the house and up to my room. Janey Louise waited for me in the dark. She was awake, as she had been every night, but that night she pretended to be asleep. Finally, when I had brushed my teeth and washed and washed my mouth, she said, "What happened?"

"Nothin'."

"You *lie*," she said. "Something happened."

"Same thing," I said. "Same thing happening every night with that ole preacher."

"I don't see why you going to see him *every night*."

"He makes me feel real good." I turned toward Janey Louise who faced me from her own bed.

"What's he doing to you?" she asked.

"*You* know."

"But tonight. What'd he do tonight?"

I told her that I put my mouth on him.

"No you didn't."

"I *did*."

"You're a *nasty* thing."

"No I'm not. It was good."

"Would you do it again?"

"Sure." I turned away wanting to end the conversation. "But he's leaving tomorrow. That's why I did it."

We were quiet awhile. "I've heard of people doing that," she said.

"You have?"

"Yeah. And once I heard my mama talking about it with Joe Sugar."

I could hardly bear to think of Volusia or of my own mother doing such a thing. I wondered if my daddy ever asked my mother for that kind of love.

"Oh well," I said. "Let's go on to sleep."

"Evie?"

"What?"

"Will you tell me sometime how to do it?"

"Sure." I felt proud and sinful all at the same time. I felt as though I'd earned something by my act, and I was glad I wouldn't be seeing him again.

The moon was full that night and though we usually sat at the window or went outside into the yard on the full-moon nights, we did not mention doing so. Later, when I couldn't rest, I sat near the window. Janey Louise's breathing was steady and full of hard sleep. I sat on the floor so the moon could hit my face, the way the sun did in springtime.

Some nights I could crawl into the moon and live for a short time in its reflected light. Private secrets were being kept in the pockets of my robe, and a certain signal from outside, a bugle sound from a new bird could release my hunger from its hurt world. I wanted to ask someone for food.

The next day I opened the closet where my mother kept August's old clothes. Was she saving them for him? Until a year ago, I could still smell him on the sleeves of his jackets. My mother's clothes were in the closet next to Tucker's and mine. A dress that belonged to Volusia and two shirts of Janey Louise's were at the end. One dress hung beside another, and my father's jacket touched a dress and shirt. Shadows and forms of people being friendly in a way that the real bodies could not.

I kept thinking about the ways I gave my love to people and how they didn't know what it was. I decided not to love anybody for a while. Except the moon. I would love the moon, and feel valued by it. But I made a decision not to lie down with anyone again until I felt the love I wanted to feel.

I took out some paper and wrote to August. I hadn't written to him in almost a year.

Dear August,

I know you are surprised to hear from me, but I have not gotten a letter from you in a long time either. So I guess we are even. I wanted to tell you that things here are fine. Last week I went to hear a preacher. He was in Mercy for a whole week, and I went every night. I gave my life to Christ.

I believe that I know now what I want to be when I grow up. A teacher. I want to teach Biology—teach people to look at everything around them, the way you taught me. I like my Biology teacher, Mrs. Kirby, very much. She has taught us about spiders (Arachnidae), and what good architects they are. We spent one whole class period watching a garden spider (Epeira diadema) spin its web.

Mrs. Kirby set the spider on an upright stick with water beneath him, and he dropped—fast—not by a single thread, but by *two*. I was amazed. When he got to the surface of the water (just before he reached it) he stopped short, and somehow broke off one of the threads. The thread floated in the air and was so light it moved like a breath. Mrs. Kirby put a pencil to the end of the thread, but it wouldn't stick, so she let the spider step onto the pencil and wrap the thread around until it was taut.

Then there was a kind of floor on which the spider went back and forth. When I see a web now, I cannot tear it down. She is teaching me more that I will write you about.

I am also sad, and miss you very much. The other night I walked to the front of the revival tent, and gave myself to God. But I am thinking now that I was *already* God's, wasn't I? Like the spider? The spider can't give itself to God. All these things are going around and around in my mind, and I can't tell anyone about it. But I can tell you. If we could start writing again, I would like it very much. Also, I would like to think that I could come back to the Sea of Cortez and visit you there. You have not seen me in a long time.

Love,
Evie

30

One night in late April, I heard a loud banging commotion at our front door. I went to the top of the stairs to watch my mother ask who was there. When Albert said his name, she opened the door. I could see Albert leaning against the post of the door. He was breathing hard, as though he had been running.

"My mama here?" he said.

"She is."

Mama Agnes led him into the hallway, but before she got there, Volusia called to see what was the matter.

"Albert's here, Volusia." She spoke in a whisper. Volusia came out and took Albert to her own room.

My mother saw me on the stairs. "Get back to bed, Evie."

"I want to see him."

"This is none of our business." She tucked me into bed. Janey Louise had slept through the banging commotion, but woke up when I came back into the room.

"Whatchu doing?"

"Albert's downstairs."

"No he idn't."

"He is. I saw him."

Janey Louise jumped out of bed and ran downstairs without her robe. She stayed gone a long time. When she returned, I pretended to be asleep, then pretended to wake up at that moment.

"What happened?" I asked.

"Somebody's been threatening him. They broke into Latham Street, messed it up bad. Tried to burn it down. Albert's got to leave for a while."

"Where to?"

Janey Louise didn't answer. She waited a long moment before she said, "He say not to tell. Even you. He say not to tell even you."

"Okay." I thought about all the ways we couldn't tell each other things, all the ways we couldn't talk. "Albert came in this house and still I didn't get to say who I was to him."

"He knows you. He knows your whole name."

"He does?"

Toward the end of the school year the National Guard was removed, and everyone's anger had gone underground or settled into acceptance. Janey Louise still wouldn't speak out in class, but she made As on almost every paper. I was proud of her.

On the bulletin board were announcements for tryouts for the spring play. I decided to audition and won the part of Julie in *The Pajama Game*. Everyone said I had a good voice, loud and belting. Janey Louise helped me memorize my part and showed me large gestures to make when I said certain phrases.

I practiced for the play on Saturdays, and since that was the day I usually spent with Janey Louise, she began to ride her bike to Corny's Pond alone. Volusia thought she went over there too much, and I wondered if she *was* meeting with Duke.

"She's gonna turn dreamy if she don't watch herself. And there is no sense in somebody turning dreamy in this world."

One Saturday morning I left for rehearsal, and Janey Louise left for the pond, but when I got home at two o'clock, she wasn't back. We thought maybe she had taken her lunch with her, but by three Volusia said for me to go looking for her. She would get Mama Agnes and they could drive along the road and meet me at the pond. I was told to check the bike path in case Janey Louise was already on her way back. I could tell that Volusia had a bad feeling.

I rode my bike to the edge of Corny's and looked around the pond for Janey Louise. I called, but there was no answer. If she had drowned in the pond, I would be able to see her, because the pond wasn't that deep at any point. I kept calling her name, then I heard a voice, not Janey Louise's, but somebody else.

"Eee-vey." My head went dry and my feet carried me, sleepwalking, to the place of her voice. I heard it again.

"Ev-ie." Weak. Hurt.

Janey Louise had been dragged into the bushes and left there. Her jeans lay on the ground torn at the crotch and her underpants were muddy with blood and dirt. Her shirt was bunched around her waist. She didn't see me. Her eyes looked straight at my face, but she didn't see anything. Her gaze was turned into what had happened to her. She was seeing that.

My head grew up, and I couldn't speak.

I'd seen Janey Louise undressed many times before, but I'd never seen her so naked, her face so raw. She covered herself with some leaves, but she left her shirt bunched around her waist. There was blood between her legs.

"Janey Lou," I said. "Janey." I stroked her head and pulled the shirt to cover her breasts. I'd never called her Janey, but wanted to change her name. "Who did this to you?"

Her face appeared washed clean, as if her head had been scrubbed from the inside, and she said in a voice that whispered toward my ear (as though somebody else might still be there and watching), "Get me out. Get-me-out."

I said, "I can't. I can't lift you up." But I tried anyway. She outweighed me by almost fifteen pounds.

"Get-me-out," she said. She did not mean the place, she meant out of herself.

"Volusia's coming," I told her, then felt immediately guilty, as though I'd told on her and gotten her into terrible trouble.

"No. No." She said.

I tried again to lift her up, to carry her a few feet from where she was. Leaves fell from her chest.

Then we heard Mama Agnes and Volusia pull up in the car beside the pond. They ran into the woods where they saw me struggling to lift Janey Louise. I heard Volusia speaking as she ran toward us.

"OhLordGodHaveMercy, OhLord Jesus." She swooped down like a big hawk over Janey Louise, and scooped up her body, running toward the car. Mama Agnes looked at me but didn't ask what happened.

I picked up the muddy underpants and left my bike beside the pond. I looked around for the other bike. All the way home Volusia chanted the "LordJesus, JesusHaveMercy" prayer. She was yelling. The prayer sounded like a demand coming from her lips.

They carried Janey Louise into the house and Volusia swept every-thing off the dining-room table onto the floor with one arm. Nothing broke. Janey Louise still hadn't spoken. She closed her eyes, and they stretched her out. She couldn't look straight at me. She thought I could not know this thing that had happened.

Volusia removed the rest of the clothes from Janey Louise's body. She spoke slowly, her voice soft, saying things like: "Now, I take off this blouse so we can cool you with some water Mama Agnes getting ready, and Volusia cool your shoulders and your neck with a nice rag." She removed the leaves and dirt from her mouth and face. She pulled the shirt down around her legs, and Janey Louise's body stayed stiff like a corpse. I knew this was the way a dead body was washed for bur-ial. Volusia murmured as though she was speaking to a small child get-ting ready for bed.

She washed Janey Louise and gave Mama Agnes a rag to clean her arms. Mama Agnes did everything Volusia told her and she began to speak, imitating Volusia's way, but without the smoothness.

"You gonna be fine now, honey." She washed one arm, soaping the rag in the big pan of water. My job was to keep bringing a new pan of warm and soapy water, then another one with no soap at all. I ran back and forth from the kitchen with bloody and clean water.

Volusia washed Janey Louise's legs, and when she did this, she let a light film of soap stay on her legs for a short while and she said, "This gonna make you clean." She hummed, and washed her thighs and crotch and bottom. She washed her breasts.

Janey Louise had bruises all over her body, and Volusia said out loud, but not to be answered, "What that man do to my baby-girl? Why he have to hurt my baby?" She cried and sang and asked these questions, but Mama Agnes and I stopped saying anything, because we did not know how to comfort Janey Louise.

When Volusia rinsed her off, I brought in a new bright towel to cover her body. Soap and water ran off onto the floor, but no one cared. Then, Volusia went to the dressing table in Mama Agnes's room. She took some Madame DuBarry face cream to rub onto Janey Louise's shoulders, her arms and legs. Mama Agnes took the jar and dipped out large amounts to rub onto her feet, massaging it into her toes and heels.

A few hours later when Janey Louise began to speak, she said, "Is something wrong with me?" Volusia and Mama Agnes told her that nothing was wrong anymore, and that the man who did this was wrong. They asked who it was. Janey Louise didn't know who it was. She said she'd never seen him before.

Volusia grew silent throughout whole days, and Mama Agnes was afraid she might wish to die. Not that she would kill herself with a knife or gun. But that her sadness might kill her.

Nothing anyone said made a difference.

We assumed the man who did this to Janey Louise was a drifter, someone walking along the railroad tracks. My mother had called Doc Beryl to look after her, but Volusia wouldn't let Janey Louise go to the hospital. She didn't want the town to know what had happened.

"Everybody'll treat her different," Volusia said. "It's bad enough as it is." Volusia wanted Janey Louise to go back to school as soon as possible. "It's the only chance she's got."

"She can't go back like this, Volusia."

But Janey Louise stayed out of classes for nearly three weeks. Doc Beryl confirmed that she had whooping cough. I brought her homework home each night and we worked at the kitchen table. Miss Bright came by the house to see how Janey Louise was getting along. She told stories about things that had happened at school. She was the only one who made Janey Louise smile.

Volusia asked Mama Agnes if she told Miss Bright what happened, and Mama Agnes said no. But we could all tell she was lying.

Janey Louise missed twelve days of school and when she came back her teachers said she seemed like she wasn't well yet.

"She's going to have to have some help with this, Volusia. She's barely talking." My mother was worried.

"We gonna help her ourselves. We know what to do."

Toward the last weeks of school Janey Louise seemed to improve. There was also the hope that the men from NAACP were going to get Albert out of jail. He had been in jail without the privilege of counsel since that night he came to our door.

"It's the beginning of summer," Volusia said. The wetness of spring was finally gone, and the air had a smell of dry wild onion. Flying squirrels lived in our chimney and sometimes swung from curtain rod to curtain rod. The smell of the ground was strong, and clung in the air like soot.

31

By the time school was out we were already going to the lake or the river to swim every day. Janey Louise and I rode on our bikes everywhere, but sometimes she spent whole days at home in bed. My mother said to leave her alone on those days, but she worried and told Volusia over and over that Janey Louise would need to see another kind of doctor.

On the Fourth of July my mother offered to drive us to Sardis Lake twenty miles away. We knew this lake, a place teenagers went on weekends. We hoped an excursion like this might cheer up Janey Louise. The lake had a wide beach, and one section where colored people swam, not far from the whites.

Volusia and Joe Sugar rode behind us in Joe's Ford station wagon. Tucker invited his best friend, Arnold Pepper, to go with us, and though Arnold had seen Janey Louise before, being in such close proximity to her made him love-smitten.

Arnold nudged his way into the backseat between me and Janey Louise, and hardly said a word all the way to Sardis. By the time we arrived, Tucker was disgusted.

Tucker's leg had gotten stronger over the years—or rather he used it whether or not it was strong. His left leg was smaller and he still had his limp, but he swam, ran, and kept up with those around him, even though he often appeared awkward. His smile looked completely normal.

Sardis had bathhouses, but Janey Louise and I decided to change clothes in the car. Arnold hung around wanting to watch us undress. I changed fast, but Janey Louise wouldn't take off her clothes.

"Tuck, get Arnold away from here. Make him stop hanging around us."

Janey Louise held her bathing suit up close to her chest. She didn't want him to imagine her in it. "He just wants to *see* us," she said. "He's not fooling anybody."

"He likes you," I laughed.

She smiled. "He probably likes *you*."

"He's been staring at you all day. He can't take his eyes off you."

"Well," she protested, "he won't look long. He won't see anything I got, because I'm not taking off my clothes for him to gape at."

"Stop gaping!" I yelled out the window of the car.

"Come on, Janey Lou. You're gonna go swimming aren't you?"

"*May*be."

"Come on, Janey Lou."

She finally changed on the floor of the car while I stood guard.

We stayed until after nightfall, watching the fireworks over the lake. Sardis had the best fireworks in two counties. We ate supper from a huge basket of chicken, potato salad, deviled eggs, biscuits, johnny-cake, baked beans, fresh pears, and homemade fudge.

That night after we got into bed Janey Louise and I talked about Arnold, and how little he was.

"I wish Dake Durrene would look at me the way Arnold does," she said.

She hadn't mentioned Dake since her rape. I knew who she meant, but asked anyway.

"Who?"

"Dake. I told you, the boy who lives on Bedford Street."

"Tell me."

"I kissed him the first time in February. We went to the movies, and he kissed me in the movies."

Janey Louise grew very still, quiet, so I asked her, "Do you love him?"

"No, it's not that." She paused, then said, "I might."

"What then? You're not telling me something."

"Well, he kissed me the last time just before my 'accident,' and I keep wondering, I mean, I'm thinking if maybe somebody might get pregnant from *kiss*ing somebody."

"Uh-uh. You have to *do* it."

"But we never did anything but kiss. He kissed me real hard one time though, and he put his tongue in my mouth. You think that could do it?"

"What are you saying? You saying he made you pregnant? He couldn't have, Janey Lou. Not without *doing* it. Are you telling me you're pregnant?" My first thought was what Mama Agnes and Volusia would say, but she must have read my mind.

"My mama and your mama already know. I'm already showing a little bit."

"You are? Let's see."

She turned on the light and let me see the pooch of her stomach.

"Gah! I thought you were just getting fat." I touched her brown belly button. "Gah!"

"I hadn't told anybody, but Mama Agnes guessed. They weren't mad or anything. They never even asked about who it was."

"But it couldn't be Dake, because he didn't do anything but kiss you. It has to be that *man*."

"What do you mean?" She lay back down and covered herself.

"It had to be that man who hurt you. In the 'accident.' He's the only one who *did* anything."

"No." She spoke quietly, breathy, but it seemed as if she had spoken loudly. "No," she said. "No, I thought a baby had to be born out of loving somebody, and if you didn't love somebody, then you couldn't get big."

"I don't think so," I said. "I don't think love has anything to do with it."

The stark quietness of the room left me with the terrible realization of what I'd told her. I planned to talk with my mother the next day, but when we woke up, Janey Louise said, "Don't tell anybody about our talk last night, hear?"

I didn't answer.

"Evie, promise you won't tell anybody about what we said."

"Okay, I promise."

"Swear?"

"I swear."

A week later in the middle of July, when the heat had risen to 100 degrees and my mother walked around the house in her slip, Janey Louise announced that she would take a cold shower. It was four o'clock. She'd been staying in her room most of that day, and when she came out everybody hoped she might feel better after her shower. We hoped she would come out demanding that we all do as she had just done. We kept waiting for the day when she turned back into her normal self. So when she suggested the shower we hoped that the moment we had waited for was here. She left the room, her dark face a mask.

Yesterday she asked me if she was pretty, and I said, "Of course." Anybody seeing her would think so. "Look in the mirror," I said, "see for yourself."

"I can't see myself anymore," she said. "I can't look myself in the face."

"It wasn't your fault," I said. "If you're pregnant, it's not your fault. I shouldn't have said anything."

Then I suggested we sit at the dressing table in Mama Agnes's room. I had the idea that if she could see herself exactly as I saw her, she'd be all right.

At first, she resisted the idea, but I took her by the hand and led her to the bedroom. For a long time she couldn't take her eyes off her feet. Then, she turned her face up to see herself, with me standing beside her.

Her face was not afraid or sad. Her face was not anything. She had the blankness of air and the expression of someone who had seen nothing of any significance. But she smiled at me in the mirror and I could see that something had changed. So I thought it was a good sign.

But as Janey Louise walked to the bathroom for her four o'clock shower, nothing seemed right.

"Maybe I'll come, too," I said, because at times when we were younger we took cold showers together on hot August days, but we hadn't done so in several years.

"After me," Janey Louise said, and her voice sounded good, regular. I said okay.

We heard the sound of water running for a long while before the screaming began. She called our names, but the door was locked. Volusia tried to bust it down, but couldn't, so we ran around the outside of the house to a window. The window was too small for Volusia to get through, so she called for me to climb in. She lifted me up.

The room had filled completely with steam. I couldn't see what was going on inside, but could hear, and the sounds from Janey Louise were like those of an animal caught in the teeth of a trap. Nothing could make me forget that sound. Our lives would be different from this day, I knew. Mama Agnes had called our neighbor, Mr. Marsh, and he tried to bust down the door with a two-by-four. The door was nearly split open by the time I climbed through the window.

Janey Louise was no longer screaming when we got in. She wasn't calling anybody's name, but had passed out and lay face down in the scalding water. Her face and shoulders and breasts were badly burned, as if fire had done it instead of water. The water still ran, landing on her legs. The room was full of steam, but Mr. Marsh rushed in to turn off the faucet and he scalded his own hands getting Janey Louise out. He and Volusia dragged her into the hallway. No one cared that she was naked, but I got a towel to cover her body. She didn't seem so naked because of her skin, which was raw now, rough like a fabric.

She looked completely different from the person she had been a few minutes ago, or yesterday, and I imagined that that was what she wanted: to be different. I began to imagine how the day might have gone if she had *not* seen herself in the mirror. Or if I hadn't told her that love didn't matter.

Janey Louise was taken to the Milledgeville State Mental Hospital. The Colored Ward. One doctor said she needed to be committed so that she wouldn't hurt herself again. The Colored Ward was small and in a separate building. And though they were mostly full, they took Janey Louise because of Mama Agnes and Doc Beryl. I'd heard about people who went to Milledgeville and got shock treatments, and I thought of horror movies we'd seen about people tied down and tortured in this way. I did not believe they would do this to Janey Louise.

No one mentioned how long she might be gone or if she'd be back in time for school. "We'll take care of everything," Mama Agnes said. We planned day visits to Milledgeville. Sometimes Volusia went alone, sometimes Mama Agnes or Tucker or Joe Sugar went with her. Sometimes Volusia took just me.

Dear August,

Every night I pray to the moon and the stars for Janey Lou. I take offerings to a place in the woods that I know. It's where we found the squirrel's nest when you took me and Tuck to the north section. I haven't prayed since I was converted, but now I'm back into it and I hope God won't notice how long I've been gone, or that I've come back just because I want some help. I can't stand friends who act like that.

Janey Louise is not much better, though we hope she'll snap out of it. The burns on her face are healing, and the doctors say her skin is young and that she'll look pretty much the same. She must have turned her face away from the water at some point, because her neck and one side of her head were burned.

I try not to think about how I could have stopped her. Volusia says Janey Louise is headstrong stubborn and that she won't listen. Volusia is a "tower of strength," Mama says.

I haven't heard from you in a while and wonder what new project you have started in the Sea of Cortez. I would like to come out there again sometimes. I hesitate to ask, but I'd like to come by myself, without Tucker. This might be possible because Tucker is so happy now. Miss Rice was made principal when Miss Bright died, and Tucker has become what people call popular.

At the end of the school year each class elects officers for the next year and Tucker was voted Treasurer because he's so good in Math. Boys don't tease him anymore, or if they do he doesn't care. I think that's what Miss Rice taught him. No one minds that he's crippled, or that he is a year older than everybody in his class. He is the smartest person in school. His face is getting handsome and Mama says he looks more like you every day.

Albert is in jail, but men are coming from Washington to help get him out. He is in the news all the time now. Joe Sugar says when Albert gets out of jail in a few days he's going to marry Volusia. I wonder if they'll have a big wedding, and if he will live here with us. I have not asked.

Love,
Evie.

32

Patients at Milledgeville looked like carnival people.

They looked as though they weren't real, as though they might be getting ready to put on a show about a place like this. Nurses and large men sat stationed in particular doorways on the weekends.

Each Saturday before we left for Milledgeville, Volusia made turnip greens or creamed corn—something that was Janey Louise's favorite food. We sat in the room with her while she ate, but hunger and appetite were one and the same to Janey Louise. She ate as if she couldn't distinguish or satisfy either one.

Tucker and I took turns riding over there with Volusia. The drive took forty-five minutes, and Volusia never said much going over. If the day was sunny, we took a walk. Volusia let me and Janey Louise walk around together, though she kept us in her sight.

When it rained, we sat in a dingy parlor with an out-of-tune piano that we usually tried out. We sat in third-grade chairs around a small table. Sometimes Janey Louise and I played cards at the table. Volusia brought hats to work on while we played gin rummy, or crazy eights, or poker. Her presence was like a big rock.

Wherever Volusia sat became the center of Janey Louise's world. She came and went as though a rope was tied to her mother's chair. The doctors said that even when Volusia wasn't around, that Janey Louise would imagine where Volusia was sitting, and her movements circled around that chair. The doctors described Volusia's presence as a promise, and I thought about how she was the same thing for me.

During the first two months at Milledgeville, we kept looking for evidence of normal behavior, but we saw no sign. For a while when I visited her room, the skin on Janey Lou's face and arms made her look tough like an old man, but her hair was still thick and bright, and combed in a nice way around her face. She looked kind of pretty sometimes when I came in and she was asleep.

Volusia always wore something bright to Milledgeville, and she urged me to do the same: a red sweater or bright blue ribbons in my hair. She wore a gold bracelet that she put on Janey Louise's arm when she got there and took back when she left. I liked the ritual, but didn't ask her about it.

One day, Volusia suggested that I walk with Janey Louise past the far trees. Milledgeville looked like a campus. She always let us go down the path to a gate and come back, but on this day she let us move for a time out of her line of sight. But after a moment we saw her running flat-footed behind us, catching up to a place where she could see us again. We laughed when we saw her running and for a moment felt like "us" again.

A wild bonnet of clouds hovered over the mountains. I tried to talk to Janey Louise about things that were easy: movies or the swing in the side yard. Whenever I asked her what it was like at Milledgeville, or if she knew anybody, or what the doctors said to her, she grew quiet and wouldn't answer. I said that some of the people here looked funny, and she nodded and rolled her eyes.

To say something about the other people brought her outside the oddness. I thought she might comment, but she didn't. I hoped she wouldn't feel ashamed. I tried a few times to take her hand, but she pulled away.

Once while we walked, she let our clothes touch. Then she asked me if I thought she was going to be crazy forever.

"No," I said, and meant it. "No crazier than you already are."

She looked down at her large swell of stomach. "Do I look fat?" she asked.

"Yes!"

She laughed. "I am *huge*," she said. "I can't even sleep on my stomach anymore."

"You are different," I told her. When I spoke, her face looked like rain, and she jumped up onto a bench. She crouched, and I was afraid I'd said the wrong thing.

"How you mean?" she demanded.

"You act jumpy all the time. Mama Agnes says you are *frantic*."

She stepped down off the bench. I helped her.

"I'm not frantic," she said. "I'm just tired."

On the way home Volusia asked about Janey Louise. "What she talk about to you, Evie?"

"She wants to come home," I said, though it was more what I wanted for her. "And she asks about Albert. Says she wants to see him." I had my learner's permit and sometimes Volusia let me drive part of the way home. I wanted her to let me drive now.

"You tell her where he is?"

"Uh-uh. I think she forgot he's in jail. I talk about him like he's free. Can I drive?" I said.

"After we stop at the country store," she said. "We need some milk and a loaf of bread."

We stopped at the store every trip and got an orange Popsicle or a Grapette. I wondered what Volusia would do if *I* smoked a cigarette.

"I want a Grapette," I said the minute we got into the door. Volusia picked out some bread, milk, and crackers. I opened the large cooler where they kept cold drinks. Grapette was the smallest bottle, but the best taste.

"Get out the money," said Volusia.

"What money?"

"Evie, I told you to get that money off the kitchen table at breakfast." She wanted the man behind the counter to know she was honest. "I told you to keep it in your pocketbook."

"But I didn't bring my pocketbook."

"Now we can't pay for these things we got."

"Are you folks gonna pay or not?" The man behind the counter turned to the woman beside him. She kept the smirk that has been on her face since we walked in. There were men near the door listening to a baseball game.

"I guess we won't buy anything," Volusia said to the man, and she left the food on the counter. I followed her outside.

"I'm sorry, Volusia. I know I should've brought it."

"That money still back on the kitchen table not doing us one bit of good where it is. Just like some people I know."

"I'm sorry," I said again. "Can I drive?"

"No."

I got in the passenger side and took out a package of peanut-butter crackers from my pocket.

"Where you get that?"

"Stole 'em," I said. "From that store."

"Stole 'em?" We were driving fast down the road, throwing up dust and rocks. Volusia was mad, embarrassed. "You stole something back there from that crotchety man? They catch us, we be in jail with Albert."

I opened the package and gave her one. We were both hungry. She chewed it slowly savoring the peanut butter with her tongue.

"Mmmmh." She smiled straight ahead. "Seems like they taste a little better stolen." Then her expression turned serious. "But now you listen here, let that be the first and last time you ever take anything like that. Just because I'm smiling and eating these crackers won't mean I think you did the right thing." She ate another one. "But now when you get to be old as I am, you can remember the time you stole something, and this can be it. And it be the *only* time." Her voice sounded strict and quiet.

"I know. I won't do it again. That man, though, he just made me *so* mad."

"Sure tastes good," said Volusia and reached her hand out for another one. "Stolen, I mean. Sweeter, or something."

I gave her two more and saved two for myself. We ate slowly, enjoying each bite.

"We been all day without money," she said. "No telling what could have happened." She pulled to the shoulder of the road. "You wanna drive for a while?"

"Yeah." I kept thinking how I wished I'd stolen the Grapette, too—to go with the crackers. "A Grapette would sure taste good right now," I said.

But Volusia wasn't thinking anymore about food. She asked the same question she asked after every trip to Milledgeville. "Did Janey Lou say anything to you about the man who rape her? She tell you the name of any man?"

"She didn't say anybody to me," I said. But I wondered if Janey Louise had named someone, if I would tell Volusia.

My room at home, without Janey Louise, felt like living inside a cube of ice. The whole house seemed a geography of cold ground. Mornings began with a marginal world of fog, and time drifted into slow afternoons. Birds browsed around their branches, and evenings grew musky as the wind shifted.

I lay in bed at night with the windows open and heard the rise and fall of insects. The owl's sound descended like a blessing. Everything I heard felt like a prelude for the time when Janey Louise would be home.

I prayed, fell asleep, woke, and sat up murmuring.

The mysterious bond that had sprouted between me and Janey Louise hung inside my head like the memory of salt. No one could come into her place.

33

School started again and Janey Louise was still at Milledgeville. "She'll be back before Christmas," my mother told me. "She has to stay until the baby's born."

"Will she bring the baby home?" Tucker asked.

"We'll cross that bridge when we come to it," Mama Agnes answered in a way that encouraged us not to ask more.

"You could give the baby to Joe Sugar," Arnold said. Arnold stayed at our house all the time now. He thought of himself as belonging to our family.

"What's Joe Sugar want with a new baby?" Volusia said. She liked Arnold. She never reprimanded the boys, though when they got noisy Mama Agnes yelled for them to quieten down, or if it was raining she told them, "Get back in this house." My mother spoke to them without patience, but Volusia made huge sugar cookies and they would sneak downstairs to eat them in the middle of the night.

On nights when Arnold slept over, I saw him with Tucker in the yard. They carried buckets and one of August's old fishing nets. They looked for crayfish in a stream behind the house.

I missed Janey Louise even more at those moments, and knew that what best friends did was sneak out together in the middle of the night and do something fun under the moon.

I went back to bed and began to think of the holidays leading toward Christmas: Halloween, Thanksgiving, then Janey Louise would be home, then Christmas. I thought of presents to buy for her, and for the baby. The baby would have to have presents. I didn't believe they would not bring the baby home, but I was thinking that a colored baby would have to be in a colored house.

Joe Sugar had asked Volusia to marry him, but she refused because she wanted to think only about bringing Janey Louise home and keeping Albert safe.

Maybe next year, she told him.

The entire autumn of 1957 was warm. Our first frost arrived on November 7th. All the leaves were gone when the policeman came to our
house with Albert.

Albert had been arrested for fighting, they said. Before taking him
to jail, the policeman brought him by our house. I saw the police car
stop. One man stayed in the car, but the other opened the car door and
took Albert by the arm. Albert was handcuffed.

Volusia opened the door, and I stood behind her with Tucker. She
said something unrecognizable and my mother came around the side
of the house, running. The day was not yet dark, the sun was down and
light in the yard fell silvery.

"Volusia?" the policeman said. "Albert's asked to speak with you before we take him in. He's been arrested."

Volusia nodded and made a deep noise in her throat.

"It's a serious charge this time." The policeman looked at Albert,
who didn't look back at him. "He hit someone with a bat, or something like a bat. Might've killed a man."

"Who was it?" my mother asked. "George, tell me who it was."

"Sand Jackson."

"And just what did Mr. Sand Jackson do to make Albert strike out
like that?"

This was the first time I'd seen Albert up close. I'd seen him on
Latham Street that day, and tried to wipe his arm, and I'd seen pictures
of him in the newspaper. I hardly ever saw him around town.

My mother repeated the question, "Tell me, George, what did
Sand Jackson do?"

"Now don't get all riled, Mrs. Bell. Sand was leading a group
of men into the meeting where that N-A-A-C-P was deciding
about more integration—like in restaurants and movie houses. Sand
Jackson says they got enough as it is, but they have to just keep
on pushing. This meeting was about that. Don't get into this, Mrs.
Bell."

"Is that a threat, George?"

"No, ma'am. Just warning you."

Volusia reached out to touch Albert's face. Albert was looking at
my mother as though he hadn't expected this behavior from her.

"Hey," I said, then said his name. "Albert. Hey."

I'd been standing half-hidden behind the doorjamb, but now I was in front of him. "I'm Evie." I was almost as tall as he was.

"I know you are," he said, his voice calm and sweet. Then "How's Janey Louise?"

"She's fine. We saw her last Saturday."

Volusia interrupted. "Albert," she said.

"I'll be all right, Mama. But I think you better call Joe." Then Albert reached out his hand to his mother. When she took it, I saw a register of surprise on Volusia's face, as Albert passed something into her hand—a tiny piece of paper no bigger than a postage stamp. He pressed it into her palm.

"I just wanted to tell you that I'm going to be all right. I didn't want you to worry when you heard about it."

"Well, you know how I can worry." She patted his arm and put her other hand into the pocket of her apron. "You be all right. I know you will." Her eyes filled. "Oh, honey."

My mother didn't see the piece of paper passed. She followed Albert to the police car saying how she would get to the bottom of this.

As they drove off, the light on top of the car flashed around and the siren was heard for miles. They wanted to make a noise as they brought Albert B. Davis into custody.

Volusia began to cry. In all the years she'd lived with us, I'd never seen her actually cry, though I'd heard sounds, like crying, in her room. I expected her to say something to us about the piece of paper. I expected her to look at it immediately, but she excused herself and went to bed.

"What're we going to do?" I asked my mother.

Tucker said, "Did he kill Mr. Jackson?"

My mother held a towel in her hand, twisting it around and around. "If he's hurt Sand Jackson, he's in real trouble. I'll call Judge Wilson and Mary Willingham. Mary can find a good lawyer."

"Mama," I said, "Albert handed something to Volusia."

"What're you saying, Evie?"

"Albert handed her something—a tiny piece of paper." I held up my fingers to show how big the piece of paper was.

"Well, I don't know anything about that." She paused and took hold of my shoulders. "And neither do you, you hear?"

I shivered, the way I did as a child whenever anyone yelled at me suddenly. She hugged me into her.

"Oh, please," she said. I was almost her height, but it seemed at that moment I would never be as tall as she was. I breathed in the smell of her hair and dress.

"This is the first time Albert ever spoke to me," I said. I couldn't wait to tell Janey Louise that I'd spoken to Albert and that he asked how she was.

"He seems real nice," Tucker said.

Men in expensive suits were due to arrive from Washington and New York, so the town of Mercy was again in the news. Albert had assaulted someone prominent in town, so bail would be high. The men in suits would try to get him out.

Volusia went by the courthouse to speak to Judge Wilson, and he gave her written permission to visit Albert in jail. Volusia made pies and cooked a whole meal to take to him. She asked me to come along with her. I had no idea why she asked me.

Two officers on duty told Volusia to go back home. They said Albert was sleeping. None of us knew what was happening to Albert, but Joe had been informed that Albert had been beaten, and that he was kept from using the toilet for long periods of time.

Volusia took out a note from Judge Wilson, and said that she'd made all this food. She hated to see it go to waste. She took out two peach pies, and offered to give one to the guards.

I stood outside the door, but walked in when I heard Volusia arguing with them. The two guards sat in an outer office playing cards. One shadeless lamp threw shadows on the opposite wall and made the room seem inhabited by more than just those two bodies.

Volusia balanced a pie in each hand.

"I brought y'all a peach pie and one for Albert. But I wanted to take it back there to him." The smell of warm cooked peaches filled the room—fighting against the other smells of sweat and stale food. Both men moved toward Volusia's pies.

"Sure smells good, 'Lucia," said the one I knew as Orin Land. Orin took a pie from Volusia. "We're not supposed to let anybody back there."

"I brought a knife you can use for that," Volusia said. Her voice came out as sweet as I'd ever heard it. Janey Louise told me once that coloreds had one voice for whites and one for themselves, and asked me if white people did that, too. I said I didn't think so. "Well, you should," she said. This, now, was Volusia's "white people's voice" and I could see how it worked.

"Now, I sure will be disappointed if I can't see my only son just a minute or two. Give him this pie. You can see for yourself how good it is, and I brought two whole ones all the way down here. One for you, one for him."

She sliced perfect pieces of pie into generous portions, then looked around the office for a plate. She was going to serve these fat, sweaty men as though they were somebody.

"Orin, I can't see what harm she'd do. We just won't tell anybody she's here. She got that note from the judge, anyway."

"Won't make any difference to Sheriff Jernigan what she has," said the other man, but we could see that he was relenting. "She could take him back a pie, I guess, then whatever's left," he smiled, "we can find use for it later." He dug a dirty fork into the pie plate Volusia had handed him.

I didn't know this man's name, but I could smell him.

"Now you have to leave that knife out here," he told Volusia. "You know you can't take that back there with you."

"Oh, sure I do" Volusia smiled. "I'll just slice it up first and leave the knife out here with you. I'll visit with him a few minutes and come right on out."

Orin still had a doubtful expression. "Okay, but you know he looks kinda rough now. He got in a fight or something. Can't figure out why you folks are always fighting."

"Law me!" said Volusia, nervous, still smiling.

"He got that before we found him." Orin turned to look at the man whose name I didn't know. "He idn't fully healed yet. He come in here looking pretty bad. I just want you to be ready."

"Yes sir," said Volusia. She sounded contrite, sorry about Albert's fighting. I walked toward the door that Orin was about to open, when the other man said, "That girl can't go back in there."

"No sir," said Volusia, still sweet, "I don't think she should go back there either. You stay here, Evie."

"Yeah. You stay here. We'll keep a eye on you." The other man winked at Orin. Volusia didn't turn around to see me as she walked to the back part of the jail. Orin led her to the cell where Albert was kept, and I saw them down the long bleak corridor, as he unlocked the cell door and let Volusia in.

Volusia's body grew rigid when she saw Albert. I could only imagine what she saw. She never mentioned afterward what Albert looked like or what she said to him.

When we went back home, I said, "Did he eat the pie?"

"Oh yes," Volusia had the smile of someone who was sick.

"Did he like it?"

"He say it's his favorite kind. He say nothing ever tasted so good."

We left with two empty pie plates, but not the knife. I asked Volusia if she saved a piece for me, and she promised to make another pie tomorrow. When I told her we forgot the knife, she said she wasn't going back to ask those dirty men for anything.

34

The week of December 11th through the 15th was a week of crises. The first day Albert had come to our door with the policeman and was taken to jail. Three days later Volusia took me with her to visit Albert. Then Albert escaped. He could not even wait for the men from Washington to find a way to release him.

Mama Agnes told me that Orin Land went back to check on Albert. Orin was drunk. Albert had a knife, and threatened Orin. He locked Orin up, and escaped at around one o'clock in the morning. When Mama Agnes told me this story, I had a new respect for Volusia.

Joe Sugar had known the exact time that Albert would escape, because he was waiting for him outside the jail. They drove off. No one knew where they went, and no one (except us) knew that Joe Sugar had taken him off in the truck.

On Wednesday of that week Volusia broke down crying, and couldn't stop. We had to get Doc Beryl to bring a tranquilizer out to her. Mama Agnes said she was having a nervous breakdown, but it just lasted for a day. She was more afraid for Albert, she said, now that he had escaped. She said she wished, now, he was still in jail. She said they could kill him if they wanted to, and she hadn't thought how much danger he would be in if he got out.

Nobody could mention Albert's name to Volusia until Doc Beryl came back on Thursday. On Thursday, someone reported having seen Albert near Jefferson, Georgia, so we thought they would be bringing him back. But at six o'clock Joe Sugar told us that this was a false sighting.

Then on December 15th the doctor at Milledgeville called to tell Volusia and my mother to come immediately.

"Her water broke," my mother said. I tried to picture it, and what came to mind was her stomach popping like a big balloon. "I'll take Volusia over to Milledgeville and be back home tonight. You stay with Tucker and Arnold."

"We'll decorate the tree," I said, but I wanted to go with them. I wanted to be there when Janey Louise had her baby.

We had put up the Christmas tree in the corner of the living room, and my mother had laid out the traditional ornaments. "I'll save something for Janey Louise to put on."

"Fine," she said. Volusia waited in the car. She honked for my mother to hurry.

"When will you bring back the baby?" I asked.

"Now, Evie, we don't know that Janey Louise can keep that baby, so don't say any more about it."

"Why not? Does *she* know this?"

"Yes. She knows."

"We won't have a baby at all? Not even for a while?"

"Not even for a while." My mother touched my face. She had to leave. "Evie, you'll have Janey Lou back though. She'll be happy to come home."

My mother got back home at 12:45. She took off her coat slowly. Tucker and Arnold were already asleep, though they had not been in bed long.

"Evie." She moved as though her body was hurting. "The baby was born dead. Volusia's staying to help her pack up everything. Doc Beryl will sign her out in a few days. Then she'll come home."

"Born dead?" I said. "All that for nothing?"

"What do you mean?"

"All that getting big, and not sleeping, and pains in her back. All of it for nothing."

"Evie," she looked too tired to talk, "we won't speak of this again. We'll put the whole ordeal behind us. Don't talk about this to anyone. Not anyone, you hear? Maybe soon she'll seem like her old self again."

"Does she know Albert's in so much trouble?"

"All she knows is that he had to go to jail."

"Will we tell her?"

"Directly."

Two days before Christmas Janey Louise got out of the car in front of our house and came up the walkway calling my name. She looked so pretty. Volusia had bought her a red-and-green taffeta Christmas dress, and stockings. She still wore her old beat-up flats, but her dress looked beautiful.

"We'll have a Christmas party," I said. I led her into the living room where the tree was.

"Close your eyes." I leaned to plug in the tree and at the same moment said, "Now, open them."

Janey Louise's face brightened, but she looked more like a woman now than a girl. "Oh yes," she said. "We had a tree at the hospital, but it was a tiny one on a table, and it had ugly decorations on it."

"We have icicles this year." I gave her a handful and she put them on one by one.

"We're going to Grady's for dinner tonight," my mother announced. Grady's was the one place in town that allowed colored people in, so we sometimes went there with Volusia. They even greeted Volusia cordially. But when Mama Agnes made this suggestion, Volusia made a counterproposal.

"I have a better idea," Volusia said. "Go to the store and get some steaks and some potatoes, and I'll make a pie as fast as you can get back home."

"Yes," said my mother. "I suppose that *is* better."

Later I told Janey Louise that I had spoken to Albert and that he had asked how she was. She said she knew that I'd spoken to him.

"Did Volusia tell you?"

"No, *he* did."

"*He* told you?"

"He came to see me, Evie. I know all about how he got away. He got away to come see me. Joe helped him."

We were in my room with the lights out. We could see lights from the street shining into the room the same way it had always done. We liked the shadows made by those lights.

"Albert got out and drove to Milledgeville," Janey Louise told me. "When Joe told me that Albert might be coming to see me, I watched for him every night out my window. I spent hours full of hope for the first time—just to see Albert. That hope probably got me as well as anything. I was *practicing* hope, then one night I saw him out in the trees.

"He looked up at my window, and I thought at first it was some kind of dream. That it might not be Albert at all but just my same old *wish* to see him, because I'd wished for it so many nights in a row. I sent him a letter and Volusia took it to him at the jail—that night with you."

"I didn't know," I said.

"I don't remember now what I wrote, but Albert came with the letter in his shirt pocket. I could see him out in the trees in a light bright shirt, and I tried to think of him in Korea in the war and what it would be like if I'd been there with him. I tried to think how he won his Distinguished Cross."

She shifted on her bed, and I turned to watch her talk, the outline of her head moving against the light of the wall.

"I cried about everything in that place." She whispered. "I cried about *moonlight*." She snickered, embarrassed to cry about such a thing. "And on that night there was a full moon, and Albert standing out there so sad. Then he came toward my room, walking, coming up the steps to the side door and he looked up to the window where I was standing, though I don't think he could see me. He used a ladder from the truck, and he climbed up to my window.

"When I saw him coming towards me, I went different places in my head. Oh, Evie. In my head, my mama came in the back door—not of your house, but of ours—carrying a load of clothes from the line, and she folded the clothes on the kitchen table, making separate piles in my mind. All of this: Mama coming in the back door with the clothes, and Albert coming in my room—my mind trying to make our life good again.

"Sometimes when Mama came to the hospital to sit with me, she'd say, 'Girl, when you gonna come back? When you coming back to the living time?' I remember exactly how she said it. 'That body of yours acting like it being a cage to keep you in. It don't matter what that man done to you. We can handle that. What matters is this day. Here. Right now. And, girl, you not even in it.'

"She said all that, but I kept coming and going like a shadow in myself, hearing you, and Mama Agnes, and Tuck, and Mama. Hearing you talking about hats and the possibilities of wigs."

"But what happened?" I asked. "I mean, what did Albert do?"

"Well, he came in and I turned toward the wall. Then he came up behind me and held me. Lord, he held me for the longest time. I hadn't let anybody hold me, but Albert's arms felt so strong. He held me hard and whispered in my ear, 'It's all right, Jane. It's all right now.' That's the first time anybody ever called me Jane."

I saw her mouth close over her teeth, a firm closing to punctuate what she had just said. "Then he took me over to the bed, and he said lie down, and I did and he pulled the covers over both of us, lying there beside me, my stomach big as a house, my back to his chest and his arms around me.

"Sometimes we would be like this at home at night after Mama was asleep. Since Mama loved Albert so much, I thought if Albert loved me, then I was the one most loved. That I was the best. And I slept all night safe in his arms, safer than I'd been since we were kids, or would be again.

"He stayed till just before daybreak, must've stayed awake all night while I slept. He looked all beat up, but wouldn't talk about it. He left the next morning early, said he was heading for Tennessee. He didn't know where."

"Maybe he made it," I said. "I hope he got away."

I could tell by her voice that she was smiling when she said, "He sure was something. You know, I bet he *did* get away. I bet he's riding on some Tennessee road just laughing to beat sixty."

"I bet he's stopping somewhere right now for chicken," I said, "and complaining because it's not spicy like Volusia's."

"I bet he is, too."

We slept that night in the same dream, and woke in a mood to ride our bikes across the whole country.

35

Albert was found after a week and brought back to Mercy for trial. Sand Jackson died, and on that day Mary Willingham hired a lawyer for Albert. Mary Willingham had been to law school herself years ago, but she'd never practiced law. Instead, she worked all her life for social causes, and used her money for those who needed to hire good lawyers. She had already hired a well-known Atlanta man for Albert, and all week she had been receiving hate mail. A few of her windows had been broken by someone throwing rocks.

When my mother asked Mary if she was afraid, she said, "I'm seventy years old. What're they going to do to me? *Kill* me? But I *am* afraid for Albert," she added. We sat at the kitchen table. Albert's trial was scheduled for the end of January.

Volusia had Tucker on her lap, even though his legs hung down as long as hers. Tucker was twelve, and he sat on her lap now as a joke.

"This is what I've heard," Mary Willingham said, keeping us informed. "If you've heard something different, tell me. But this is how it's being told."

We all got quiet. Mary would tell us exactly what had happened.

"There was a meeting at the Ninth Street Baptist Church on the Friday night Albert was arrested. Two hundred people showed up, and the city council was getting nervous, so they wanted some of their own members to go to the meeting. They'd been watching that church for weeks, and expected something to happen because men from the NAACP had already arrived. So that made everybody stirred up.

"During the first part of the meeting they discussed a plan to continue integration—restaurants, stores, and other schools besides just the high school." She stopped to see if we wanted to ask anything.

"They planned for a few children to go into the elementary school, but somebody from the city council said they thought things were moving too fast. Some of them wanted to see how the integration at

Mercy High was going to work out first. But they were just stalling, and everybody knew it.

"Then Albert, he stood up and made a short speech about the success of the program so far, and how the press was starting to praise Georgia instead of criticizing it. He appealed to their sense of state pride.

"But Sully Cantor, who's been on the council for five years, made a remark about Janey Louise, which Albert heard. He said that everybody knew she was in Milledgeville and that she wasn't smart enough to keep up with the white kids. He said this proved the point he was making all along."

"Why can't we tell them what really happened?" I asked. "Why wouldn't it *help* to say what happened to Janey Louise?"

"No!" Volusia exploded. "Nobody's gonna talk about my girl in the way they would if they knew she had been pregnant. They'd never believe somebody did it to her. They'd think she got herself into this trouble. They'd blame her for that baby." She lifted Tucker off her lap. "Why she even thought it herself. Thought it was her own fault. Thought she got pregnant from Dake's kiss. Lord, now, she *knew* better than that. But she never thought she could have a baby from such a terrible thing. She's had to learn too much in her life."

Tucker shifted upward, and my mother urged Mary Willingham to continue. But Mrs. Willingham's voice grew level, so I was afraid of what she was going to say.

"The meeting went for about an hour before Sand Jackson came in with his boys. They stood in the back and spread themselves around the doorways. Turnbull, with his brothers and nephews got up to join Sand Jackson's group. They knew what was about to happen. A few of the women tried to leave the church. The men blocked the doors, but allowed the women and a few men to go out.

"When all the women were outside, the men brought out billy clubs and knives. Sand Jackson's boys had baseball bats. They started to threaten Albert saying if this meeting didn't break up, there could be real trouble."

Volusia made the same sound in her throat that I heard on the night Albert was brought to the door.

"A man from Washington stood up and said these people had the right to have a meeting here. He said the men who came to break it up had no rights. Then the man standing beside Sand Jackson hit the Washington man with his bat, hit him in the side like he was swinging at a ball. That's what Albert said."

"You been talking to Albert?" Volusia asked.

"He doesn't look good, Volusia. He needs medical attention. I sent Doc Beryl over there this morning."

"Bless your heart," Volusia said.

"Anyway," Mary Willingham sighed, "the place began to break into fights and it went on for several minutes before the police came. But before the police arrived, Albert took the bat and he hit Sand, then he hit the man beside him. Sand got the worst blow, and his heart's been bad for years. He didn't die of the blow to his head, he died of a heart attack in the hospital. But nobody'll ever see it that way." She spoke directly to Volusia.

"Volusia, all of this is just an excuse. They hate Albert. He's stirred up their hate, which Lord knows, didn't need much stirring." She looked down at the table, her face a study in concentration. "Joe Sugar goes down to the jail to check on him every day. He tells me how things are."

"We need to plan for this court date," my mother said. "We have to make sure the Turnbulls don't use this incident to stop Albert for good."

The ceiling fans were high and barely stirred the air. The day was January 28th, but not very cold. Winter never completely came to Mercy, Georgia, and the sun was warm enough to have the tall windows open at the top. The room buzzed with voices, whisperings, and ladies brushed back hair from their faces nervously.

Albert waited at a long table between his white lawyer and a policeman. He rubbed his wrists where they had just a few moments before removed his handcuffs. Everyone stood when the judge came in, and we noticed that we did not have Judge Wilson as we had expected.

The bailiff called the court to order. Albert was the only colored person on the lower level of the courtroom, except for Volusia who sat next to my mother. All other coloreds stayed in the balcony—even Joe Sugar and Janey Louise. The court bulged with reporters and people who wanted to see what would happen to Albert Davis, the war hero.

Albert's accusers came forward in groups: the Turnbull brothers and their nephews, Tom Hill and Sully Cantor, Sand Jackson's friends, and some Klan members from other towns.

Mary Willingham's lawyer earned his money by trying to discredit each witness. Then he brought in witnesses of his own: Negro men from New York City—lawyers and university professors. And though these people were convincing, they only stirred up more hate because of their articulate manner.

I had the uneasy feeling that Judge Wilson, the lawyer from out of town, and Mary Willingham were losing their power. The whole courtroom carried a stench of indifference, like old roses in a corner.

At noon, the court broke for recess. When I returned to my seat, there was a furor in the front part of the court. A policeman had come in, running, with news whispered to the judge and to the lawyers. They were all talking at once.

Volusia sat forward on her seat, hopeful. For a moment I thought she might kneel and pray.

"What is it?" my mother said to no one.

The judge turned to the room full of people.

"Shhhh," my mother told people around her. Others said, "Shhh."

"A few minutes ago," the judge stated, "Albert Davis escaped. He was seen running into the woods where he got into a truck and was driven away. One of the guards was shot and other shots were fired, but we believe that Albert was not hit."

Volusia leaned against my mother. She made a crying noise that sounded like a cow's moan.

My mother put her arm around Volusia's shoulder and helped her stand. She led her out of the courtroom.

"Due to these circumstances," the judge said, "the court is adjourned."

The room buzzed again, not with whispers, but with voices of reporters who shouted questions to the judge and to the lawyers. Reporters were in charge now. They raced each other to find Volusia, but my mother had whisked her toward the rear of the courthouse. Tucker and I followed. We saw Janey Louise running ahead of us. We did not see Joe Sugar. Tucker yelled to Janey Louise and we hurried down a back street toward our house.

Tucker, though, wanted to speak to the reporters. He wanted to tell them how nice Albert was.

Janey Louise and Volusia stayed the night at Mary Willingham's house, so when reporters came by we sent them away.

That night in bed, in the dark, I felt like Alice in Wonderland wandering into a heap of things tall and small. I kept trying to remember Volusia's dark moon, Janey Louise's large belly, Albert's low voice when he spoke to me at our door—his swollen face in the courtroom. I looked behind memory, opened it up wide.

Behind the memory door, I grew seven feet high or turned tiny-small. I became a hard-shelled daisy, an ugly squash, something yellow gone awry. The things I'd dreamed of had gone so far off course that I felt a jinx on my life.

36

Albert had been gone for two weeks, when Joe Sugar's truck drove up to our door. We were all in the kitchen. The day was cold and the weatherman had predicted sleet and ice. Mama Agnes saw Joe's truck and jumped up from her chair. She screamed something to Volusia.

Before Joe had a chance to climb out of his truck, Volusia grabbed her coat and ran outside. Mama Agnes got the car keys, threw a coat to me, and one to Tucker. Janey Louise ran out to catch Volusia, so I brought a coat for her.

When Mama Agnes backed out, I shouted, "Wait! Wait!" I wanted to get in the truck with Janey Louise. I wanted to give her her coat. But Mama Agnes told me to stay in the car. We drove to the courthouse without speaking.

People came out of the hardware store, barber shop, and restaurants to see the spectacle on the courthouse steps. They stopped in the middle of what they were doing to come outside. Everything they did looked like an emergency.

Somebody yelled, "They found him. They found the bastard!"

I could see Volusia climb slowly out of Joe Sugar's truck. Joe tried to keep her from looking. Our car drove up and Mama Agnes called to Volusia, but nothing stopped her. Janey Louise followed with Joe's coat around her shoulders. People stepped back from Albert's body as though they were being polite. Janey Louise went straight toward the body, and I think she didn't know yet who it was, or what she would see. Volusia walked more cautiously, but her movements still had the effect of hurrying, stumbling. She wanted to believe he was alive.

Janey Louise stood beside Albert's head, as Volusia knelt and put his head onto her lap. Every part of his body was bloody and ragged with skin. He had been dragged and didn't seem like a real person. When I saw him I hoped he was dead, but when I saw his face, I knew he was alive, though barely. He looked at his mother, and tried to say something, but could hardly get it out. The crowd around us yelled, so Volusia leaned down and put her ear to his mouth. She left it there a long time, and when she took her head away, Albert was dead.

Janey Louise knelt too, imitating her mother, touching Albert's arm. I went to stand behind Janey Louise. Volusia got up, letting Albert's head bounce off her lap. She didn't feel gentle anymore. She turned to the crowd. They were going to let her speak.

"All my life," Volusia said. Her arms were stiff and curled into fists at her sides. "I've been a peaceful woman all my life—but no more. I did not know this could happen. I didn't know you could bring him here like a dog. All my life I been peaceful, but I want to say that the men who did this thing, those men will not outlive me."

Mama Agnes whispered, "Vo-lu-sia." She took her arm and tried to lead her away. Joe Sugar stopped my mother. He wanted her to leave Volusia alone.

I took Janey Louise's coat and handed it to her. I looked down at Albert and studied his clothes—the gravel embedded in the cloth of his pants. His clothes were half off, the skin on his chest and thighs scraped raw. His head was matted with bloody hair, and his face I could not believe the condition of his face. So I looked away, so as not to see it. Joe and Janey Louise did not look away.

Volusia still spoke, but the crowd moved off. Some were sad, so they lingered without knowing what to do. They had stopped yelling, but returned now to the barber shop, or hardware store, or whatever they were doing.

Volusia called for them to come back, to listen to her.

"I'm telling you something," she said. "I'm telling you," and she turned to Janey Louise to look straight into her daughter's eyes. "Now, now we've got to learn to hate," she said.

That night we heard a wild sound coming from downstairs.

Janey Louise stayed in the room with her mother, but when Volusia began to scream, she went to get Mama Agnes. We all ran downstairs. Volusia stood in the middle of the room flapping her arms as though she were drowning. She talked, but she wasn't talking to us.

My mother tried to hold her, but Volusia pushed her away. She tried again, reaching around her. Volusia pushed, and finally they wrestled each other to the floor. The two women cried. They spoke—though not really to each other—more to the grief of the moment.

Mama Agnes sat on the floor with her legs splayed out and Volusia's big body between her legs. My mother's arms wrapped around Volusia's chest, holding her, rocking her in big swaying motions. She told me to take Janey Louise upstairs, and that we could all three sleep in her bed.

But she stayed the rest of the night with Volusia.

As the three of us lay in Mama Agnes's bed, with Tucker in the middle, I thought of Volusia and my mother sitting all night, swaying with grief. Over the years, they had learned how to be each other's friend.

37

On the day Tucker and I had seen Volusia's body at Joe's store, Jane promised she would come by the house again, but I didn't see her anymore that day. I picked up August at the airport, and in the evening when she still hadn't called, I dialed her number. No one answered.

Then, late the following afternoon, Jane phoned, asking me to meet her at the cemetery. Her voice sounded nervous, shaky. She said that she wanted to visit the grave before the service the next day, but she didn't want to go alone. So I walked to the cemetery, going along the same path that we had walked to the river in the summertime.

Before I reached the grave, I saw Jane standing beside a freshly dug pile of dirt. A suffusion of afternoon light fell over her, and the dirt. A shovel lay propped against a tree. Whenever we walked here as girls, we liked to pretend to be scared. We never went to the graveyard at night.

Jane stood beside a headstone. The inscription read: *Volusia Finehold Davis, 1914–1978.* She threw flowers into the grave. They landed in a puddle of water at the bottom, and floated. I hated to think of Volusia lowered into that grave water. I stood beside Jane, and threw in a fistful of dirt.

Jane took a long insuck of breath. "Joe came out here this morning," she said. "He told me I should come."

"I'm glad you called me," I almost took her hand, but stopped myself. Her voice sounded nasal, as if she were holding her nose.

"I've got to ask your help, Evie."

"What is it?"

"It's about Bandy and the boys."

I expected her to ask me to pick up Bandy at the airport. I expected her to say that he was arriving today with Max and Sammy, but her voice was too urgent for a small request.

"My life's been falling apart since March," she said. "And it keeps on falling." She continued to pitch flowers into the grave, tearing the petals and throwing them in separately.

"Bandy left me in March, Evie. He took the boys with him. Right before I came here."

She waited a moment for me to respond.

"He left?" I said. "I didn't know you were having any trouble." My comments felt stupid on my tongue. Jane was breathing heavily.

"He took the boys," she said, repeating the hard fact. "But there was a reason."

The petals were gone and Jane held nothing but an empty stem. Her purse was slung over her shoulder. "I had an affair and Bandy found out. The man was somebody at work." She turned away when she said this. "I don't know how it happened. I've always loved Bandy."

"Where are they?"

"I don't know. All I have is this."

Jane reached into her pocketbook to lift out a letter. The envelope was greasy from being handled so much. The letter contained large third-grade cursive script.

Dear Mama,

Sammy cries for you at night, and I do too. Daddy takes us sometimes to the place where he wurks. But we cannot go there at nite, so he gets a nabor laddy to stay with us. She is not nice as you. She does not let us eat on the bed. When you come back from Grandmama we want to come home with you. Daddy says you can call us at this number — 1-312-786-1309. Thank you ver much.

Love,
Max

As I read, Jane leaned forward and held her head. I placed my hand on her back, and when she looked up her eyes were without hope, blank as a pair of doors.

I knew the debilitating effect of someone's leaving. And though I had felt relief when Lowell Hardison left after only two years of marriage, I remembered how I could not lift my arms without effort.

To brush my teeth, to get out of bed, to make a phone call—everything required enormous strength. Ty was only a few months old, but I knew that the constant physical care he required would bring me back into the world. And I knew that Jane's care of Volusia had done the same for her. But now Volusia was gone. I handed back Sammy's letter, and she tucked it into her purse.

"The reason I'm telling you, Evie, is because people will ask where Bandy is. They'll be asking about the boys. I want you to make excuses for them." Her face grew tremulous as water, not blank at all. She made a vague gesture indicating that we should walk.

I was glad she thought to ask for my help. "We'll say they wanted to come, but the boys were sick and you thought it might be easier to handle all the details of the funeral alone. People will understand that."

Jane nodded, and we passed familiar markers along the cemetery path. We passed Albert's grave, and Finney's. Then Jane pointed to one that said Twin Babys.

When we were girls and saw this marker, I told her that Babys was spelled wrong. But neither of us could get over the idea that two people might be buried in the same coffin.

Janey Louise had asked if I thought they were in there together, if their bones were touching. I believed she liked the idea of them not being alone.

"Husbands and wives get buried together all the time," I told her. "So do twins," but my unformed mind could not imagine how this was done.

"Not in the same coffin," Janey Louise had said.

"Maybe if they died at the same time," I told her. "Maybe if you died with somebody at the exact same time that they die—then they let you be in there together."

We made immediate plans to share a grave together, and promised that even if our deaths came at separate times, we would make the graveyard man open the coffin and put in whichever one came second.

"But what would the marker say?" I asked Janey Louise.

She thought for a moment. "Two girls," she told me.

It did not occur to us then that we would not always be girls.

The clouds had turned red and the sky looked like rain, but I said a silent prayer for a mild funeral day tomorrow. I wanted something to be easy.

"Max and Sammy don't even know Mama died," Jane said. She looked on the verge of tears again. "Bandy knew she was sick, but he doesn't know she's dead."

"Why don't you stay with us tonight," I suggested. "Stay at the house."

"No." Her eyes receded. "Capp keeps running off. He ran off last night and I had to go looking for him. He cut his head. Fell on something in the woods and cut himself pretty bad. I took him to the emergency room."

Two squirrels looped from tree to tree, moving the branches and speckling the light on the ground.

"Capp doesn't know how to grieve," Jane said. "He thinks Volusia's alive somewhere and that he can find her."

My mother had already expressed concern about Capp's erratic behavior. She said we needed to get him under control.

By the time we closed the graveyard gates, the moon was up, though daylight still had several more hours. As we left, we had our arms around each others' backs, and I felt that Jane through her confession had opened a way for me to come back into her world.

In our early life we couldn't walk like this in public. People would see. Though sometimes in this cemetery for coloreds, we could walk like friends and I could feel connected to Jane's whole world and believe she was connected to mine.

We always ran home from the cemetery, chasing each other under the thrill of being frightened. We would run into the kitchen where Volusia stood planted at the sink.

"You girls almost made me drop this pot of beans," she said. "You want me to drop this whole boiling pot on you feet?"

"Evie's trying to scare me."

"I was *not*."

"Why y'all always going through that cemetery? Seems like you could leave those dead people alone. They dead. Leave 'em alone. I can't see why you always going through that cemetery. Anyway," Volusia had turned toward me and I was sure she would reprimand me for trying to scare Janey Louise, but she said, "that cemetery's for *coloreds*, not for *you*."

She had singled me out. She had sided with Janey Louise over me, and with one swift blow had ousted me from their world.

"That's not true!" I hissed. "I used to be! I *used* to be a colored person!"

I was convinced that this was true, and that I had been, and could remember being an actual colored person. I didn't let my eyes fall from Volusia's face. I didn't want her to think I was lying. But I could not determine, or even translate, the force of the expression that Volusia gave back to me.

For over one hundred years the Charles Street cemetery had been set aside for blacks. Albert and Finney were buried there, now Volusia, and someday maybe Jane.

"That man was white, Evie," Jane said. Her voice so quiet. "That's what got to Bandy. If the man hadn't been white, maybe Bandy could've taken that."

Of all the things I ever expected Jane to say, the last thing was that she had chosen to sleep with a white man.

"They'll come back," I told her. "I know they will."

As we passed again the marker that said Twin Babys, I couldn't tell exactly what Jane was thinking, but I knew she was thinking of us, and maybe our own cold graves side by side.

There were moments, and this was one of them, that I felt a whole world between us. For one fleeting second I had let my mind acknowledge that I didn't want to be buried here.

After I left Jane, I decided to go to Bowdin's Drugs. Bowdin's still had booths, and was one of the few drug stores left that had a lunch counter where old-timers came in at eleven o'clock for the daily special.

As I walked in I heard the familiar jingle on the door. A young man named Bailey owned the store now, though he had not yet changed the sign outside. Charles Bailey was a good-natured man who grew up in Alabama, lived for a short time in Vermont, and came back down South. He loved the tree-lined streets of Mercy, the warm winters, sidewalks, and bike paths. He liked that Mercy was a landmark town in Georgia for early integration in the fifties. Charles Bailey was a black man. Last year someone put him up for mayor.

When I walked through the jingly door, he called my name, and though I'd never been introduced to him he knew who I was and I knew him. I asked if this store still served a cherry smash. He prepared it himself with two cherries floating on top.

I bought a magazine and heard someone mention Adele Turnbull's name, then Margaret's. They said that Margaret was in town. They had seen her at the Turnbull house.

I left Bowdin's before I'd finished my fountain drink.

When I arrived back at the house, my mother showed me the evening paper. The article on the front page had large headlines and a picture of Robert Turnbull. He had been murdered in his bed the previous evening.

38

The river grew wide with the rains, and people walked along its sides, afraid of the overflow. There had not been a flood here in twenty years, but those who could remember the last one passed down stories of enormous loss, and some of the sadness still lingered in many of the families.

A young black preacher carried himself with stiff pride along the river's edge. He didn't walk with the crowd, but stood slightly apart. He led them to the grave site.

Volusia had asked that her service be held graveside, rather than in the church. The request surprised many of the townspeople, who preferred the Mt. Zion Church of God. Joe Sugar suggested that everyone meet at the churchhouse, then walk to the graveyard together. He liked the idea of a procession.

Volusia's plot had been bought years ago. Joe planned to be buried beside her   Jane too, if she wanted it. My own suspicion (though I did not know this for sure) was that my mother wanted to be buried near Volusia.

I'd never asked directly about my mother's choice of funeral arrangements, but a few years ago she told me she planned to be buried in a place the rest of us might not want to go. I didn't ask what she meant.

I walked to the bridge at the end of town and leaned over the railing to study the current. When I looked up, I saw Margaret and Adele Turnbull at the back of the procession.

To my surprise I felt angry at seeing them. The morning papers— both Mercy's *Morning Herald* and the *Atlanta Constitution*, reported Robert Turnbull's death, calling it a murder. The police had a suspect, but didn't mention a name. They said an arrest was imminent.

The black community walked together separate from the white folks. Judge Wilson, in his nineties now, walked among them. Capp walked beside the judge. Capp's face and arms were the color of cocoa.

He loved to walk with people, and he loved being anywhere near the woods.

Capp came to these woods as if it were a room. He knew where to find an owl's nest, where beavers lived, and foxes. One summer when Capp was almost nine, and I had come back to Mercy for a few weeks, Volusia suggested I walk with him to the river.

We walked through the forest, past Corny's Pond, all the way to the river. Whenever Capp showed me something, I told him the name of it. I told him the name of different lichens, trees, and birds, until Capp learned them all, as though we had named it for the first time. He never forgot me for that.

When I returned to Texas, I sent him a book with pictures and labels. My mother said he took it to the woods, and could identify plants by sight and picture.

When Capp was in the woods, his face turned alight with power. He knew everything around him. He was aware of sights and sounds. Sometimes in traffic, if a horn blew, Capp became so startled that he didn't know where he was for a moment. He would spin around or lose his balance. But in the woods, noises did not frighten him. Each sound was an element to which he listened attentively.

Capp carried his piccolo and could make forest sounds that mimicked the real thing. Birds answered his quick notes, and townspeople called Capp their Woods Scholar.

As we crossed the bridge to the grave site, I could see Capp lean to peer into the water below.

The day had started out sunny, but now the clouds blew sideways and our mood changed with the disturbance of weather. My mother pointed to some policemen lined up along the path that led through the cemetery gates. August walked behind us, and made a comment about security. My mother had not directed the question to August, but still he answered—trying to feel included. After all these years, I thought, he finally wanted to be included.

Then we saw Margaret and Adele walking along the edge of the crowd.

"Why are they here?" my mother said. Neither Margaret nor Adele would look at us. They stayed along the fringe of the procession.

We saw four more policemen. I couldn't imagine why so many policemen were present. The black preacher began to slow the procession's pace.

Looking at the sky, I was afraid we'd get one of those drenching showers we sometimes got in summer—a hot, steamy downpour. But as we gathered at the grave and the preacher began to speak, the sun came out again—not bright, just gold. The day was getting toward evening.

If it had been years ago, Volusia's voice would have called us in for supper. We would have heard her from the yard, and if we didn't hear, she'd ring a cowbell that could make its sound go all the way to Corny's Pond.

When we heard the bell, we raced home. First one back got an extra roll at supper.

The preacher began the service with a hymn. Then he spoke: "When Volusia Finehold Davis came to our church thirty years ago," he said, "I wasn't even born. She was here before I'd even thought about being a preacher. We remember her because of who she was and because of the things she did for us in hard times."

Then he named the hard times.

"Marie Fisher remembers when Volusia rode through a bad storm to help deliver her third child. When she came that night, Marie says Volusia's clothes were blown nearly to smithereens. She brought Marie and Jolie's boy, Buddy, into the world."

The preacher had known Volusia for only a few years, so he told stories that had been passed down. But he told them impersonally, as if he were talking about a remote, distantly remembered woman. I resented him, and felt the instinct to shout.

"She found a wet nurse for Hank Stokes' youngest boy when his wife died in childbirth. And she made coconut cakes for our bake sales that brought in more money than our Easter pledges."

People laughed, so the preacher added, "And, you know, we all wear her famous hats." He held up his own famous hat, as did others around the graveside. The gesture looked like a salute.

The young preacher's name was George Eustis. He took advantage of this moment to speak to the white people of Mercy, quoting Martin Luther King Jr. He ended his speech by mentioning Capp. He called him Cappadocia.

Capp stood next to Joe. His head had a bandage that kept falling over his eye, and he kept pulling at it. But he smiled when the preacher said his name.

When my mother was given a chance to speak, she moved to the head of the grave. Squirrels barked in a nearby tree, and the sky turned a hard metallic gray.

"I don't really know how to say what I feel." She took a deep breath. "Volusia lived in my house for eleven and a half years. We raised our girls together, and Tucker. And Albert." She stopped. "Albert, though, stayed in the house of Latham Street."

Jane's face looked surprised at my mother's assertion.

"Jane and Evie slept in the same room for most of those years. They shared clothes, and sometimes when I bought a shirt for Evie and Tuck, I bought one for Jane. When Albert turned up dead, Evie and· Jane went every day to his grave taking flowers or whatever they could find."

She paused, and covered her face. She wept, soundlessly.

"We lived through some things," she said, not wanting to say everything. "And there were times when I didn't understand." She hung her head, and I believed she was going to pray.

Then she lifted a piece of paper on which she'd written something to say. She read, "I see the shreds of my life through a lens Volusia gave to me, and whatever I know about the world, or about myself now, I learned from her. My heart without her is torn."

She put the paper down and looked into our faces. "All our lives people said we were enemies." She tried to think of what to say about that. "But our old hearts called us friends."

My mother moved to sit down between me and Jane. Jane took her hand and held it. Until that moment, my mother had held back most of her tears.

Then Joe Sugar went to the head of the grave and called Capp to come stand beside him. Capp had turned into a young man, and I liked his face. I liked his short, hopeful name.

"I see her everywhere," Joe said, his expression looked bored with grief. "I see her on the porch of the store, in her rocking chair. I hear her calling to me from the door, from the ground. All the years of my life flow into her, and I bring her voice and her face back—at random times.

"And it's like I'm seeing inside a big machine, hoping to step in there, too. I don't feel nothing much—just sad and useless. I been dispossessed of a precious thing, and I'm confounded, like my head's full of paint fumes, like I'm a bull."

Joe ran the back of his hand over his eyes and wavered slightly. To me, Joe looked like a burned-out man, like someone who had just come out of a fire. Capp knew how to steady him. Joe stepped backward. "Something's got hold of me and I guess it's old grief."

He looked at Capp, and wanted to say something about him for Volusia. To let Volusia speak. "Capp's a good boy," he said. Capp smiled and held Joe's arm. He was taller than Joe.

"When we found him he was a frizzled little thing—his head a tangle. Volusia said they didn't bathe him right, or at all. He look so thin and mangy. We hadn't visited him in a year, then we came in unannounced, and saw how he was. Volusia took him out and brought him to live with us."

Joe shifted his weight, then touched his genitals, not a conscious gesture. Tenderness welled up in his eyes, and he had forgotten what else he wanted to say, so he began to speak from his swollen heart.

I remember the days when summer was thick with blueberries and air felt sweet to the skin. I remember all the days. And I am grateful for my Volusia and her whole life. She made all the rooms of my heart come alive with the light. He was woozy with speaking.

Joe had stepped over a boundary—away from politeness into meanderings. I wanted to stand up and bring him down to the grass beside me, but as soon as Joe paused, Capp began to play "Now the Day Is Over" on his harmonica.

Then, before anyone could stop him, he played two verses of "She'll Be Coming Around the Mountain When She Comes." When he was finished, everyone clapped. He had made us smile at one another.

We stood in a circle around the opening in the ground where Volusia would be lowered. I could see the flowers that Jane had thrown earlier into the grave water. The mound of dirt beside us was red with Georgia clay.

Each year in March, Volusia brought bowls of red spring mud to the kitchen. She liked to urge me, Janey Louise, and Tucker to touch and smell it, until spring had completely arrived.

As we sang the last hymn, Jane drew herself up into a thin line. Her body resembled a pole. Everything about her stance instructed us not to touch her, though everything in me said she needed to be touched.

Six big men lowered Volusia's coffin into the ground, with her rose-sleeved dress, her hat, and Albert's letters. When she was in the grave water, the only movement came from clouds pulling back from the sun. A breeze disturbed the high tops of trees, and the sun washed us in a coppery light. Volusia would have liked this day's rusty smell of wet, red earth.

Less than a year later, Agnes Bell collapsed on the road to Atlanta. Her heart stopped on a Friday afternoon as she was driving Capp to the doctor. The police found her body slumped at the wheel of her car, and Capp had been standing by the road for half an hour trying to get someone to stop.

My mother was buried as she had asked to be—in the grave next to Volusia.

39

As we left the cemetery, Tucker looked in his rearview mirror. "What's going on?" he said. "The police are following us home." My mother was riding in Mr. Shallowford's car, but Jane and I rode home with Tucker and Becky. We sat together in the backseat.

At the house, we saw a squad car in the driveway and two plain-clothes policemen on the front porch. My mother and Mr. Shallowford got out first and I heard them ask, "What's the matter?" Tucker got out with them.

Becky turned around to ask me what I thought was happening, but I kept watching the policemen talk. We watched their mouths move, then my mother's hand went to her face.

"Oh, God," Jane said.

As they walked toward the car, Jane's expression made my arm hairs stand on end. She slid from the backseat as if everything in her body felt sore. A policeman took hold of her arm and began to read her her rights.

Jane jerked away.

"Someone identified you at Robert Turnbull's house Monday afternoon around the time of his death. We have to take you in."

"Am I being arrested?" she asked.

They said yes.

Tucker and Mr. Shallowford argued with the policemen. All their voices gave me a headache, bad. I eased myself from the car. So did Becky.

In the police car behind us I heard someone say the word "nigger." My mother heard it too, and looked around the yard as if she were seeking help. She kept repeating herself, saying that they were making a mistake. That this was all a mistake. She asked how could they do this, just as we returned from a funeral.

The police captain said they'd known about the funeral, and for that reason had waited until the service was over.

When I asked if I could ride downtown with Jane, the captain said no. They walked Jane to their car and took her away.

Inside our house tables lay covered with food from well-meaning neighbors. I began to prepare a plate to take to the courthouse, thinking it might be a way to see Jane for a few minutes. "I'm going down there," I said. Tucker offered to drive me.

My mother called Judge Wilson, who gave us the name of a good Atlanta lawyer. Mr. Shallowford wrote down the name of the man and the law firm.

When they got off the phone, I covered the plate in Saran Wrap, and Tucker added a slice of cake to her supper.

At the front desk the sergeant told us that we couldn't go into the room where Jane was being questioned. Tucker threatened to stay until we got to see her, and I showed the sergeant the plate of food.

"She hasn't eaten anything all day," I said.

The sergeant lifted the plate from my hands and walked down the hall. He closed a door behind him, but when it opened again, Jane stuck her head out and waved. Her eyes looked haunted, even from a distance. She mouthed "thank you" for her supper, and motioned for us not to wait for her.

To see her down the long hall, her head poking out of the door—shadows of people milling around—made my position in the world seem neutral. All the angles of the hallway, all the shadows made me feel dizzy and droopy-eyed.

What I didn't know, but what the sergeant soon told us, was that someone had seen Jane go into Robert Turnbull's house between 5:30 and 6:00 on Monday night. A neighbor woman saw her go in, and never saw her leave. And she saw the car that Jane had been driving for all these weeks in Mercy.

So there was an eyewitness—someone who actually saw Jane go into the Turnbull house. At that moment I couldn't think of any reason for Jane to be in his house. I couldn't imagine any excuse that I, or anyone else, would believe.

The desk sergeant suggested that we go home, but when I asked what time the questioning might be over, he said, "Well, just let me say this, she won't be going anywhere tonight."

When we got home, Mr. Shallowford had gone and my mother told us to sit down. She and Becky had been discussing what they could do. "They're saying that somebody broke into Turnbull's house," my mother said. "Somebody just came in, though I don't think any of the doors were actually locked. Did he say the house was locked?" She turned to Becky, but didn't wait for an answer.

"Nothing was stolen," she said. "It could've been anybody." She looked as if she was trying to think of who it could be.

"His neck was broken," Becky said. And the fact that Becky spoke shocked me as much as what she had said. "They said that he was smothered first, then his neck was broken."

My mother walked nervously around the kitchen. She couldn't find a place to set anything down.

I took a chicken wing and a piece of Lorraine Hitt's lemon pie. At the edge of my mind's eye, I saw Albert's young self in Mercy's same jail. I saw myself walking beside Volusia with a knife and two pies. And I thought about how one situation could resemble another—like people who bear a resemblance around the nose or mouth.

Then Becky thought of something. "Didn't you tell us that Jane was taking care of Capp on that night?" She directed the question to me, and I tried to remember what Jane had said.

"When you came home from the cemetery with Jane, didn't you say Capp had hurt his head and that Jane took him to the hospital for stitches?"

I grew excited thinking that this might be Jane's alibi.

"Did she take Capp to the emergency room?" my mother asked, hopefully.

"Yes, that's what she said. Joe can probably verify it."

My mother nodded. "I've tried to call Joe several times. Nobody answers."

I tried to call Joe's number. When he answered, I said, "Where've you been? We've been trying to get hold of you."

"Capp ran off again. I leave him alone for one thin minute and he's gone, seems like. I been looking for him. I'm afraid he's gonna tear out his stitches. He keeps messing with that bandage."

"Did you find him?" My mother had gone to the extension phone.

"Yeah, we found him. He's all right." Joe cleared his throat. "What'd you want me for?"

40

The next morning I rose early. I hadn't slept well, and wanted to get up before anyone else. I wanted to begin thinking in a practical way.

By eight o'clock my mother and Tucker had come downstairs, but no one fixed breakfast. We were sick of food. I waited on the porch, hoping for someone to come out and sit with me. I could hear my mother scrambling around in the kitchen.

But before anyone came out, the phone rang. I answered, expecting it to be either Joe Sugar or the lawyer, but instead I heard August's voice. He had read in the morning paper about Jane's arrest, and though he had planned to leave in a few hours, he was calling to say he'd be willing to stay. My mother motioned to let me know she didn't want his help.

"Everything's under control," I said. "Jane has a good lawyer. He came in last night from Atlanta. If you want, I'll drive you to the airport."

"What did he think he could do?" my mother asked.

"He's just lonely," I said.

"Wonder why he never married that woman."

"Melina?"

"Was that her name?"

The phone rang again. It was Joe Sugar. "I'm going to see Jane this morning. The lawyer wants to talk with me. Can you go this afternoon, or tonight?"

"Sure. I'm taking August to the airport in a little while, but I planned to see Jane later. Did you see the paper? What's that lawyer saying?"

"We meet with him tomorrow at his office on Tenth and Broad. He'll tell us something then."

While still on the phone, I saw a blue truck come around the corner at the end of the block. I told Joe good-bye and got up to go inside.

My mother saw the truck, too. She told me to come to the kitchen. "Quick!" That's how I knew she'd seen the truck.

We stood at the kitchen window. A few minutes passed before we saw it again.

"See? I told you I saw them," she said.

The truck held four men. Two rode inside, two in the truck bed. They drove slowly by the house.

"What're they doing?" I asked.

The two men in the back of the truck looked in our direction, then drove off. We didn't see the truck again before I left to pick up August.

I waited for August outside his motel. He came to put his suitcase in the car, then went back in to pay his bill. I hadn't waited in a car for August since the year spring came late, when I was seven, and I waited outside Heck's Grocery for him to return to the car with eggs and milk.

That was the year spring came on a Friday morning, and we got up to the new-green smell of wild onions, animals coming out of the ground and into the house, bumblebees flooding the yard. August had announced that spring was here, and that he would take us to the river for a cookout breakfast.

I loved for him to excite the house with his moods. As I waited for him in the car that day, I saw a bumblebee climb up the window. The bee climbed and jumped down, climbed and jumped. I thought it was falling.

The yellow and black fur moved very close to my eye, and I studied the hunched body, huge. August had already explained to me the impossibility of the bumblebee's actual flight. Scientifically speaking, he said, their bodies were too large for their wings to hold them up. I delighted in the idea of seeing this bee do some science-defying feat.

As it climbed the slick window, I studied its wings and legs. I saw the "minuscule-ality" of its parts. August had taught me the word *minuscule*, but I liked the sound of "minuscule-ality." I liked the made-up-ness of it.

When the bee climbed again, I rolled down the window slowly. The bee always fell away at a certain spot, so I rolled the glass down to a little lower than the place where it always fell. When the bee reached the falling place, it found the lip of the window, climbed onto it, and flew off. I considered mashing it quickly against the glass, and though I liked to see the blood of small things, I wasn't able to destroy him just to see the blood.

When August came back with his bag of groceries, I told him about the bee. He gave me five new facts, and said to memorize them.

At home on my windowsill, I kept a parade of baby-food jars holding different insects. August required that I know five facts about each one.

"What did you notice?" he asked, wanting me to come up with a fact of my own.

I pictured the bee in my mind. "At the place where the yellow fur ends and the black fur starts, there's a tiny groove."

"Good."

"And," I said, "his wings come out of the place where his ears are supposed to be."

August lifted a box of animal crackers from the bag and handed them to me. I wasn't supposed to eat cookies this early in the morning, but I opened the box and the waxed paper, and ate a camel. August ate a rhinoceros. We finished the box before we reached the house.

We drove to the airport on back roads, and August read aloud from the newspaper: one article about Turnbull and two about Jane. I tried to change the subject, but couldn't, until I mentioned teaching. August was always interested in what I taught, and whether or not I was teaching the same methods he had taught me. He fished for a compliment.

"I loved going places with you," I told him. "I loved all the reading you made me do before we even stepped out the door." He smiled. What I didn't say was how much I missed all that when he left.

I used to go to August's room, before Volusia took it over with her hats. The shelves were a repository of rocks, bird nests, pieces of robin's eggs, a brown-speckled shell, sea conchs, and specimens of butterflies and moths pinned to a board and labeled. My own study at home duplicated his room with tennis shoes, hiking boots, rubber boots lined up in a closet for different kinds of searches.

"You used to write me such long letters about what you saw," he said. His voice cracked.

That's when I noticed his face looked like a vacuum—his neck shadowy and clammy. There was no help for him inside his own body. I knew, everything in me knew, that he was behaving like a man who was sick, but didn't want anyone to mention it.

"We could start writing letters again," I suggested.

He contented himself with a nod, and rolled up his sleeves to the middle of his forearm. I touched the rolled-up part of his sleeve. His face had a light behind it, like a candle in a jack-o'-lantern. Light came through his eyes and his skin glowed.

I loved him. I loved him as much as I did the year spring came late. I kept thinking "I love him," as if someone else had said it—an aunt talking about someone remembered continuously.

He checked his bag at the curb, and the way he leaned down looked old. His baldness made me sad. As we headed for Gate 24 my eyes burned, but before we got to the gate he said good-bye, and kissed my jaw. As he bent toward me, he smelled like somebody's father.

I went to Joe Sugar's store before returning home and found him in the back room moving boxes with Capp. Capp shook my hand, then went back to work. He had a fresh bandage on his forehead.

"How is Capp's head?" I asked Joe.

"You take your daddy to the airport?" Joe lifted a box and handed it to Capp.

I nodded.

"The lawyer's gonna set bail," he said. "Don't know how much yet." He shook his head.

"What's wrong? What happened?" I hated the way he was shaking his head.

"I been hearing about a necktie party—not for Jane, but for me—anybody, I guess. Something's about to hit."

At that moment we heard someone come into the store. A man, a white man's voice.

"You stay back here," Joe said, "out of anybody's sight. No sense in anybody seeing you here."

I heard men, more than one, talking to Joe.

"Idn't it a little late in life for you to be getting militant around here, Joe?" one man asked. There were two, maybe three, men in the store.

"I don't think of myself as militant," Joe said. He moved some papers from one part of the counter to the other. "Nobody's ever thought of me as a dangerous man. I'm just working with what's rightfully my own."

"And you think this store is rightfully your own?"

"Yes sir. I inherited it from my papa's money."

"And you think that boy in there, that Capp, you think he's rightfully yours?"

Why would they mention Capp? Was that a threat?

"Not mine, exactly, but part a my family." Joe moved to maybe get the papers of adoption, to show them, but they told him to stop.

"And you think this dirty tomato is yours? You think all you sell in this store is yours? Or you think this town's been good to you, letting you sell your goods all these years?"

"They been good to me. Yeah. But what I sell is good, too. That tomato you got there's as good as any you might eat. You just take a bite. See what you think."

"I will. I'll do just that." They turned to leave.

"Why y'all come by here?" Joe asked. I couldn't decide if this was a brave question or a stupid one. "Why y'all coming in here?"

"We're just seeing if you were expecting Jane over here, or if she's gonna stay at the Bells' house when she gets out. I'm telling you right now, we don't want her out. You hear me?"

"I hear you," Joe said. "I didn't know she was gonna get out anytime soon. But if she does, she'll be staying over at the Bells all right."

When Joe came back into the room again, I said I had to leave. I wanted to get out, fast.

"You be careful now," he told me. "They can be mean to you now, well as me. The ones that be mean, be mean to anybody."

Capp dropped a box on his foot and made a sound of pain—not a loud sound, but a gar-ru-umph of air that was forced out. A lung sound. It was the first noise I'd ever heard from his mouth.

41

I couldn't see Jane until almost five o'clock, because she had been talking all day to her lawyer, Lamar Pratt. I'd heard Mr. Shallowford say the lawyer's name and tried to picture what he might look like.

What I couldn't picture was what Jane would look like in a jail cell. She was being kept in Mercy's oldest jail, which had only three holding cells. This jail housed criminals before they were sent to the prison near Athens, Georgia. If the judge decided to hold Jane over for trial, they would take her to the prison, and I imagined visiting her there in a cubicle with a Plexiglas shield between us.

Jane was the only person in any of the three cells. As I went in I knew that this was where Albert had been kept—where Volusia had brought me the night we took Albert his pies. The room where the sergeant sat had been refurbished, but the three cells looked exactly the same. I'd seen these jail cells, not when Albert was here, but once when our school had taken a field trip to Mercy's courthouse and jail. I recognized the smell of it. My heart began to race, and my whole body wanted to leave.

Jane was sitting on a metal cot with a thin mattress. Light came from a high window with bars, and made the cell look like something we might have seen in an old western movie.

When she looked up, I saw that she was wearing glasses. I had never seen her in glasses before. Her expression showed several emotions.

"Are you all right?" I asked. She looked at me a long moment without answering, as if she were trying to recognize someone she didn't remember very well.

She wore a pair of orange pants and shirt, too big for her. A few books and magazines lay scattered on her cot and there was a small lamp not turned on. When she saw me, she reached to turn it on.

The sergeant wouldn't allow me to enter the cell, but he brought a chair so that I could sit outside the cell door. When he left, Jane came and reached her arms through the bars. We held each other, our foreheads touching. Then Jane pulled back and brought her own chair up close to mine.

I had brought a handful of candy bars, all kinds. Jane smiled, as if we were being mischievous. She pushed her glasses onto her head.

"When did you get glasses?" I asked.

"A few years ago." She was holding some papers and I assumed they were from her lawyer. "I am so hungry," she said.

Some of the candy was broken from my being searched.

"Wanna hear a joke?" Jane said.

"I guess." I didn't.

"A man walked into a chicken place in north Georgia and asked to speak to the manager. When the manager came out, he said, "Tell me, how do you prepare your chickens?"

"'Ohh-h, we don't do much,' the manager said. 'but we *do* tell them they are about to die.'"

We laughed, then we laughed at our laughing. The sergeant could see us. When we settled down, Jane said she felt like that chicken, and my heart poured out of itself. I leaned forward.

"Jane," I said. I wanted to ask everything.

"I can't talk, Evie. The lawyer told me not to say anything."

"But listen," I said, "I keep thinking of things you could say." Jane began to shake her head, and she kept shaking it until I was through. "Did you tell them you were with Capp? Did you say you took him to the emergency room, and that's where you were?"

"I told them everything," she said. "It didn't make any difference."

Jane opened a Milky Way and handed it to me. A guard saw her reach toward me and asked what we were doing, so I held up the candy. They were watching all our movements.

"I'm so sorry this happened," I told her.

"What does that mean, Evie? What does that mean, 'you're sorry'?" The tone she used was something I hadn't heard in her before. "I wish I could call Bandy," she said, "and tell him about all of this."

Jane had received another letter from Sammy and one from Max.

Bandy had called her twice, and she believed that that part of her life might be healing.

"You want me to call him?" I asked.

"Not yet."

At nine o'clock the sergeant told me I had to leave. I went out to his desk and asked if he would let me stay a while longer. He said I could, so I returned to the cell with two cans of Coke and several packages of peanut-butter Nabs.

"You're back?" Jane said. "They arrest you now?" She was trying to sound lighthearted.

"I can stay awhile longer," I told her. "Unless you're tired. Unless you want to sleep."

"I won't get much sleep in here," she said. She reached for the Coke and popped open the can. We unwrapped the packages of Nabs and ate silently.

We could hear each other open our crackly papers. We could hear the lifting and putting down of Coke cans. Then Jane went back to her cot, turned off the lamp, and lay down, but not to sleep. When we talked our words went back and forth, as they did at night in our childhood beds.

"What has happened, Evie?"

She didn't want an answer.

"Has anything changed?" she said. "I mean, did it ever change?"

I stayed quiet.

"Didn't you hear me?"

"I heard," I said quickly. "It's changed." I didn't want her to lose hope.

"Are people saying I killed Turnbull?" she asked. "Is that what they think?"

"Some say it. Some *want* to think that."

"God knows, I've thought about it enough times," she said.

I'd never heard Jane say she wanted to kill anybody, though I'd seen her face become a shadow and close up tight when Albert was lowered into the ground.

"Have you talked with my lawyer yet? Have you asked him about bail?"

"We meet with him tomorrow," I said. "I'm sure he'll get the bail reduced. Anyway, I know we can scrape up several thousand. If the bail's too high, we'll get a bail bondsman." I was making the only promises I could.

"The lawyer's good, I think," Jane said.

We began to sound hopeful, our words moving like a bird through the bars, and only a small light coming down the hall from the sergeant's desk.

"Jane?" But she didn't answer and I thought she might be drifting off. I settled back to let her doze. Then she spoke.

"What you never got, Evie," Jane said, "was the fact that whenever we were together—walking in town or through the cemetery, anywhere—there was never any doubt in anybody's mind about who was servant and who wasn't. I was always there, because I was with you. I'd like the day to come when I exist for myself, the same as anyone. I'd like for the issue not to be a part of people's minds. I'd even like for it not to be very interesting."

I felt as if my years with Jane had been a test, and that I'd failed. I tried to imagine a world in which I had not failed—what would have been different?

She said, "I *do* want to get out of here. And I *do* want whatever bail you can bring together. And I am grateful. But I tell you, Evie, I hate the thought of *again* being 'saved by the Bells.'"

At first I thought she was being funny, so I laughed, but she wasn't joking. The phrase sounded like one she'd said many times before, but not to me.

"Look at us," Jane said. "We grew up in the same house, but look how different our lives are. Our lives are as different as *this*." She pointed with her whole arm at the bars between us.

I couldn't see much in the darkness of the cell, but heard her move to sit up.

"First thing I did after I was raped," she said. (I'd never heard her use that word.) "First thing I thought of was Dake. You remember Dake? I just kept hoping he would still love me."

I nodded, but I didn't imagine she saw me.

As children, when we talked at night, we said everything. We said more at night than we could say in the daytime. We took pictures of the moon and planned one day to go there. When we told our mothers about our plans, they brushed us off with a flip of a hand. "That's just night talk," they'd say, as if what we'd been saying had no meaning. "That's nothing but night talk."

But now it was night, and our talk was taking root. I kept listening.

"Dake was the first boy to kiss me. You know that. But before I had a chance to love him, I was torn apart at the river. I nearly died when I had to go to Milledgeville." Her voice sounded brittle, angry.

"You remember what that year was like for *you*, Evie? Remember that preacher? What he did to you? We were hurt, both of us, you know? But the hurt that came at me was different."

I couldn't say anything.

"Do you see that?" she asked again. "How what happened to me was so *diff*erent from what happened to you? It always *has* been," she said.

Once at Corny's Pond I walked up on three fish sleeping in the shallow edgewaters. They were still, their tails barely moving in the force of the current. The air was hot, and I squatted a long while to watch them sleep. I could've reached down and caught one in the palm of my hand, but I didn't want to wake them. Then something happened, a lizard moved itself into the mud and disturbed the water's edge. The fish woke, quickly, as anything awakens—all at once. The act of waking made me know for sure that they'd been asleep.

I felt that now. I felt startled awake. Until that moment I had not known I was sleeping. I saw how I had fooled myself, and I was clobbered by a slap of recognition. What Jane had just said, she had always been saying. I wanted to stand up. I wanted to make everything different for her.

"If I were you," I said, "I'd never forgive this. Not ever."

"I don't think I can." She nodded.

I had to get out of the moment. "Okay," I said, "I never knew what to do, Jane. Don't know now. But was it wrong? Everything we did together—was it *all* wrong?"

Jane sat very still. There was no hardness in her body. She was listening. For a moment I thought we could live forever.

I said, "I do love you, you know? I love and hate you the way I love and hate Tucker, and Mama, and August, and Volusia. I want to change the whole world for you. I want to change myself."

"Oh, Evie." Jane spoke my name like someone who was tired and had given up.

Then she did the strangest thing. She walked to the jail cell door and reached her arms through the bars. She pulled my head toward her chest, and held it there. I could hear her heartbeat. She held me for a long time, and I sat stiffly, like a desperate child.

Whatever happened in this world would not outlast the force of habit that had charged our lives—our mothers' lives. And I knew that, even though the Bells might save Jane from jail, Jane had already saved this Bell from sleep.

When I walked to my car, it was midnight. A summer rain gave the July air a respite from the heat. A cool breeze came in from the east, and I could smell the brisk scent of fall—what it would be like in a few months.

42

I carried two packs of cigarettes to the bedroom, along with the phone, a box of Cheez-Its, and a Diet Coke. I closed the door and sprawled onto the bed, lighting one cigarette before dialing. I hadn't smoked in seven years.

"Johnny," I said, my voice did not hide my distress. "I won't be home as soon as I thought." He made a noise that indicated he knew this would happen. "Jane's still in jail, and they've set a hearing date for next week. It's a preliminary hearing."

"Could she get off?" he asked.

"Maybe. Her lawyer says they have to establish probable cause. He told us that since a witness saw her go into the Turnbull house, they already have enough to support an accusation. Now, they have to find ways to keep her from being held over for trial."

"Have you seen Jane?"

"Every day. I take clean underwear to her, and bring something good to eat. We're trying to get the bail reduced."

"What's it set at now?"

"Fifty thousand."

"Whew!"

"We can get a bail bondsman, but Tucker still thinks the lawyer will get it reduced."

We met Lamar Pratt for the first time in an old Victorian house that had been turned into lawyers' offices. He was a short, squat man, with tiny hands and feet, a high forehead, and a beard. His face was mostly forehead, which made me feel that he was very smart and capable. He had the reputation, in Atlanta, of being a young hotshot.

His beard had tinges of red on the chin and around his ears, and the more I looked at him, the more I realized that his beard kept him from being an ugly man. He was not calm, though he seemed steady, and appeared to be someone with a system in his mind.

Lamar Pratt had been described by Judge Wilson as gung ho, which is a word I had not used, or heard, in a long time. The judge said he was a gung ho lawyer.

He shook hands with each of us, as though we were in a receiving line. Then he informed us that bail would not be reduced before the preliminary hearing, though he planned to petition the court. He made us feel hopeful about the chance of bringing Jane home.

As he shook my hand, he admonished me. He knew that I'd been with Jane at the jail until midnight. "The policeman on duty said you stayed past the regular hours," he said. He suggested that I not do this again, and repeated his promise to get the bail adjusted. When he mentioned his fee, my mother nodded, indicating that whatever the fee was, it would be paid.

"Don't discuss any aspect of this case," he urged me. "It's critical that this case not be discussed with anyone."

My knowledge of the law came from television shows. I wondered how accurate it was. So far, the police made complaints and accusations as though they were in front of a camera. The same could be said of Lamar Pratt.

"Let's have a plan," my mother said. "We've got to make sure we're consistent in what we do or say." Tucker nodded, but we couldn't think of a plan. I hoped Lamar Pratt would tell us what to do.

"Jane has got to be exonerated," my mother said. She wanted Mr. Pratt to know what she was paying him for.

Pratt nodded. In my mind I was already referring to him by his last name. He urged us again not to speak about the case, but he looked directly at me when he said it. He did not know if Jane had told me anything, and felt that I had intruded upon his territory.

"I want to emphasize," he said in a voice so mixed with formality and seriousness that I wondered if he spoke to his wife in this way, "that you not attend the meeting tonight held at the school auditorium."

"What meeting?" my mother asked.

"Some of Turnbull's friends," Pratt said, "his cousins and nephews—men mostly. They're meeting in the auditorium of the high school at eight o'clock."

Tucker seemed to know something about it. He nodded as if he knew.

"I hope you'll stay away from it." Pratt looked around the room for an air conditioner. The room was hot. Ceilings rose high and floors had a precarious wobble. Pratt switched on the air conditioner, and a steady, cold blast of air cooled us in minutes. He took a notebook from his briefcase, and told us that he hoped he might be able to get the case dismissed so that Jane wouldn't have to face a trial. When he said it, my whole body soared, because I thought maybe he already had the kind of information that would provide dismissal.

"How would you do that?" I said.

He closed his notebook. "Jane was in the Turnbull house," he said. "She went to get Capp. She hadn't planned on going into the house, but the door was open, and she thought Capp had gone inside. She said she heard something upstairs, but came back out immediately. She was scared of Turnbull, has been scared of him for years. She claimed she wasn't inside the house more than three minutes."

"How is this going to help?" my mother asked.

"The witness claimed she saw a light on in Turnbull's room at five o'clock, and Jane heard someone moving around. This means that Turnbull was alive when Jane was in the house. Then we have proof that she was in the emergency room with Capp. It's not much, but it's a start."

He shook our hands again, energetically, and with a final nod put on his hat and left the room. He forgot to turn off the air conditioner.

I didn't call Johnny again until after eleven o'clock that night, but he answered the phone on the first ring. "Tell me what's going on," he said.

I told him the hearing was set for Tuesday morning, and I told him all that the lawyer had told us.

"I wish I could be there," Johnny said. He wanted to believe he could help.

"Me, too."

"Want me to catch a plane? I could be there tomorrow before the hearing is over."

"You hate to fly, Johnny, and anyway I want you to stay there with Ty." I waited, wondering if I would change my mind. "But part of me wants you here," I confessed.

"What part wants me?" he asked. "Exactly which part is that?"

"The part that makes this bed so wide without you," I said in my whispery voice. I rubbed the sheets with the back of my hand. "I stuff pillows on your side, so I can pretend you're here."

"Sounds to me," he said, testing, "like you want to get married."

"Maybe you're right," I told him.

"Evie?" He wanted to know if I was teasing.

"Yes," I said. "Ye-es."

"Yes?"

"I even have a wedding hat."

What I didn't tell Johnny was that Tucker, Becky, and I had gone to the school auditorium. We didn't go inside, but at nine o'clock we went to the back of the building and tried to hear what was being said. We had told my mother and Mr. Shallowford that we were going to a movie. I think they believed us.

A man was stationed at the back door of the auditorium to keep out unwanted visitors. He stopped us.

"You can't go in," he said. "This is a private meeting." I didn't recognize him.

"This is a public place," Tucker told him.

"I'm telling you all. You can't go in there."

Someone—Sully Cantor—was speaking in a heated voice, but we couldn't tell what he was saying. I could see Margaret and Margaret's husband and Adele Turnbull seated in chairs facing the audience. For some reason I hoped that Margaret would see me, but everyone focused on the speaker, and also on one or two other men standing in the front.

Becky had snuck around the side of the school and found another entrance. The man stationed at the door hadn't seen Becky, and didn't see her motion to us. Tucker and I followed her to a side entrance and listened to the rest of the speakers.

"We can't let all these problems come up again," Sully Cantor said.

Sully had married one of Turnbull's sisters, and grew wealthy off the Turnbull family. Before becoming part of the family, Sully had worked at the filling station. But after only a few years of marriage, he bought a Cadillac, and his stomach began to hang over his belt.

"I don't think she ought to get off scot-free," he said, and another man agreed. "Not when she killed a man."

"That's for the court to decide," said a voice that sounded derisive. "That's for a jury of our peers to decide."

Everyone clapped. The meeting ended at ten, so we drove around until time for the movie to be over. I didn't tell Johnny any of this part.

When I went to bed, before going to sleep, I took my wedding hat out of Volusia's box and put it on. When I placed it back inside, I saw at the bottom of the box a letter.

The letter was addressed to Jane, but another note was attached to it, and neither envelope was sealed. The note was to me:

Dearest Evie,

I have wrote this letter many years ago, but I have put it in a new envelope. It is Jane's letter, but it is from me. Your Mama thinks I should not ever give it to Jane, but I do not think that is right. Your Mama will have nothing to do with what I am telling, though she has had so much to do with all these years of a secret.

Evie, I have to ask you to read this letter. Then I want you to pick the time it is right to give it to Jane. I think she must know *what* has happened, but I cannot say *when* she must know. When you read this you will be confuse. I hope your Mama and me has done the right thing. I hope Jane will be glad for what we did.

Thank you, my dear sweet Evie. I have love you, and I have love your child. As I have love Jane and her children. When you find out this thing, you will know something more about all of us. That is all.

Love,
Volusia

III

FORCE OF HABIT

But soon we shall die and all memory of those five will have left the earth, and we ourselves shall be loved for a while and forgotten. But the love will have been enough; and all those impulses of love return to the love that made them. Even memory is not necessary for love. There is a land of the living and a land of the dead and the bridge is love, the only survival, the only meaning.

THORNTON WILDER
The Bridge of San Luis Rey

43

For a period of time in the late fifties Adele Turnbull and my mother were friends. Adele had come to our house for bridge club for years, but around 1956 she showed up at our house on other days. I would come home from school and find my mother and Mrs. Turnbull talking together on the porch or in the living room. They talked quietly, seriously, until I walked in, then their voices turned falsely cheerful.

Their friendship lasted nearly a year, then ended as abruptly as it had started. Mrs. Turnbull still came to bridge club, but she no longer showed up at our house at unexpected times.

At about the same time my mother and Mr. Shallowford began to talk about marriage. Jane had graduated from Mercy High School and planned to leave the next year for nursing school in Chicago. I would attend the University of Georgia in the fall, with Lowell Hardison.

During that same year Volusia married Joe Sugar and moved in with him over the store. She came back to our house for dinners, and holidays were often spent with my mother. Tucker was the only one whose life did not change in the midfifties, but Tucker had already learned to experience drastic change.

Adele Turnbull had always been, and still remained, a mystery to my mind. She was a woman who seemed to have more spunk available to her than she had revealed to the world. When I saw her in town yesterday afternoon with Margaret, I kept waiting for that spunk to become visible.

As soon as Adele arrived in town, she called our house asking to speak to my mother. But my mother wasn't home when she called, and had not yet returned the calls.

"Adele Turnbull called again," I said, as my mother came through the door with two sacks of groceries.

"I keep putting off calling her back." She let the sacks sit down hard on the counter. One sack spilled over. "Where's she staying? Did she leave her number?"

I pointed to a piece of paper beside the phone. We began to put away the groceries. "I have something to show you," I said. "It's a letter Volusia wrote."

She stopped in midmotion, laying the carton of milk on its side, not even bothering to put it in the refrigerator.

"What do you mean?" she said, but she already knew. I handed the letter to her. I had read it a million times. As my mother took the letter, her expression told me she knew what it would say.

My Sweet Jane,

I have love you for so long. You do not know how much I have love you. You always believe I love Albert the best, but I just had him more in my thoughts because he was far away, or always in danger. I never thought you would be in danger.

Then you were hurt by someone I didn't know who it was. And when a baby came in that dark Milledgeville place I wanted you to be free. So I told you he was born dead, but he was not. Mama Agnes and me took care of the child ourself. At first he stay in a foster home in Jasper, Georgia. I know this will come as a shock to your mind, but Capp is your own blood child. The baby born to you is not dead. It is Capp. I know this might be hard for you to take in, but it is the Truth.

Capp is grown up good now. People in town like him and help him to get along. Things have work out all right—you being in Chicago with your family and your job, and Albert lying safe now in his grave. Evie and Tuck have grown up to be fine people too. Soon I will be gone, but I am glad we have our Cappadocia. I could not leave this world and not tell you about him.

Next to Joe Sugar and yourself, Capp is the sweetest thing in my life. When he plays his music he make me cry everytime.

He is one of the best child I have ever saw. I think God hisself could not love him more than I do.

With All My Heart,
Mama

"Have you shown this to Jane?"

"Not yet."

"But you will? Have you decided you will?"

We finished putting away the groceries, and I said that I couldn't keep this from her, but I didn't know when would be the right time.

My mother nodded. She picked up Adele Turnbull's number and took it to her room. I had the feeling she would return the call today.

44

On the first day of the preliminary hearing the courtroom was hot. Women wore sandals and sleeveless dresses, with sweaters thrown over their shoulders for the air-conditioning. The court was called to order and Fred Martin, the district attorney, asked Francine Hawkins to come to the witness box.

Fred Martin had been Mercy's chief prosecutor for ten years. When he called out Francine's name, his composure was of someone who felt sure of his case. I could see Jane shifting in her seat.

Francine Hawkins walked to the witness box, and the bailiff told her to hold up her hand. He asked if she promised to tell the truth. Francine said she would, and added, "I don't have anything to hide."

Judge Harold Few instructed the witness not to embellish her answers. From Francine's expression, I doubted she understood what Judge Few meant.

"How are you today, Miss Hawkins?" the D.A. said.

"I am fine," said Francine.

"I'm sure you would like to get this over with as soon as possible, so we'll ask you a few questions and you can go home."

"Okay," she said.

The courtroom was still filling up. Not all the chairs were taken, but by lunchtime people would be standing in the back against the wall.

"I want to ask a few questions about the day of Robert Turnbull's death."

"Yes, sir," said Francine. "I sure do . . ."

"If you don't mind, I would like to ask the questions and then you can answer." He smiled agreeably.

Francine nodded.

"Now tell us what you saw on the evening of June 19th?"

"I saw a woman, who I believed to be, who I recognized as Jane Davis. She went into the back door of the Turnbull house. That was about five o'clock in the evening."

"You saw someone who seemed to you to be Jane Davis go into the Turnbull house?"

"Yes."

"Then what did you do?"

"Well, I was sitting on my porch, just about to go in and cook myself some dinner, when I saw a car drive up."

"Can you describe the car?"

"It was a Chevrolet—I know the car because it's the one Jane's been driving ever since she came back to Mercy to look after her mother. I work at the hospital and I would see her there sometimes. And I saw the car she drove."

"What kind of work do you do at the hospital?"

"I work in the cafeteria. I help to cook and plan the meals. But sometimes when we run short of help, which is pretty often, I take meals up to the wards."

"When you go on the wards, do you see the nurses?"

"Yes. I see them and a lot of them recognize me. They know me from the other cafeteria workers because I take the meals to the patients."

"Did Jane Davis recognize you?"

"I don't know if she knew my name, but, yes, she recognized me when I was on her ward, and she usually spoke to me."

"So when you saw her outside your house on the night of June 19th, you had no doubt that the woman you saw was Jane Davis?"

"No doubt. Of course she wasn't wearing her nurse's uniform that day. She just had on her regular clothes. But I remember thinking how sad it was to see her, because I knew her mother had died."

"On a scale of one to ten, how sure are you that the woman you saw was Jane Davis—ten being the absolute surest point."

"Ten," she said.

The D.A. turned the witness over to Lamar Pratt and sat down. Pratt went to the witness box and stood a long moment before speaking.

"Miss Hawkins, have you always wanted to work in a hospital?"

"Yes, I have."

"And did you want to be a cafeteria worker in a hospital?"

"No," she hesitated, thinking she was about to get caught at something. She looked at Fred Martin. "I wanted to be a nurse."

"And what happened to that dream?"

Francine explained that she never finished nursing school, and Fred Martin made an objection.

"Judge Few," Pratt said, "this goes to the credibility of the witness." He was allowed to continue.

"The fact is—you flunked out of nursing school, is that right?"

"Yes."

"What did you think when you saw Jane Davis, someone you had seen all your life in Mercy, someone with whom you had attended Mercy High School in the fifties—what did you think?"

Francine Hawkins turned red hot in the face. "I thought she had made it."

"Made it?"

"That she was successful, you know, she'd made it."

"Were you jealous of what she'd been able to do?"

Before Francine could answer, Lamar Pratt had approached the witness box, walking up close to Francine, then turning away again, he spoke to the audience in the courtroom. "Can you tell me what you said to your coworker, Sally Headrick, about Jane Davis? What you said concerning her nursing degree?"

Francine got very still, then she burst out, pushing forward into her chair. She poked the air with her fingers, like a politician trying to make a point.

"I said that it was a shame how somebody black could get to be a nurse over somebody white. I said that we were in school together and I never thought she was so much smarter than me, yet she had the job and I didn't. I said that this fairness thing works two ways, and I got the short end of that stick."

No one had expected her outburst, and the courtroom silence accentuated her explosion of words. She folded her arms and looked sheepishly at the D.A. who did not look at her, but was leaning over to talk to someone else at the long table.

He stood up, objecting on the grounds of relevancy, but Judge Few overruled his objection.

Pratt continued. "So you were angry at Jane before you saw her at Robert Turnbull's house on the evening of his murder?"

"Just because I was angry won't change what I saw."

Lamar Pratt said that he had no more questions and sat down. I wanted to clap.

Fred Martin stood up to ask one more question, "Miss Hawkins, did you see anyone else go into Robert Turnbull's house that evening?"

"Yes."

"Who did you see?"

"I saw Cappadocia go in, but he went in all the time, because he worked over there on certain days. He worked for Turnbull in his yard, and sometimes around the house. He's been going in and out of there for almost twelve years now."

"But you saw him enter the house *before* Jane Davis went in?"

"Yes, but seeing Capp go in was nothing. Seeing Jane was."

An objection was raised and sustained.

Lamar Pratt asked for a sidebar and the three men talked for a few minutes.

When Fred Martin came back, he said that he had no more questions, but Mr. Pratt asked Francine if, since Capp had entered the house before Jane, Jane could have gone in to look for Capp?

"Speculation," said Fred Martin, and Pratt withdrew the question.

I called Johnny to tell him about the hearing, but he wasn't home. I believed in Jane's ability to sway people's minds, and I wanted Johnny to hear what I'd pieced together.

I knew that Jane went to pick up Capp at Turnbull's house. I knew she heard Turnbull moving around upstairs before she went to see if Capp was in the shed out back. When she left the house, she found Capp on the road. His head was bleeding, so Jane took him to the emergency room. I knew that people saw her there.

I tried Johnny again, still no answer, so I went to bed. The sheets felt cold and my arms branched out stiffly to my sides. I wanted to have Johnny next to me. I wanted to taste his neck, and mouth. Before I slept, I brought to mind the smell of him—like grass. Thinking about him in this way made me want to chew on something.

45

The next day Lamar Pratt called Jane to the stand.

When Albert was tried, this same courtroom had ceiling fans. The fans still hung above us, turning the air, but the atmosphere in the building was controlled now by a system that kept each room the same temperature all year round.

Jane looked very nervous, guilty even. As soon as she took her seat in the witness chair, I began to worry. I hoped Pratt knew what he was doing. I wondered if Jane had told him everything. These were my first thoughts.

Jane's lawyer asked if she was comfortable. He seemed solicitous, and the way he spoke made everyone in the room feel solicitous, too. I began to see clearly the manipulative ways of lawyers. His first few questions established how long Jane had lived in Mercy, and her strong ties to Georgia.

He asked how she knew Robert Turnbull, and I imagined he would lead up to Jane's arrival at his house. But that is not how the day went.

"As you know," Jane spoke clearly, enunciating each word in a nervous but slightly pretentious way, "my mother and I lived with the Bells for most of my growing up years. Those years were good, and what wasn't good was not usually the fault of the Bells."

"Did you know Robert Turnbull?"

"I knew who he was in the town and I'd seen him, but not to speak to. Then one day when I stayed home sick with a fever, I met him," she said. "It was March, during that first year of integration at Mercy High." Her face went inside itself. "I'd been part of the integration process since September, but on this day I stayed home. My mother was in her workroom making hats when I heard men come into the house."

"Was one of those men Mr. Turnbull?"

"Yes." Jane shifted slightly in her chair. "This was not my house on Latham Street. I expected trouble to happen there." She was looking at the judge. "This was the Bell's house. Agnes Bell was downtown at The Hat Shop and my mother, as I said, was in the room where she worked during the morning hours.

"It was just before noon when four men came through the back door. I'd seen them from my bedroom window, but didn't know who they were, except for one. Robert Turnbull was someone I had been hearing about, because he hated Albert so much. Albert was my brother."

I began to grow nervous for Jane. I believed she might be creating a motive for herself, and the courtroom was so quiet that I wondered if everyone else felt the same way.

"What happened when the men came into the house?" Mr. Pratt had his back to Jane, and faced the courtroom. He wanted to gauge their reaction. Reporters took fast notes.

"They came in without knocking or asking to come in. They came upstairs and broke open the door of the room where my mother was working. They told her—I could hear them because they were shouting and didn't know I was in the house—they told her that Albert had better not bring any more trouble to Georgia. Albert was involved with the NAACP, and people from Washington came to help him with rallies, or to get him out of jail. They said he could get hurt if he kept it up. This was the real threat to my mother—I mean, the threat about Albert. They kept asking her if she understood."

Jane stopped and took a sip of water from the glass beside her. She seemed to be expecting the lawyer to ask a question. When he didn't, she went on.

"I was on the landing of the stairs, and heard them yelling at her. I went back to my room. In a few minutes someone opened my door. It was Robert Turnbull. I ran past him to the bathroom and locked myself in. I was so afraid. I heard him say something like, 'Don't worry, little girl, we've come to see your mama this time,' and it was the 'this time' that sent a chill up my back."

Jane turned toward the judge. "I didn't know then how men could come into a white person's house the same as they could a black's."

The judge urged her to continue telling what happened without the benefit of side remarks.

"He left my room and . . ."

"Mr. Turnbull?"

"Yes, Turnbull." She could not call him mister. "He left and went back down the hallway where I could hear my mother's voice. I heard her begging. But then they said something I couldn't hear. Something that made her angry enough to fight, because I heard her tell those men to get out! saying they had no business in the Bell's house.

"Then I heard a thud, and another one. The men were leaving, so I ran down the hallway to the sewing room. But I stopped, because one man had stayed behind. He stood over my mother holding one of the boards she used to cut out hats.

"He lifted the board over his head and brought it down hard. My mother's arms flew up to block the blow, but that board broke on her arms, and I slid behind the door as he went out. The men didn't close the door downstairs when they left. I could see it still open.

"I called to her and she made a groaning sound, so I knew she was alive. I wanted first to go down and close the door, to lock it. I imagined they could come back, do worse. I returned to my mother with a rag and some warm water. She was already trying to stand up.

"I told her we had to call Mama Agnes—which is what I called Mrs. Bell in those days. Still do sometimes." People gave a little shudder of laughter that stopped abruptly when Jane spoke again. "But my mother spoke to me in a way that made me do what she said. She said we had to be quiet about what happened. She said if we told anyone, Albert would be killed for sure.

"I argued with her, because I thought she needed to see a doctor. Her eye had begun to swell where the man hit her, and her arms were bloody from the board.

"She told me that we would explain her wounds by saying she'd fallen on the back steps. She could wear a long-sleeved blouse to cover her arms."

I remembered that March day when I came home from school and saw Volusia's face half blue and swollen, one eye almost closed shut. Her arms were covered, though the day was almost eighty degrees, and too warm for long sleeves.

"What happened to your face?" I asked her.

"I fell down those rickety steps y'all have out back. Fell flat on my face. Seems like to me you'd tear those things out and build you something sturdy."

"You look awful," I said.

"You would too you fell down like I did."

"Where's Janey Louise?"

"Up in the bed where she's supposed to be."

Going up the stairs I could smell the presence of men in the house. I could smell their sweat and shoes. Leather and dark clothes. But I never mentioned it.

That night my mother called me to her room. "Wonder what happened to Volusia?" she asked.

"She told me it was the back steps."

"Looks to me like somebody hit her. Her arms are sore." She turned down the covers of her bed. The sheets looked clean and white. "You want to sleep in here with me tonight, Evie, since Janey Louise is sick?"

I said I did and slid between the cool sheets. "What do you think happened?" I asked.

"Some man, I guess. They get like that sometimes."

"Like what?"

"Sometimes they hit their women."

Lamar Pratt moved around to a position beside the witness chair, so that he and Jane faced the courtroom together.

"So these men beat up your mother and threatened you, though their main threat was toward your brother?"

"Yes."

"Was this a threat they eventually carried out?"

What was this lawyer doing? I couldn't figure out his strategy.

"Yes. They were constantly harassing Albert, then when Albert escaped, he was brought back dead. He'd been dragged behind a truck for miles." She could have said that the truck was Robert Turnbull's, but Lamar Pratt had urged her to leave that part out.

Jane's fear of Turnbull was becoming firmly established, but I didn't believe this line of questioning would be enough and I saw from Tucker's tense expression that he didn't believe it either. All I could think was: There must be more.

"Did you go into Mr. Turnbull's house on the evening of his murder?"

"Yes. I did."

"Can you tell us why you went in?"

"I was looking for Capp. Capp had been running away every afternoon. He went off into the woods, or walked the highway, or sometimes he hid in the shed behind Turnbull's house. He'd run off that day. But Joe said that Turnbull had called Capp to come over. He asked me to go pick him up. When I got to the house, I saw the door open. I looked in."

"Did you see Capp? Did you call out his name?"

"Not loud. But I called to see if he was in there. I was afraid for him. I was afraid he might just walk in, so I went in the door and walked down the hallway and out the back door. I wanted to look in the shed. I would've gone straight to the shed, but I got curious when I saw the side door open." Jane paused for a moment.

"I wanted to get Capp out of there as quickly as possible," she said. "I didn't want him to get hurt."

"What made you think Turnbull might hurt Cappadocia? Had he ever hurt him before?"

"Not that I know of." Then she said, "But he had hurt me."

"He hurt you?"

The air in the courtroom crackled with expectation. Jane's voice grew shaky. "He hurt me beside the river," she said. "When I was just sixteen."

There was a gasp that came so loud that people turned to look at my mother. She was shouting, at whom it was hard to tell, but she wouldn't stop. Her interruption of the court procedure broke up the courtroom. The judge called for a recess. No one, not one person dared look directly at Adele or Margaret Turnbull. Both women sat as stiff as two mannequins.

46

By two o'clock the court reconvened and Jane continued.

"I went to the river almost every day after school. I liked to fish there, and had a special spot where I went on a regular basis.

"But on this day Turnbull was waiting for me. I don't know how he knew I went there. He didn't speak when I walked up, though I spoke to him. I was frightened when I saw him, but I didn't believe anything would happen to me. I felt protected because of the Bells. I thought I would be safe because of their name."

Everyone could hear my mother crying softly. My brother couldn't get her to stop. Adele Turnbull turned all the way around to look at her.

"He didn't speak," Jane said. "He just pulled me off my bike and tore my clothes. I screamed, but he wouldn't stop. Then he ," she didn't want to say the word, "He raped me," she said. Her face looked like a statue, which was the only way she could tell it. "He put a stick or something inside me, something rough to break me open, then he put himself in me." She paused. "I was sixteen years old."

Margaret stood up to leave the courtroom. She urged her mother to come with her. But Adele Turnbull wouldn't leave. She jerked her arm away from her daughter. She was determined to stay, to hear it all.

I believed in that moment that Mrs. Turnbull had always known the truth, but had kept it inside herself. I believed she had confronted her husband during their life together, and now, instead of being shocked, she felt vindicated.

"I must've passed out at some point, because I don't remember when he left. I just remember hearing Evie call to me, and somebody lifting me up." She turned to look at me seated on the second row. "I remember being washed."

We could hear a door close in the back as Margaret left the courtroom.

"Can you remember anything else?" Lamar Pratt's voice was quiet and gentle.

"He warned me that if I told anyone that no one would believe me."

"Robert Turnbull warned you?"

"Yes. He said I would be in more trouble than he would. And I believed that part."

My mother's face could not be settled. She could not be touched, or spoken to. She had turned around to look at Joe, but Joe had not moved a muscle. I knew, as Adele Turnbull knew, as my mother and Joe Sugar knew now: Capp was Turnbull's child.

Tucker didn't know this yet, and neither did Jane.

"So when you entered the Turnbull house to look for Cappadocia the other night, you dreaded going in?"

"It's the last place I wanted to go. During my first years after moving to Chicago, I wouldn't return to Mercy, because I didn't want to see him. I didn't want to see his face.

"I told my mother and the Bells that the man who raped me was someone I'd never seen before. They never knew who it was. I got pregnant and had a baby in the Milledgeville State Hospital, where I stayed for almost seven months."

"Did you graduate from Mercy High School?"

"Yes."

"Then where did you go?"

"I went to nursing school in Chicago. I met a man there, Bandy Johnson. We've been married now for nine years, and we have two sons. I am a nurse at Chicago General Hospital."

Fred Martin stood up and addressed Jane as Mrs. Johnson. "Mrs. Johnson," he said. Until that moment everyone had referred to her as Jane Davis.

"That is your married name, is it not?"

"Yes."

"You are married to a policeman in Chicago named Bandy Johnson and you have two children, is that right?"

"Yes." Jane's eyes clouded as she mentioned this.

"Where is your family now?"

"They're in Chicago. I asked them not to come."

"They are home?"

For the first time Jane looked afraid in the witness chair. She'd seemed nervous, she'd seemed sad; but now she looked afraid. This prosecutor knew something. We didn't know how much he knew.

"My boys are with my husband. My husband and I are separated, so they're with him until we can work things out."

Lamar Pratt sat upright. He hadn't known about this.

"And what are these problems centered around?"

Jane knew now that Fred Martin would bring it out.

Lamar Pratt stood up, objecting; but the judge allowed the prosecutor's line of questioning. He reminded Mr. Pratt that this was a hearing, not a trial, and that he would allow leniency on both sides.

Jane hadn't answered the prosecutor's question, so he answered it himself with another question.

"Isn't it true, Mrs. Johnson, that you had an affair? And that your affair was with a white man at the hospital where you work? Isn't it true that your separation was due to the affair?"

Jane was crying. She nodded.

"Please give your answer for the court reporter."

"Yes, that's true." Jane said.

"Have there been other white men in your life besides this recent affair and Robert Turnbull? Have there been more than that?"

He was making Turnbull's attack on Jane seem as though it might have been Jane's choice. I was shocked at how quickly the prosecutor could turn material against her.

"No," Jane said. She spoke louder. "No!"

At that point Adele Turnbull stood, and everyone thought she was going to leave. She did leave, but first she spoke to the judge. "I have something to tell the court concerning my husband's actions," she said, "and his death." Her face looked like a block of ice as she spoke. Then she left the room.

Lamar Pratt sat down, settling into his chair as though he'd been dropped from a high place.

The whole courtroom buzzed, and Judge Few declared the court in recess until tomorrow morning. He asked the lawyers to meet with him in his chambers.

My mother didn't want to leave her seat. Her whole face was a question. Jane was being led away by a policewoman.

When we got back to the house, Tucker and Mr. Shallowford argued over what Adele Turnbull might say, and whether the knowledge of Jane's rape would provide defense or motive. Mr. Shallowford thought it provided motive. He said that Jane was sure to be held over for trial.

I told them both to shut up. I told them if they didn't shut up I thought I would go crazy.

I couldn't sleep, and at 2 A.M. I went downstairs and opened the door to Volusia's bedroom off the kitchen.

I believed, though I had never admitted it to anyone, that when somebody died the spirit hung around for a while. And I knew if Volusia were still around, she might be in this room.

I lay on her bed, putting my head down on her pillow. This was not the good bed we had bought for her. It was her first bed—the one she hated. But the sheets were hers, and the bedspread was the one she had used.

Lying there, I believed I could smell smoke from her Old Gold cigarettes. I convinced myself of her presence. "Jane's in trouble," I said. I wanted her to know this, to help us.

"Jane's in so much trouble."

Then I fell asleep wrapped in the arm of her old room.

47

Jane's trial was set for the first week in July, and Pratt's petition for reduced bail had been successful. Jane would be delivered to our house by four o'clock tomorrow.

Tucker, Becky, and I sat down to dinner with my mother and Mr. Shallowford. We spoke of Jane being with us the next evening, and were startled to hear a rattle of garbage cans outside the kitchen door.

Mr. Shallowford looked outside. Two raccoons were rummaging through the garbage. As Tucker got up to shoo them away his chair scraped the floor, and Becky screamed. She'd seen a man's face at the window, and so had I.

Everything seemed to happen at the same moment—the chair scraping, raccoons, Becky's scream. Then the dining-room window was shattered by a rock wrapped in a white cloth. The rag was on fire and the room suddenly had a strong odor of gasoline.

Tucker put out the fire by covering the rock with part of the dining-room rug. He scorched his hand, and the floor shimmered with broken glass.

My mother ran out into the yard, though Tucker and Mr. Shallowford told her not to go. A blue truck pulled fast out of our driveway and into the street. She yelled as the truck moved onto the main road.

"You see who it was?" I asked. I dialed 911 for help.

"Turn off the light, Tuck," my mother said.

He flicked the light switch and Becky turned off the kitchen lamp. We could hear men yelling toward our dark house. We caught only a few words, but they were something about Jane. The men were drunk. They called her a whore.

They stayed inside the truck for a few moments, but as Mr. Shallowford stepped out the door and walked toward them, they drove off. When we turned the lights back on, I saw that my mother had opened the gun case in the hallway.

I'd never seen the gun case open. My mother never allowed it to be opened, saying it belonged to her grandfather and that the only reason she kept it in the house was her sentimental feeling about him. Now it had been opened, and she had lifted a dusty shotgun.

"Put that back," Mr. Shallowford yelled to her. Tucker and Becky picked up shards of glass, and a police car pulled into the driveway, with its blue light going around.

My mother and Adele Turnbull spoke several times. After they had talked, my mother came to my room.

"Adele was the only other person who knew about Capp," she told me. "She was a good friend during the time when Jane went to Milledgeville and Albert was found dead. Volusia almost collapsed under the burden in those days." My mother was confiding in me in a way she had never done before.

"Adele had to sneak over here to speak with me. She knew her husband had been part of Albert's death, though she didn't say much about that. She must've known about Jane, too. I mean, she must've known it back then." She was shaking her head.

"What did she tell you?" I asked.

"She's going to testify, Evie. She's going to speak for Jane. She can't withdraw the charges, because Turnbull didn't die of natural causes. But she can speak what she knows. And what she knows will help Jane."

"You think Jane will plead self-defense?"

"It's more than that." And my mother proceeded to tell me how Robert Turnbull had been trying to force Adele to come back to the house to take care of him. Adele wouldn't come. They argued over a period of months, and during one of those arguments, Adele told him she knew what he'd done to Jane. Turnbull defended himself by saying that Jane was no better than a whore. Then Adele said, 'Well, whatever she was, you got her pregnant, and she has your son. And he's living right here in Mercy. It's Cappadocia, and if you don't leave me alone, I'll tell everyone that Cappadocia is yours. They'll believe me, too.'

"Adele said he was furious. She said he was sick, weak, but his fury brought back strength and purpose. He called Joe's store to ask if Capp could come by the house and get some money he owed him. Joe said he called several days in a row trying to get Capp to come over and get his money.

"Capp never went into anybody's house—not upstairs. Adele told me that Turnbull made a threat on Capp's life. He said if she didn't leave this matter alone that Capp might just disappear suddenly."

"So Capp could plead self-defense. Is that what you mean?" I asked.

"It's not over, Evie. But Adele Turnbull is the one who can set us back on course." My mother's whole face grew calm, and she looked young again. "I believe Capp will be okay."

"Does Jane know this?"

"She'll know by the time she gets here tomorrow. Adele's talking to the lawyers now."

Everyone in the house felt calm all night, even with the unsettling intrusion from the previous night. Police would patrol the neighborhood for the next few days, and by tomorrow at four Jane would be home.

The first thing Jane wanted to do when she got home was to take a long hot bubble bath and put on soft pajamas. We ate dinner on the porch. Tucker and I wore pajamas too.

"My skin feels scraped," Jane said. She talked as if she had no audience. Her face had a light to it, not a honeyed light, but silvery, as if it were coming from the center.

My mother, Tucker, and Becky kept conversation going while Jane seemed to enjoy being a silent part of the evening. We sat for a long time with the dishes in front of us. In fact, for the next three nights we sat on the porch, well fed and lazy, like rich people.

On the third night, Mr. Shallowford left early, as did Tucker and Becky. My mother decided this was the right time to show Jane the letter.

"Jane, Evie has something to tell you."

I stood up to get the letter. I was gone for a few minutes but I could hear no talking on the porch. I returned and handed Jane the envelope.

"It's from Volusia," I said. "She wrote it a long time ago." I also handed her the note that Volusia had written to me. "Read this first," I said.

Jane read the note slowly, her face a puzzle. Then, without looking up, she read the letter from Volusia. The tears that fell down her cheeks did not seem like crying exactly, more like weeping. Before this moment I'd only read about people weeping.

When she finished reading, she folded the letter and put it carefully back into the envelope. She took a long time doing so. She turned her head sideways and listened to the sounds outside.

"Crickets don't sound the same way in Chicago as they do here," she said.

My mother looked at me. She didn't know what to say, but I did. "Not in Texas either," I said.

Jane held her fingers together, creating a cage. "I think I'd like to bring the boys down here again," she said, "so they can hear it. I think I'd like for them to see what these summers are like."

My mother got up to leave us alone. Fireflies were beating against the porch screen. "Ty likes to come back," I said, "but the person he liked to see most was Volusia. I can't tell my mother that."

Jane smiled weakly. She started to speak again, but we heard another beating sound against the screen. Strong, like somebody's hand. Jane gave a shivery cry, but I recognized the sound as the flutter of a Luna moth.

I opened the screen door to let in a huge swallowtail moth with pale green wings and body. It landed on the table next to the lamp. The wings were large and sweeping with a tiny spot on each segment.

"You gonna let it stay?" Jane asked.

"Listen," I said. We grew quiet and listened to the moth fly from house to porch. We didn't speak, but I imagined our voices had metamorphosed into this flutter of wings. I wanted the moth to land on me for a moment. I wanted the pale green fluted edge of swallowtail to land on my face, or Jane's heart.

"It never occurred to me, Evie," Jane said, finally. "Isn't that something? That it never even occurred to me that that baby might be alive?"

The night spread out vacant before us, and present time on this porch grew strong like memory. Maybe this was the true meaning of the word *memorized*.

"I know." We listened to the wings of the Luna moth. "Me neither." We listened the way we did when we sat on roadsides together and pretended the sound of traffic was the ocean's waves. Time on this porch became old, like a story we'd lived in.

"I don't know what to do now," Jane said. "I don't know how this is supposed to change my life."

"I don't think you need to take him back to Chicago with you," I said. "Capp would hate that."

"You think so?"

"I think he wants to stay where he knows people. With Joe."

The Luna wings kept up their tiny whispers, and the next thing I knew it was morning.

I awoke on the porch in the same chair, stiff and aching. Jane was not there. During the night I had dreamed that I was wrong about something. As I awoke I couldn't bring to mind the events of the dream, only the deliberate caution of being wrong.

As I went upstairs I passed Jane in the hall. She was fully dressed in her nurse's uniform, and was standing before the long hall mirror. She appeared completely surprised.

"What're you doing?" I asked.

"I had a dream that Mama was still in the hospital and that I was going in to see her," she said, staying inside her surprise.

"Every morning, Evie, I have gotten up and dressed in my nurse's uniform. She was so proud of my uniform. So when I woke this morning, I put on everything, even my shoes." She pointed to her shoes. "Then I realized I was acting from my dream—and I knew that she wasn't alive at all."

Jane sat down on the floor and buried her face in her hands. I told her I would fix breakfast. But before I left, I saw the Luna moth lying on top of the hall table—its wings spread wide. Moth dust was sprinkled around the perimeter of its body.

I felt shocked to think that we'd sacrificed this lovely creature for our wish to be memorized. Its body kept itself completely still, and I didn't know if it was dead. I didn't want to know.

48

The trial would begin in two more days and we had every reason to be hopeful. But we wondered privately what would happen if Adele Turnbull decided at the last minute not to tell what she knew.

We'd had a full week of rain, and gloomy weather kept us wary. My mother and I washed the last of the dishes, and put them away. Tucker and Becky hadn't come to the house for dinner in several nights, and Mr. Shallowford was playing poker at his house down the street. Whenever he played poker, he stayed at his house all night.

It was almost nine o'clock, and the rain had let up. Jane excused herself to go upstairs, saying she was going to bed early. I could see the end of a dark sunset from our kitchen window. I hoped the rain was over and that tomorrow would bring sun.

But as I put away the last dish, I saw a blue truck move slowly by the house. I could see the outline of four men in it. As they drove by, they turned off their headlights, and the truck moved along the street like a boat on water.

I pointed to it, so my mother would look. One man had his arm out the window. They stopped a little past our house, and we heard them get out, slam the doors of their truck.

"Is Jane upstairs?" my mother asked, but before I could answer, she had run down the hall to the gun cabinet. She lifted out a shotgun that I imagined had never been used, though it looked now as if it had been recently cleaned.

"I'm calling the police," I said.

"Okay." Then my mother stopped me by my arm. "Wait, Evie. Wait." Two men walked across the yard. The other two men remained in the truck. "Listen," she said.

They stood shadowed by our house, and called for Jane to come out. Their voices sounded simple. I recognized one of the men as Sully Cantor.

The men weren't armed. I knew Sully owned a gun, and a gun rack with several shotguns was perched in the cab of the truck. I wanted to go to the door and tell them that Jane wasn't here, but my mother had a different idea. I'd never seen her with such an expression of grim determination.

"Raise the window, Evie," she said. Then she yelled to the men outside. Without moving from her stance in the kitchen, she faced the doorway, her legs apart and the shotgun pointed at where she imagined them to be waiting.

"They're just standing there," I said, but then they began to move toward the door.

"Leave-Jane-alone," she yelled, each word separate and clear. "I'm warning you, Sully. Go home. Let this be handled by the police."

"Sully's cousin *is* a policeman," one man called.

"They're almost to the door," I told her.

"Open it," she whispered. "Open the door."

When I did, a shot sounded and surprised me so completely that I thought one of the men had gone to the truck and gotten his shotgun. But the sound came from my mother.

She shot, blowing open the screen door, ripping the curtains on the nearby window. The kitchen filled with a chemical smell of black smoke, and the air around me grew distorted. Everything in my body wanted to run, but I couldn't think of any place to go. The house silenced itself. The back porch was covered with debris.

My mother breathed hard. I could hear her breathing, though the moment of my own breath had stopped. She'd blown down the door and hit Sully in the leg with buckshot. My own heart came to a halt until I said, "Mama?"

"You all right, Evie?" without waiting for an answer, she said, "I hit Sully. I think I hit him. *Did* I?"

I saw Sully on the ground, but he tried to stand up. "He's hit, but okay, I think."

The men dragged Sully to the blue truck. One man fired Sully's gun several times into the air to scare us.

"They're leaving," I said.

My mother lifted her gun again in response to the shots. This time the door exploded. The blast cut off part of the molding and sent splinters of wood across the yard. My first thought (though I'd seen her shoot), my first thought was—"Have they shot *us*?"

The screen lay across the railing, and three men pulled Sully into the bed of the truck. The truck backfired as they sped off.

My mother ejected the empty cartridges and slid two more into the chamber. Her movements seemed as practiced as a sheriff.

She yelled to the men, even though they were gone. "You keep away from us. You hear me? You keep away from my house."

Someone ran around the side of the house, and my mother lifted the shotgun again. I took it from her as Mr. Shallowford bolted around the corner. His shirt flapped open, and I could see his barrel chest, his sinewy arms. In his hand he carried a knife. By the time the police car pulled up to the front of the house, the blue truck had moved completely out of sight.

Mr. Shallowford had called the police. They inspected the damage done to the door and porch. At first everyone assumed the damage had been done by Sully's men.

My mother's face was wild, primitive. Her hair stood on its short ends, and she looked beautiful to me.

I propped the shotgun against the counter. What stayed in my mind was that the men were still out there, and that they would probably come back.

"You get those men who're doing this to us," my mother told the policeman. "I know who they are. I saw them. Tom Hill, two of Turnbull's nephews, and Sully Cantor. You make them stop."

At eleven o'clock Tucker and Judge Wilson came to the house. Not until then would Jane come downstairs. The judge walked with her into the living room, and Jane sat down beside him. She sat as though her weight might break the wood of the chair.

"They'll be back," the judge said, without any thought of comfort or distress. "That's a dangerous enclave of men, Agnes. They'll be back. We have to get some protection for you."

My mother collapsed into Mr. Shallowford's arms. I tried to think of the last time I had seen my mother lean against a man, crying. Maybe never.

49

The next day reporters showed up to get the story. News of Sully's actions spread through the community. Even those people who felt sympathy for Sully were surprised that he had threatened Jane in the Bells' house. The tide had come in too strong, and was beginning to turn. Sympathy for Jane was taking hold even in the least sympathetic remnant of Mercy.

After the reporters had left, and the curious had drifted away, Jane and I sat on the front steps. I offered her a Pep-o-Mint and took one for myself. We sucked the mints and looked out over the yard.

"When did this place turn into such a madhouse?" I asked, half-jokingly.

"About a hundred years ago," Jane said. She tucked the mint into the side of her mouth. She was growing tired. She shifted the mint and rolled it around on her tongue.

The trees on this street were large and shady. Their branches hung over the road. Jane and I used to climb them and peek into people's houses.

"My mother almost killed a man for you," I said. I didn't know if she knew that.

Jane's face in the late afternoon light turned black, black. How often had I seen a shadow cross her face like that? How many times?

The next morning the yard lay unusually quiet, not a bird or any sound came from the trees. Light slanted over the tops of houses, and heat even this early in the day made everything look hazy.

From the kitchen my mother and I saw Joe Sugar, Adele Turnbull, and Capp walk toward our house. Capp had the amble of a comfortable man. Adele walked stiffly beside Joe, and Joe's face looked blank. Capp saw us at the window, and though he usually smiled when he saw someone, he didn't smile at us. Only his gait was comfortable.

Jane had not seen Capp since she read the letter.

"Does he know?" she asked. She meant did he know that she was his real mother.

"I don't think 'knowing' will have much meaning for him," I said. "Volusia was his mother. Mama Agnes, too. He called both of them Mama."

As they came up the back steps, I held the door open for them. Joe kept his hand on Capp's back and seemed to be saying something to him.

"Hello, Cappadocia." My mother's voice sounded more cheery than I knew she felt. Capp hugged her, and nodded to me. When Jane came into the kitchen, he nodded to her too. Capp headed straight for the living room and sat down. He had been told to do this. Adele Turnbull also sat down, but Joe stood, and so did the rest of us.

We waited for Joe to speak.

"Cappadocia's got something to tell you," Joe said.

Capp stood up and took a woman's handkerchief out of his pocket. I recognized it as one that had belonged to Volusia, a soft, limp cotton edged in lace. Capp had carried it in his pocket until the edges had grown dirty and ragged. Lint fell from it onto the floor.

"Now tell them," Joe said.

I thought for a moment that we might hear Capp speak for the first time, that maybe Joe had taught Capp to speak and had chosen this moment to reveal his accomplishment. But Capp didn't speak, he gestured.

He pretended to open a small bottle of pills, pouring them out, then shaking the pretend bottle to show how empty it was. With great tenderness, he propped up an imaginary head and administered the pills. He gave water, then more water. He mimed the whole scene for us, walking back and forth between the imagined bed and the imagined sink.

When he sat down again on the sofa, I realized he was still inside his gestured language—his hands moving. So I got up to bring him a plate of cookies from the table. He took a cookie and ate it. I felt odd offering food to someone who had just confessed to ending Volusia's life, but it seemed to me something Volusia herself might have done.

Joe nodded. Capp didn't look up, but he also nodded.

"Now the other thing," Joe said. "Show them the piece of paper I gave you."

Capp stood up again, as though he might be giving a lecture. He lifted out a folded sheet of paper and handed it to Jane. The paper was his birth certificate. Jane read it, then nodded toward Joe, so he would know she understood, and that she already knew who Capp was.

"Show them what you did," Joe said.

Capp grew distracted. He moved toward the door, and his anxiety was so contagious that I reflexively looked out the window for the blue truck.

Then Capp moved so suddenly that I was afraid he might run outside. I grabbed his arm, but he pushed me away. Then he leaned over a chair where no one had been sitting and he began to shake it. He lifted the chair and banged it against the wall. My mother moved to stop him, but Joe said, "Let him show you."

He was showing us something. His dark arms muscled up hard beneath his light shirt. Then he stopped and picked up a pillow. He held it tight against the back of the chair. He was smothering the chair. He dropped the pillow, put his hands around an imagined neck, and made a snapping noise in his throat.

When he sat down again, he pulled at the scab above his eye. He no longer wore the bandage, but he kept pulling at the scab and making it bleed. He looked exhausted.

It was Adele Turnbull's moment to speak. She said that she wanted us to know these things before we saw it in the courtroom. She said Capp had gone to the house because her husband had been sending for him.

"Robert called me last month saying that I'd have to come take care of him and if I didn't he would write me out of the will. I told him he had no right to do that. Then he threatened to write Margaret out as well. I grew furious. I told him what I knew about Jane, then I told him that Capp was Jane's child, and that the child he thought was dead had lived."

She turned to look at Jane and said, "I am so sorry, Jane. I'm sorry about then and now."

"I'd seen the birth certificate," Adele said, "and I told him if he didn't do right by us I would tell the whole town. The next thing I knew, he was dead."

Jane went to sit down beside Capp. She took hold of his hand and held it. He wasn't looking at anyone, but he looked at Jane, then bowed his head. They could not stop bowing their heads.

50

I imagined the night at Turnbull's like this:

Capp never entered anyone's house alone. He would go downtown alone, to the woods alone, even ride in a cab when he needed to, but never went into anybody's house. So as he entered Turnbull's hallway, he looked for Jane. Jane was supposed to pick up Capp when the big hand was on the 12 and the little hand on the 5. Capp was going to get the money Turnbull owed him. Capp, though, was in the habit of running off at night, so Joe had asked Jane to get him, bring him home. But Capp had come early and Jane was not there. He felt troubled, disobedient.

The hallway did not have much light, but a light was on in the bathroom. Capp went into the bathroom and urinated before going upstairs. Still, he continued to look around for Jane. He was confused about what he was supposed to do.

Then the door of Turnbull's bedroom opened. Turnbull was anticipating him. He had heard him downstairs. He waited for Capp behind the bedroom door. When Capp came in, Turnbull hit him with something blunt and cut his head above the left eye.

I imagined Capp growing furious with the blow to his head, I imagined him rushing toward Turnbull to keep from being hit again, then pushing Turnbull down onto the bed. I imagined him lifting a pillow.

Capp had seen Joe Sugar smother animals in this way.

Once when a fox got caught in a trap, Joe tried to free it, but the fox bit him. Joe's hand was bleeding, so he lifted a sack of grain and pushed it down onto the fox's head. He and Capp watched the fox struggle until it was limp.

Capp tried this. He lifted the pillow and pushed it down hard. But Turnbull's arms and legs flailed and knocked off the clock and a glass tumbler on the bedside table. Turnbull pulled at the sheets, so Capp threw off the pillow and took hold of Turnbull's neck with both hands.

He bashed his head once against the brass head rail, and heard the bonecrack sound that Capp had imitated in his throat.

He ran outside and down the road. Jane had gone into the house. She had looked around downstairs and she had heard movement in Turnbull's room before going to look in the shed out back. When she returned to the house, all was quiet and the front door was flung open. She could see Capp running down the road.

When Jane drove her car up beside him, Capp was no longer running. He was too dazed at first to recognize who she was. Jane took him to the emergency room.

The charges against Jane were thrown out, and Capp was brought into custody. The burden of trial had shifted to him. A hearing would determine his next fate, but for the time being he was kept in the jail cell where Jane had been. Joe Sugar went to stay with him.

By the time we got home it was the supper hour, but we couldn't eat. Volusia's presence was keeping vigil in our house. The kitchen was full of images of her broad back turning, and her arms moving at the sink or stove.

Finally, around 8:30, my mother put food on the table and we sat with full plates in front of us, pretending to be hungry. My mother was the first to lift her fork.

"Turn off the light," she said. So we sat in the dark listening to one another eat—Jane and I on either side of the table, my mother and Tucker at the ends. A pale evening light covered the room and our forks went steadily to our mouths. Soon we were through, and my mother and Tucker rose to leave the table. Jane and I stayed in the dark kitchen.

When Jane spoke, her voice was deep as if she had gravel in her throat. "Mr. Pratt said he would take Capp's case. He says it'll never go to trial. It won't get past the hearing. He says self-defense will be easy in this case."

"I know," I said.

"I'm going down to the jail to stay with him," Jane told me.

"Joe's already there."

"Joe can go home. I'll stay with him. I want to."

"Then what?" I asked her.

"Then I'll go home," she said. A tremor went through her, as though the vagueness of many days had become suddenly clear.

"Bandy called me today, Evie. I told him everything that had happened, and you know what he said? He said did I want him to come here? He said he would come here or he would stay there and keep everything going till I got home. He said which did I want?"

Her words hit like a spark of light in the room.

"I told him to just keep everything going," she said.

51

July 30, 1978

Dear August,

Whenever I write to you, I plan to write at suppertime, so the day will be fresh in my mind. I've been back home now for three weeks, and I've heard from Jane each of those weeks. She stayed in Mercy until Capp's hearing was over. Lamar Pratt got Capp off on self-defense, but Judge Few will petition for Capp to be institutionalized in a few years, probably at Milledgeville. Joe will fight not to send him there. Jane says she calls Capp almost every night, and though she speaks to Joe, Capp listens on the other phone and feels that the call is for him. She calls right before his bedtime. This ritual keeps him from running off at night.

The clearing at the head of the river is filled with wild pigeons, and there are streams and inlets where fish are as tiny as ribbons, and stones as flat as ears. Today I stayed at the clearing through a thunderstorm, and made note of wild grains that let off an odor after the rain. Tucker and Jane used to run back home at the first sign of thunder, so I'm used to being in thunderstorms alone. In fact, I always thought of rain as part of an excursion, not an interruption. Did you teach me that?

Johnny and I will marry on Friday. No wedding, just a small ceremony. I'll wear the hat Volusia made for me. We'll spend our honeymoon in Santa Fe. Ty wanted to go with us, but didn't want to miss the first two games of his play-offs so we talked him into staying a week with a friend. He says he can't see what difference a wedding will make—everything will seem the same, he says. He's probably right. But he *is* disappointed that we're not having a big wedding. He wanted us to get lots of presents. Maybe you could send a nice wedding present for Ty—a baseball glove or a Boston Red Sox cap.

The days are long. The clouds today, at noon, were like streaks of wool. Sometimes I walk to the quarry to see the bizarre shapes of strata and ridges, and the subtle colors of clayey slate. I swim in the cool quarry water.

This month is hot, hot. In the late afternoon nothing moves. Sometimes, on the way home, I stop by the side of the road to hear cowbells clang against their slow grazing. I feel quiet inside. I like to sleep and lumber through the woods.

Love,

Evie

October 10, 1978

Dear August,

I talked with Tucker and Becky today, and they have set the date for their wedding—a big wedding. May 25th. Jane and Bandy will come with Sammy and Max. I plan to see Jane before May though. We've planned to visit Capp on his birthday in December. We've promised to do that every year.

Owls and porcupines have surrounded our house—since July I note their habits and I leave bits of food so they'll come close enough to observe. Sometimes when I go to other parts of the woods, I believe I see the owl or porcupine that comes to the house. I imagine they recognize me. I saw two owls today near the river, and left bits of bread, and some peanuts for the porcupines.

School has begun, and I'm starting the semester of biology by taking my students into the woods. Your letters to me are so full of information that I will use them in my class. I'm thinking that you might like to spend Christmas with us. Mother will come for Thanksgiving. Think about Christmas. Until you say yes, I will not even mention the possibility to Ty.

Love,

Evie

November 15, 1978

Dear August,

I've been remiss in my letters to you. Last week Johnny was invited to present a paper in San Francisco. He's becoming quite famous, I think. Several colleges have called to offer him a job. I wouldn't mind moving, though Ty might mind a lot.

It is not the time of year for spiders, but still I've been observing tapestries of webs. One lady spider stretched her threads from the windowsill to the porch swing. I won't allow anyone to sit in the swing for fear of tearing the web.

I bring a lawn chair and watch her spin—such an intricate architecture. But the reason she spins is not clear. Some naturalists believe that because of the spider's eagerness to drink water, she builds a web to catch dewdrops. Others say the web helps spiders to move rapidly from place to place. Still others (like myself) believe the web is just a tool for catching insects. For days, though, nothing has flown into her careful weave.

Yesterday, I caught two flies and threw them into the web. She would have nothing to do with them, so I gave up, went to town and bought myself a Mexiburger with jumbo fries. When I got home I didn't go to the porch. I didn't want to think of her still fasting. I cleaned up Ty's room, and browsed through some library books for my teaching. When I finally checked on the web, the spider was nowhere to be seen. She had removed herself, as I had removed myself—both of us going out for the day. I imagined her somewhere eating Mexiburgers with a friend.

I'm keeping notes on the habits of spiders, searching for new facts, and stories. By the time Johnny comes in, he finds me flushed with knowledge, and old Latin names. He asks, "What's for supper?" I tell him I didn't remember to pick up anything at the store. "Didn't you go into town today?" he asks. "Yes," I say. "What do you *do* all day?" This is the way the conversation goes, but then he opens the refrigerator door and takes out five eggs. He puts on a chef's hat and proceeds to make an omelette with peppers and mushrooms and three kinds of cheeses. He burns hash browns in a skillet and I heat up some biscuits. I cannot tell him how full I am from lunch. I eat all he puts before me, because I know how lucky I am to have this man who goes along with my peculiar habits.

Before I go to bed, I see the spider back in her web. I call Johnny to come out onto the porch. He has seen this spider before, and will be glad when he can sit again in the porch swing. He looks at her with interest, but all spiders look pretty much the same to him, and he says so.

"She's beautiful," he says, without prompting. He knows this creature has occupied my time for the last few days. He doesn't know how. I have taken copious notes. We watch her longer than he wants to, but he loves me, even after six years of living together, and almost four months of marriage.

And another thing: I am pregnant.

Love,
Evie

December 29, 1978

Dear August,

We loved having you here at Christmas. Ty says he's going to write and thank you for his presents. I hope he does. You were generous. I want you to come back soon.

I love winter days—the spare look of the trees and air, the light that has no color in it. I used to imagine how everything would look when the leaves and blossoms came back, but now I see only what it is.

I have a few more days before school starts again, and I'm still experiencing some morning sickness. But I'm spending the rest of my time walking to the streams, even as far as the quarry.

Love,
Evie

January 15, 1979

Dear Dad,

How do we stand what has happened? I expected my mother to live until I was old, or at least older than this. I wish she could have lived long enough to see Tucker married. Mr. Shallowford said she had been hiding a heart condition for years. We just buried Volusia, and now Mama.

Tucker and Becky will still be married at the house in May. Mr. Shallowford will postpone the sale of the house until after the wedding. Mr. Shallowford looked absolutely lost at the funeral. I'm trying to think of more ways to include him into our family. I've never really thought of him as anything but an outsider.

Capp was so confused at the funeral that Jane offered to let him fly to Chicago with them for a week, but Joe wanted him to stay. Joe has grown to depend on Capp. If Capp is sent to Milledgeville, I don't know what Joe will do. I don't know what I will do without my mother to talk to each week. I wanted her to see this baby. I wanted her to be around for a long, long time.

Love,
Evie

February 24, 1979

Dear August,

Today I am low in my mind. I want to call mother. During the past few years whenever I went to Mercy, or whenever she came to Houston, we had fun the way Jane and I used to. I like the thought that mothers and daughters can enjoy each other as adults. All of this keeps me low though. I feel gypped out of so many years. Maybe you do too.

Love,
Evie

April 18, 1979

Dear August,

I walk along the Alamara River and spot many bluebirds. The other day I saw fourteen in one tree. There were more, but I only counted to fourteen before they left. I will probably never see such a sight again. I try to lure them to my house by concocting a mixture of cornmeal, lard, and peanut butter. Last spring I watched two families of bluebirds build a nest, hatch their young, and leave. The mother bird even let me look at her eggs—so blue it was hard to focus on them. She hovered over me, but did not attack. She hopes I'll make more of the peanut-butter treat.

I'll see you next month at the wedding. I'm huge with child, as they say, but I'm not the only one. Jane is pregnant too. Did you know? At the funeral Jane was showing, so she had to tell us. She's two months ahead of me. I wish our mothers could know about this.

Love,
Evie

May 7, 1979

My Dearest Evie,

Your letters to me make me want to give you an answer that I think is long overdue. You never understood why I went away from you, your mother, and Tucker. I want to tell you now, not so much because I'm sick, but because your mother is gone and I couldn't tell you while she was alive. I don't want this to change any idea you have of your mother. I only want to change some idea you might have of me.

When I married Agnes Barstow I loved her more than anything in the world. She loved me too, I think. But as years went by, as she had babies, she grew more and more distant from me. We had no closeness between us, no intimacy—though I wanted it and asked for it. As years went by, I knew I couldn't continue to live such a life of abstinence, but I also knew I didn't want to have a "life on the side." I could not imagine being without you and Tucker. My love for the two of you kept me at home for ten years.

I'm telling you this because I read in your letters your passion for Johnny and I'm glad to see this in you. You have some of your father in you. I've given you more than just a way to love the world.

Am I sorry that I left? I don't know. There are days when I was happy in my work, happy with Melina. Melina and I lived together without marrying, though I wanted to marry. After ten years of being together she left me. What goes around, comes around, I guess they say. I regret not being around you and Tucker all those years. A man can be far away from the daily life of those he loves, and still feel the pangs of that love.

I want to say this to you, because I want you to be sure of the love you have from both your father and mother. It is, and has always been, a sure thing.

Love,
August

52

Summer began its genial season in June.

Honeysuckle and clematis rambled throughout the orchard, and the smells by midday carried sweet perfume for miles. One bright day followed another and had been doing so since the third week in April. Private gardens were wild with vegetables: small hard green tomatoes, lettuce tips, the beginnings of squash and cucumbers, peas, Jerusalem artichokes, sweet corn to come.

The wedding ceremony was over, and people milled around the yard and house. Yellow and white flowers abounded, but were beginning to wilt in the hot sun. I'd taken off the thin shawl I wore around my arms, and Jane had taken off the pink scarf at her neck. Neither of us could stand to have anything on our neck or arms on this hot day. We had removed our panty hose and stuffed them into our purses.

We sat down under the backyard oak, and watched our children chase each other, throwing pinecones, putting grass down each other's backs and fronts. Max caught a June bug and tied its legs to some string. He watched it fly around, making noise like a small plane.

"I feel like they're still here," I said. "Both of them. In the house somewhere." I was talking about Volusia and Mama Agnes.

"I know," said Jane. "It's hard to even think about this house without them inside."

A large three-tiered cake sat showcased in the middle of a long table, and food was spread around the yard at what the caterers called "stations." Ladies, who had been friends of my mother's, stood around the table and waved off flies.

They called to the children, "Y'all don't knock off that iced tea now." But they didn't care. These soft days did not inspire enthusiasm, but for children enthusiasm was already a habit. The rambunctious play did not annoy anyone, and no one remembered to tell them to be quiet, or slow down.

Max and Ty raced each other, and Sammy ran after them like a little goat. Other children began a game of cops and robbers, but the game soon deteriorated into roughhousing. August sat in a big comfortable rocker. His sickness had progressed and become visible in his face. Still, he hadn't mentioned illness to me, and seemed not to want to do so now. The day would have been too hot for him if not for the breeze that kept us in the yard.

Ty ran into the house to get his ball and bat. He wanted to start a game in the side yard, but Sammy came over to his mother and complained of being itchy. He said Ty put grass down his back.

When Ty came out with equipment, he called to Sammy and Max. Tucker took off his wedding coat and offered to join them. His limp down the aisle had been noticeable in ways it usually wasn't, and now as he ran to the side yard, his gait was exaggerated and uneven. Becky reminded him that they would dance in a little while, but she didn't care if he played ball.

Jane lay back onto the ground, so I did, too.

"My baby just kicked me," she said. She took my hand to let me feel the kicking going on inside her. I wanted my own baby to kick.

"She'll kick you awake at night, if she hasn't already," Jane said. We knew these babies were girls. We'd both been through amniocentesis.

"Two girls," Jane said. She liked saying "two girls." She liked all it implied about us.

A mockingbird called its songs from a nearby yard, then flew to the arbor covered in wisteria vines. The wisteria now was full and dripping with blooms. Two blue hydrangea bushes, full with flowers, kept guard at the back door, and Mr. Shallowford had recently added a large picture window that allowed anyone in the kitchen to look out at the huge oak where Jane and I were now.

We lay back on the ground, our stomachs poking up like hills. We laughed loud about our awkwardness. We wanted people to see us. We wanted to seem silly.

Our outside children stopped their play to look at us, but only for a moment. Johnny stood at the table with Joe Sugar. From their gestures we could tell they were talking about football. Johnny helped Capp fill his plate with food. I saw Bandy encourage Capp to stick his finger into the cake and scoop off an inch of icing to taste.

Tucker pitched the ball to Sammy, who hit it past second base, but cried because he didn't want to run. Ty helped him run, ran with him. When Sammy got to first base, I saw the first lightning bug of the evening.

On summer nights when everyone was asleep and the moon was full, Janey Louise woke me to go outside in our long nightgowns and run across the yard. We thought no one knew where we were, and we felt beautiful.

We took a Mason jar with us to catch lightning bugs and carry them around the yard, swinging the jar like a lantern. We jumped and leapt, and ran into bushes. The lace on the bottom of our nightgowns got dirty, so that our mothers knew when we'd snuck outside. We gathered a handful of lightning bugs and let them crawl into the jar, but I kept one in my palm to watch its small light go on and off in the dark. Every summer, when I saw them for the first time, my life seemed like magic.

Janey Louise had the idea of pulling off the tiny light of its tail and rubbing the light on the third finger of her left hand. When she did this, her third finger glowed and she held it out from her body to admire it, as we had seen women do, women who were engaged and proud of their stones.

"How'd you do that?" I asked and she demonstrated, putting a jewel on me. August would hate this, but I loved the adornment. We pulled off the tails of ten lightning bugs, then twenty—no longer interested in the ritual of the jar. Our hands glowed. We ran across the yard in our nightgowns and jeweled hands. We could not get over ourselves.

When we came back to the house, I saw a small orange light in Volusia's room. I told Janey Louise that a lightning bug was in the house, then we realized that the glow came from the end of Volusia's cigarette, and that she'd been watching us. Her eye brought us to shame.

The next night when we saw the orange light in Volusia's room, we caught lightning bugs without decorating our hands. We put them in the Mason jar. But before we went to sleep Janey Louise said, "Wanna make rings?"

We smeared the tiny light on our fingers and let our hands dance above our heads in the dark room. But when the moon was full again, we went outside and ran in the yard. We didn't care who saw us. We wore blue nightgowns with our fabulous rings.

The sky at the end of Tucker and Becky's wedding day turned the color of azaleas, though the azaleas themselves had already bloomed. The magnolia trees lining the street held huge flowers that looked about to fall off. Earlier in the day, Jane and I picked magnolia branches and decorated the house. We placed the branches in huge clear vases, but floated some of the larger blossoms in bowls on tables in the living room and guest rooms. I put one bowl in August's old study. Jane put one in Volusia's room off the kitchen.

The house would be sold after the wedding. Mr. Shallowford had already put it on the market, and the proceeds from the sale would be divided equally between me and Tuck and Jane.

Jane and I lay back down, but she turned her head quickly toward me, like a bird. She turned the way she did when she could read my mind, or pretended to read it.

"Two girls," she said. I didn't know if she meant us, or our inside girls. Her eyes looked watery.

"Yes." I spoke in answer to her heart.

The river's surface this time of day ran silvery and smooth. I did not have to be there to see it. I was haunted by those currents.

I placed my hand on Jane's hill of stomach and she did the same to mine. The ground was slightly damp. But beneath us something came into our bodies, into our backs and arms, feeding our inside children.

"I felt it." Jane said. "I felt yours kick."

And if our children would listen to us, if they would stay near and take note, they could breathe a life of branches into their arms. If they could speak to each other, their speech would feel like touch, and their lives would never be the same.

EPILOGUE
1991

Each year Jane and I take a trip to Mercy in December—on a weekend around the time of Cappadocia's birthday. Capp lives in Milledgeville now, since Joe Sugar's death. We alternate staying with Mr. Shallowford and Tucker and Becky. We spend the weekend and sleep for two nights in the same room. Each time we do this, when the lights are out, we talk in our old way. We are in our fifties, but in the dark of a sleepy room, we become us again.

This year we bring our daughters. Julie and Olivia are twelve, and though they've spent Thanksgivings together over the years, and sometimes a week in the summer, still our daughters are not anything but civil to each other.

These girls, whom we imagined would be close friends, are not. But they know how to tolerate each other with politeness learned from schools and politicians. They speak guardedly about their feelings, because they have been told that words can start a riot. They do not yet believe that love can stop one.

Jane and I grow so uncomfortable around these two daughters that we don't know what to say to each other when we're around them. Julie and Olivia don't know how to argue or laugh at each other. How to speak in ways that are hard. But, of course, they have never experienced anything together.

We arrive on Friday night and visit first with Mr. Shallowford. Becky and Tucker prepare dinner for us at their house. We visit all the graves, then the next day drive to Milledgeville to see Cappadocia.

The first night together Jane and I discuss our daughters and how we can help break them open. "It's too soon," Jane said. "You know what Mama told me one time? She said people won't be friends until they can cry and play together. She said they had to do both."

"We did some," I said. "Seems like Julie cries all the time though. I think she likes to cry."

"Olivia does, too," said Jane. "She wears me out with it."

When we drive through the Milledgeville gates the next morning, the girls in the backseat show no sign of being very interested. Then I point to Cappadocia working in his plot of garden. The ground is sopping wet, and nothing can be done in the garden in December, but still he's there. He wears ill-fitting clothes. Someone has chopped off his hair oddly around his ears, and I believe maybe he has done it himself. But when he hears us coming, when Jane calls to him and he turns to see us, his whole face brightens.

"Have you seen him before?" Julie asks Olivia. For an hour they have spoken like salespeople. They've been asking each other about school and friends.

Olivia nods. Olivia looks so much like Jane used to look—long legs and oval face. She wears her hair short with bangs and has on a floppy long dress.

"I've been here twice," Julie says. "I don't like to come though." This is the first statement from either of them that seems honest.

"Why not?"

"I just think about all that happened back then and I'm glad *I* didn't live in those times."

Olivia turns to her mother and I see the look.

"Say it," I tell her. "Say it out loud." I am speaking to Olivia.

But she doesn't say anything. She stays quiet to spare Julie any impolite anger she might carry. She changes the subject and from that moment the air between the girls grows more secret, more polite.

Capp approaches our car. He has learned to make a small sound in his throat that denotes pleasure, and he makes that sound now. Julie looks startled, but Olivia has heard it before.

When we get out of the car, after we have each greeted Capp, he stands beside Jane and gives Olivia a small rock he has saved as a gift. He shakes hands again with Julie, though I cannot tell if he knows yet who she is.

His face softens as he looks at me and Jane. He knows us, and he hooks his arm through our arms. He likes to walk between us with our arms linked together. His head leans slightly forward, and he urges us through gestures to talk around him. He wants us to speak to each other, and to be between us as we do so.

What I do next is not planned.

I reach to Olivia and give her Capp's hand. Jane gives his other hand to Julie. They don't know what to do, but Capp loves the moment, takes his cue, and locks arms with them.

"Talk," I say. "Talk about anything at all."

I know that if they talk around Capp, keeping Capp between them, that their talk might change. I hope it will. Capp is the pain we keep visible between us. He keeps us honest.

The girls stay polite though, hiding inside their rhetoric for a hundred yards. Then Capp runs away, fast, behind a tree. He pokes his head out, and runs again to another tree. He wants them to chase him. He runs and leaps like an old man.

At first, he pushes Olivia, trying to make her play. She's embarrassed, but she pushes at Julie. Julie is thrilled. This is the first time I've seen them touch voluntarily. Julie darts from tree to tree, and motions for Olivia to do the same. They feel silly, become rambunctious. They jump at once, holding hands. Their feet land hard on the path, and they scare Capp. To his immense pleasure he leaps and scares them back. The day is clean of pain.

If this were another time, if Volusia were alive—her face steaming with abundance, her body moving around us like a large heart—if she were here seeing these two girls, we might hear her say: "Y'all better *stop* that."

She would not mean it.

"Y'all better stop that now, else in a minute *somebody* is gone be crying."

ELIZABETH COX is the author of *Familiar Ground* and *The Ragged Way People Fall Out of Love*. She makes her home in Littleton, Massachusetts and teaches one semester each year at Duke University in North Carolina

Night Talk has been set in Adobe Caslon, designed by Carol Twombly of Adobe Systems in 1990. Adobe Caslon is one of the more accurate renderings of the venerable type cut by William Caslon in London about 1725. This book was designed by Will Powers, set in type by Stanton Publication Services, and printed on acid-free paper by Edwards Brothers.